Stories of
Little Girls
and their
Dolls

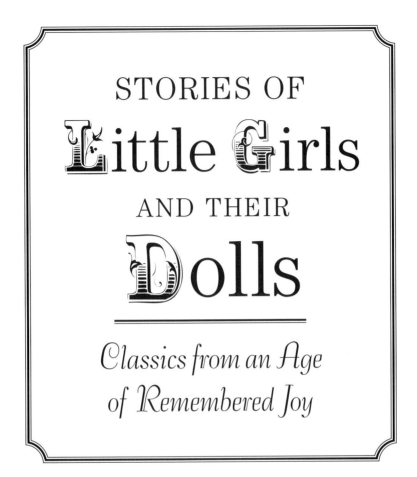

STORIES OF
Little Girls
AND THEIR
Dolls

*Classics from an Age
of Remembered Joy*

*Selected from
St. Nicholas magazine by
William C. Carroll*

BOYDS MILLS PRESS

Published by Caroline House
Boyds Mills Press, Inc.
A Highlights Company
815 Church Street
Honesdale, Pennsylvania 18431
Printed in the United States of America

Publisher Cataloging-in-Publication Data
Stories of little girls and their dolls : classics from
an age of remembered joy / selected from St. Nicholas magazine
by William C. Carroll.--1st.ed.
[192] p. : cm.
Summary: A collection of stories and poems about dolls, taken
from the turn-of-the-century children's magazine, St. Nicholas.
ISBN 1-56397-738-9
1. Dolls--Fiction--Juvenile literature. 2. Children's literature,
American. [1. Dolls--Fiction. 2. Literature--Collections.]
I. Carroll, William C. II. St. Nicholas (New York, NY). III. Title.
813.52 [F]--dc21   1998   AC   CIP
Library of Congress Catalog Card Number 98-70381

First edition, 1998
Book designed by Charlotte Staub
The text of this book is set in
ITC Century Light

10 9 8 7 6 5 4 3 2

To Margaret Ave
and all the Carroll and
Conway girls

ontents

Preface *William C. Carroll* xi

How Do You Know There's a Girl in the House? 1

The Best Loved of All *Katharine Pyle* 2

Jemima *Harriet Clark McLear* 3

A Doll Upon the Waters *Albert Bigelow Paine* 5

The Dutch Doll and Her Eskimo *Ethel Blair* 8

The Little Girl-Magnet *Clara Greenleaf Perry* 10

Trouble in the Doll's House 15

The Dolls' Complaint *N. P. Babcock* 17

The Dolls' Baby-Show *B. M. B.* 19

A Doll's Wedding *Lucy Larcom* 23

A Nightmare *Anna May Cooper* 24

The True Story of a Doll *Rebecca Harding Davis* 25

The Conscientious Corregio Carothers *Malcolm Douglas* 27

The Dolls' Convention *George Cooper* 28

Dressing Mary Ann 31

Borrowing a Grandmother *Helen Angell Goodwin* 34

Lucindy Listens *Esther A. Harding* 37

Cynthia Ann *Eleanore Myers Jewett* 38

A Fashion Parade 41

Prue's Dolls *Mary N. Prescott* 43

The Lament of the Outgrown Doll *Julia Schayer* 46

Two Little Travelers *Louisa May Alcott* 47

Parasols 49

Jemima Brown *Laura E. Richards* 50

A Year With Dolly *Eudora S. Bumstead* 51

Racketty-Packetty House *Frances Hodgson Burnett* 63

Perfect Mary Jane *Nahda Frazee-Wheeler* 77

The Dead Doll *Margaret Vandegrift* 78

How I Play With My Dollies 80

The Pine-Stick Doll *Mary L. B. Branch* 82

Maisy's Christmas *C. T.* 87

Cuddle Down, Dolly *Kate Douglas Wiggin* 89

A Warning to Mothers *Elsie Hill* 91

Mrs. Slipperkin's Family *Clara G. Dolliver* 94

Shopping *W. W. Gibson* 98

A Dolly Dialogue *Carolyn Wells* 99

Jo-An of Ark *George Merrick Mullet* 101

Week-days in Dolly's House *John Bennett* 108

Anna Belle's Christmas Eve *Josephine Scribner Gates* 110

A Dispatch to Fairy-Land *Helen K. Spofford* 116

Dolly's Lullaby Mrs. Schuyler *Van Rensselaer* 117

Little Daughter of the Revolution *Mary Bradley* 118

Only a Doll! *Sarah Orne Jewett* 120

A Book-Lover *Annie Willis McCullough* 121

A Doll on Mount Etna *E. Cavazza* 122

Queen *Faith Van Valkenburgh Vilas* 129

The Tea-Set Blue *Rose Mills Powers* 130

Kittie's Best Friend *M. Helen Lovet* 132

Hetty's Letter *Katharine Kameron* 135

The Smiling Dolly *M. M. D.* 140

An Idyl of the King *Ernest Whitney* 142

The Story of a Doll-House *Katharine Pyle* 144

Wee Mother Hubbard *A. Brennan* 147

Anna's Doll *Lucretia P. Hale* 151

The Rag Doll *Junius L. Cravens* 152

How Bunny Brought Good Luck *Susan Coolidge* 153

Busy Saturday *Fanny Percival* 158

Troubles in High Life *Mrs. J. G. Burnett* 159

A Letter from a Doll 161

The Cat's Answer to the Doll's Story 162

Rosy *Mary L. B. Branch* 163

The Doll that Couldn't Spell Her Name *Sophie Swett* 168

Dolly Takes Tea *Albert Bigelow Paine* 174

Thirteen and Dolly *Mollie Norton* 175

Preface

This volume could well be called *The Dolls from St. Nicholas*, since all of the selections originally appeared in *St. Nicholas* magazine. *St. Nicholas* (1873-1939) is the most highly regarded children's magazine that has ever been published in America, and remains so more than sixty years after it suspended publication.

St. Nicholas acquired its reputation by publishing the work of eminent literary figures, including Mark Twain, Henry Wadsworth Longfellow, L. Frank Baum, Lewis Carroll, Robert Louis Stevenson, Rudyard Kipling, Jack London, Christina Rossetti, and Emily Dickinson, among others.

Moreover, many of *St. Nicholas*'s young readers and contributors went on to illustrious careers: E. B. White, Eudora Welty, Rachel Field, F. Scott Fitzgerald, Faith Baldwin, Edna St. Vincent Millay, all the Benéts, Bennett Cerf, and Henry Luce, and on and on.

This unique collection is not without its share of distinguished authors: Louisa May Alcott, Frances Hodgson Burnett, Kate Douglas Wiggin, Sarah Orne Jewett, Mary Mapes Dodge, Susan Coolidge, and Albert Bigelow Paine.

Girls' love for their dolls transcends cultures, borders, and years. Dolls are thought to be the second-oldest plaything in civilization; the rattle is likened to be the first. Remnants of dolls have been uncovered in archaeological sites that date back thousands of years. While society and fashions have changed over the years, the devotion of little girls to their dolls has changed very little or not at all.

Although most of these stories date from the 19th century, there is a spirit of freshness and originality to them as they have been absent from public view for four or more generations. As we travel back in time to witness how Great-Great-Great-Grandmother lived and played with her dolls, we observe not only a glimpse of life in her times, but also the unaltered relationship between girl and doll which survives to this generation and most likely will endure in future generations.

It is the very special bond between girl and doll that we celebrate in this book. I hope these stories will delight young girls now in their "doll years" and bring a smile and perhaps a tear of gladness to older girls who fondly remember their precious, adorable dolls from childhood.

William C. Carroll

Stories of
Little Girls
and their
Dolls

How Do You Know—
There's a girl in the house?

By the beautiful doll with the movable eyes—
A French doll that sleeps, and that talks, walks, and cries;
By the toy-house and trunk and the stove and the chairs;
By the needle and thread, in the nursery upstairs;
By the doll-hats and furbelows made every day
For Annie and Sallie and Bessie and May;
By the soft little laugh and the sweet little song,
Which never to grown folks or boys could belong.

"And if you run up to the nursery floor,
And go to the room, and then open the door,"
Aunt Dorothy says, "well, when *I* take a peep,
And see a wee mother a-rocking to sleep
Her own little dolly, as still as a mouse—
Why, then I am sure there's a girl in the house!"

The Best-Loved of All

By Katharine Pyle

Three new dolls sat on three little chairs,
  Waiting for Christmas day;
And they wondered, when she saw them,
  What the little girl would say.

They hoped that the nursery life was gay;
  And they hoped that they would find
The little girl often played with dolls;
  And they hoped that she was kind.

Near by sat an old doll neatly dressed
  In a new frock, black and red;
She smiled at the French dolls—"As to that,
  Don't feel afraid," she said.

The new dolls turned their waxen heads,
  And looked with a haughty stare,
As if they never had seen before
  That a doll was sitting there.

"Oh, we're not in the least afraid," said one
  "We are quite too fine and new;
But perhaps you yourself will find that now
  She will scarcely care for you."

The old doll shook her head and smiled;
  She smiled, although she knew
Her plaster nose was almost gone,
  And her cheeks were faded too.

And now it was day; in came the child,
  And there all gay and bright
Sat three new dolls in little chairs—
  It was a lovely sight.

She praised their curls, and noticed too
  How finely they were dressed;
But the old doll all the while was held
  Clasped close against her breast.

Jemima

By Harriet Clark McLear

She stands up straight before me,
　　With her prim old-fashioned air,
With her ancient dress and buckled shoes,
　　And quaint, cold, wooden stare.
The little modern maidens
　　Think her "queer" and "old" and "slow,"
But most dear was she to one fond heart,
　　Just ninety years ago.

Time has not dimmed the brightness
　　Of her black, well-painted eyes,
Nor stolen the roses from her cheeks;
　　But looks of grim surprise
Replace the loving glances
　　Which she must have given, we know,
When she saw her little mother's face,
　　Just ninety years ago.

Her arms are made of linen,
　　But the rest is all of wood;
And she stands up very stiff and straight,
　　As well-bred ladies should.
She likes to stand up always,
　　For she thinks it best to show
To the ill-bred modern dolls the ways
　　Of ninety years ago.

No hair has she had ever,
　　So she quite despises curls,
And she thinks them fit for giddy pates
　　Of frivolous doll-girls.
She thinks hair is not needed;
　　For she says 't was never so
In the good old days when she was young,
　　Just ninety years ago.

She wears three caps as always
　　Made, the innermost, of lace,
And the outermost with ruffles wide,
　　Which come about her face.
The middle one of cambric;
　　They were all once white as snow,
But have browned with age since they were made
　　Just ninety years ago.

Her dress was fine and dainty,
    Of a blue and white, 't would seem,
But the blue is now a faded plum,
    The white is like rich cream.
The skirt her ankles reaches,
    And the neck is rather low;
But 't was in the height of style, when new,
    Just ninety years ago.

Her little hose were snow-white,
    And were tied with ribbons blue,
And she has small silken slippers,
    Which were bright pink when new.
She wears her red shoes, always,
    With the silver buckles, though
She has lost one buckle—careless she,
    Just ninety years ago.

She always wears a necklace
    Of small beads of shining green.
Her little mother strung those beads
    With loving thoughts between.
You plainly see that they are glass;
    But you must not tell her so,
For they played that they were emeralds, once,
    Just ninety years ago.

Her rosy cheeks are wrinkled,
    There are cracks across her brow,
And her quaint old dress is thin and worn;
    She is never played with now.
She dreams of days when no one
    Thought her "queer," or "old," or "slow,"
And she longs to be once more beloved
    As ninety years ago.

A Doll Upon the Waters

By Albert Bigelow Paine

Helen woke up then. It was her mother who was shaking her, her face filled with anxious fear.

"Quick, Helen!" she was saying. "The ship is on fire, and we haven't a moment to lose. Hurry, hurry with your clothes, dear! We can't take a thing with us. Your shoes, child! We can't button them! The boats will be going at once. Oh, Helen!"

The dazed, half-awake little girl was grabbing wildly here and there, trying to understand what was happening. Suddenly her eyes fell upon her doll—her precious doll, who had always slept with her.

"Mirabel, mama! Oh, my Mirabel!"

Mrs. Barclay was dragging Helen from the state-room.

"No, child, no! They said we could take nothing in the boat, not even—"

But Helen had broken away and was hugging her treasure to her bosom. Then came a crowded scramble up the companion-stairs, a wild, hysterical gathering on the after-deck, which the fire had not yet reached,—women crying, men calling loudly to one another,—until Helen, confused and blinded by tears, knew nothing except that somebody had lifted her, and then that she was in a boat beside her mother, with the sailors rowing hard to get away from the big, beautiful steamer, that was now pouring out smoke and flame in a dozen places. Then, all at once, she remembered.

"Oh, mama, mama, my doll! my Mirabel—she's gone!"

The other passengers stared at her—for the moment forgetting their own losses in this great tragedy.

Then came a fruitless search in the bottom of the boat—a wild scanning of the tossing waters about them—a little girl wailing sorrowfully in her mother's sheltering arms.

She could not remember. Perhaps she had dropped the doll in the confusion of the companionway or on the after-deck. Perhaps Mirabel had slipped while being carried down the ladder to the boat. It did not matter. It was only horrible to think how nearly she had been saved, and yet left to a cruel fate.

Poor Helen! They were on their way home from Florida, and in a few hours more would have been safe with papa in New York. Now they were being rowed to some unknown place on the New Jersey coast, with nothing in the world but the clothes they had on—not one of the beautiful shells or cones or palms she had gathered for papa, and oh, not even Mirabel—her own, her beloved Mirabel, who had been on the last Christmas tree, and her constant companion every day since.

The little girl was almost too grief-stricken to look at the burning vessel, which was now half a mile away, a mass of flame. Then, remembering that perhaps Mirabel was in those flames, she did look, and moaned and wept, with a heartbroken cry at last, when the poor ship, that had sunk lower and lower in the water, went down, down into the sea, leaving only a trail of smoke that floated away on the horizon.

They were less than twelve miles from shore, and soon after ten o'clock pulled into a little harbor, where a crowd of people were waiting, and where there was a big summer hotel, which, it being June, had been opened for the season. Then, several hours later, Mr. Barclay arrived from New York, with a trunk of clothes and some money, for in her excitement mama had even left her purse—the pretty purse Helen had given her, in which, fortunately, there was not a great deal of money.

What joy to see papa! even though she did not have the beautiful things she had gathered for him; and what a comfort he was when he rocked her and consoled her in her first great sorrow! Then all at once he said cheerfully:

"It is very pleasant on this coast, and is already warm in the city. I know of a quiet little hotel a few miles above here. You won't need the pretty dresses you lost, up there. I will send down some things when I get back, and I will come to see you every Saturday night."

So Helen and her mother went to a pleasant place on a little inlet, or river, where the tide ran in and out, and where there were boats and places to bathe. Helen's mother could row very well, and Helen was learning, so often they took a light skiff and rowed down to the beach at the bathing-hour, and then came back with the tide. This made rowing easy, for the swift current swept in, bringing in seaweed and foam and bits of drift that swirled and danced about the light boat, which was lifted and borne along like a piece of drift itself.

And these things Helen enjoyed. She was beginning to be contented, though down in her heart was always the grief for Mirabel. Often at the beach she would look out over the tossing water, where their good ship had gone down; and the tears would come as she remembered.

It was late in August, and they were thinking of school and of returning to the city, when, late one afternoon, Helen and her mother were coming home from the beach,—"tiding home," as Helen called it,—talking of their pleasant summer there, where they had never expected to be, and how it had all come about.

"I have had a nice time, and I should be glad to get home and all, if only poor Mirabel could be there with me," Helen said sorrowfully. "Oh, mama, wasn't it terrible that morning? I can never forget how I felt when I found that she was gone! How I— Oh, mama! *mama!*"

Mrs. Barclay turned hastily to look at the little girl, whose cry was almost exactly like that given when she had discovered her great loss. Was the child imitating the anguish of that moment? Not so, for she was pointing ahead at some object amid the whirl and drift of the tide; something that bobbed and eddied and danced up and down with the current; something white-and-black-dotted, tangled with seaweed and foam.

"It's Mirabel, mama! My Mirabel! I know her darling dress! Oh, mama, quick! Row quick, mama!"

For a few moments there was great excitement. Helen's mother had not been rowing at all. When she grasped the oars now, and tried to row very quickly, she missed the water altogether and slipped off the seat backward. Then Helen, half frantic, tried to help her up, and to row, too, and between them they came near upsetting. And all the time Helen was calling to her mother to hurry, hurry, and all the time she kept talking to the white-and-black-dotted thing, calling it her own darling Mirabel when, after all, it might prove to be only a whiff of foam on a bunch of seaweed.

"But now they were getting nearer and nearer . . ."

But now they were getting nearer and nearer, and Helen felt more and more sure. At last she leaned far out of the boat, with a little fishing-net she had, and dragged the dotted bunch closer and closer, till presently it was in the net and lifted triumphantly into the boat.

Poor Mirabel! It was indeed she! By what wind and wave had she been tossed back and forth, by what ebb and flow swung under the moon and stars all those weary wet weeks, to be borne shoreward at last on the bosom of the kindly tide, and brought, bruised, bleached, and battered, to her mistress's loving arms!

She was dead—at least, she seemed dead. She could not have been recognized save for the dotted dress and several other articles of clothing. Her strawberry marks were entirely washed away, and her features were quite beyond recognition. She would never do to play with again—oh, never, with that face! It was quite too distressing; but she was Mirabel—Mirabel, the once beautiful, the adored!

Helen held her to her bosom and cried and rejoiced, and when they reached the hotel created a sensation with the story of the wonderful restoration of the sea. Then the poor remains were made as presentable as possible in freshly dried and ironed garments, and laid away in a quiet trunk for a long-needed rest. Now and then Helen would go to take a brief look at her; but it was sorrowful comfort, and she went less and less often. When they returned to town and school began, Mirabel was put in a box with other sacred treasures which Helen was saving until she was grown.

And now, with school and lessons, the little girl became busy and partly forgot her loss. As Christmas drew near she began preparing presents for papa and mama and some of her dearest friends. She did not give much thought to what she herself would receive. Last Christmas had brought her Mirabel. This Christmas would not bring her another doll, for, as she said, she would soon be too old for such things, and she did not care to replace poor Mirabel.

But one evening, after the little girl was safely tucked in bed, Mr. and Mrs. Barclay in the library were discussing some subject that seemed to be of the greatest importance.

"He certainly does some very wonderful things," Mr. Barclay was saying. "He showed me to-day some already restored, and some he still had to do. We might at least see what he says." Then they went softly up to Helen's room and opened the box of sacred treasures.

Next morning Mr. Barclay stopped with a package at a curious little shop that had the word "Hospital" on the door. And when the little man who kept it heard the story and saw the package opened, he did not laugh, but put up his hands and said, "It iss mos' vondairful!" though whether he meant the story, or the contents of the package, I do not know.

"But the expression—it seems quite lost," said Helen's papa.

"I feex de expressione. Nevair can tell heem diffairence."

"And the eyes and hair?"

"Aivrything! I feex heem."

And Helen knew nothing of these things; but when on Christmas morning she was carried down to see the beautiful tree, behold, on the tiptopmost bough, exactly where Mirabel had stood a year ago, there was another marvelous creature! Not only that, but hair, eyes, features, expression—even the dotted dress—all, all were precisely—oh, they *must* be! It was! it *was!* for right underneath was a card, and printed on it in big, true letters:

> MIRABEL.
>
> CAST UPON THE WATERS—
>
> RESTORED AFTER MANY DAYS.

The Dutch Doll and Her Eskimo

By Ethel Blair

An idle Pixy chanced to stop
Before the doorway of a shop.

Within were dolls of every nation,
Each in its native habitation:
Cossacks, English, and Japanese,
Italians, Dutch, and Cingalese,
Spanish, Irish, and Eskimo.

The Pixy wandered to and fro
Until his eyes began to blink.
And so he shut his eyes—to think.
(You'll find that, toward the close of day,
Your father often thinks that way.)

He woke up very late at night,
And all the doors were fastened tight.
The store was quiet—the light was dim—
And all the dolls just stared at him.

(Of course *you're* brave, but even *you*
Might feel a little nervous, too,
To find yourself, all unprepared,
Locked up with glassy eyes that stared.)

The Pixy sang a faerie song,
And soon the magic grew so strong
The dolls began to breathe—to walk—
To fill the room with merry talk.

The clock struck twelve. And then, too late,
The Pixy thought about the date.
It was the day of lovers' signs—
The morning of St. Valentine's.

And as the big clock chimed above,
The dolls began to fall in love;
And then their troubles had begun,
For each doll loved the nearest one!

* * *

The Eskimo looked out to see
The Dutch Doll working busily.

He thought: "How comfy it would be
If she would come and cook for me."

(His Eskimotive may seem low,
But Iceland wives are *not* for show.)

He quickly won her for his bride,
And brought her to his hut with pride.

(The furnishings were rather few:
Two sealskins and a bowl or two.)

The Dutch Doll hadn't much to say.
Perhaps it took her breath away.

(Whale blubber in an air-tight room
Can add much to the general gloom.
And fourteen dogs around the fire
Is more than many wives desire.)

He made her household duties plain,
And soon was fast asleep again.

The Dutch Doll looked around that room,
Then went and got her little broom.

Her husband, lying on the ground,
Was waked up by the strangest sound.

You see, he didn't know the meaning
Of spring (or any other) cleaning.

She waved the little broom about,
And fourteen dogs went flying out.

Her husband, feeling nervous, too,
Informed her this would never do.

8

She heard him out. (She didn't know
A single word of Eskimo.)

Then from her pail commenced to pour
The soapy water on the floor.

(A stream of water, rightly sent,
Is a convincing argument;
And coldness of the feet, you'll find,
Will sometimes make you change your
    mind.)

The Eskimo forgot his pride,
And joined the fourteen dogs outside.

They soon could sympathize with him,
For when she got the house all trim,

She washed the dogs with soap and lye,
And hung them on the line to dry.

Then tried to get her husband clean—
But let us skip this painful scene.

He found it very hard to bear
Until she started on his hair.

She found two valued harpoon spears
Which had been missing several years;

Also a richly carved whale's tooth
Which he had lost in early youth.

She finished in an hour or more—
It left him rather weak and sore.

And now that busy little broom
Goes daily round the spotless room.

She makes her husband scrub the floor,
And (which he minds a great deal more),

She plaits the fur upon his clothes,
And ties it up with ribbon bows!

The Little Girl-Magnet

By Clara Greenleaf Perry

ally wanted a doll and a doll's carriage, a little brown bear, and, in fact, every one of the things that all the other little boys and girls had. Sally had no mother or father, but was taken care of by some kind people, who fed and clothed her. They could n't afford to give her toys, which made her so unhappy that, this morning, she had run away.

Sally had reached a lonely part of the country, and the tears were running down her cheeks, as she thought of all the good things that people were eating, for she had only a crust of bread. Just then an old woman came along, and stopped to ask her what was the matter. Sally sobbed out her troubles; she had no toys, no pretty clothes, never went to parties, never had candy, and, in fact, had nothing but just plain food and a house to live in! The old woman, who was really a very wise fairy, looked grave as she heard this discontented little girl.

"My child," she answered, "it is very wrong, and it makes people unhappy and disagreeable, to think only of the things that one can't have. You are well and strong, and have lots of loving friends, old and young, to care for you."

But no; Sally wanted more, and when the fairy asked, "What would you do with all the things that you long for?" she answered quickly:

"I would keep and use them."

"Very well," said the fairy; "everything that you wish for you shall have; but remember, you will have to keep and use every one! You shall be like a little magnet that attracts things to it, only with this difference: they shall not stick to you, but you may not be farther away from them than one hundred and one pussy-cats' tails."

Sally clapped her hands in joy, but the fairy said:

"Be sure not to wish for anything of which you may grow tired, for you can give nothing away, and must keep everything as near as one hundred and one pussy-cats' tails."

Sally could hardly wait for the old woman to be out of sight, before wishing for a doll, to find out if it were really true. To her surprise, she held in her arms the most beautiful doll she had ever seen! Its clothes were so pretty that Sally sat right down, in the greatest excitement, and took them all off, that she might admire every garment. She played a long time with "Dora," as she named her, but finally started on her way again.

Dolly grew pretty heavy after a while, and Sally

10

said: "Oh, I wish I had a doll-carriage, Dora, dear." She almost fell over one with her next step, for she had forgotten her new power of having what she wanted. She clapped her hands and wished at once for a lot of good things to eat, she was so very hungry. Immediately a basket appeared, filled with chicken and rolls, cakes, candies, fruits, and many other goodies. Sally sat down and ate until she could eat no more, then put what was left in the basket, and with that and the dolly in the carriage walked on, a very happy little girl.

By and by she came to a village, and, thinking how people would stare to see a poor girl with such a beautiful doll and doll-carriage, she wished for the prettiest dress a little girl could have. Sally held her breath in wonder to find herself the next moment clothed in just such a lovely thing, all lace and embroidery, with the cunningest soft kid slippers, while there was even a gold locket and chain. She could n't resist saying, "I wish I could see myself in a mirror!" There it hung on a tree, and Sally could hardly believe that beautiful little girl could be herself. It was a very proud, vain child that entered the village.

All the other boys and girls stared at her in wonder and envy; but presently she heard a shout and turned around to see what was the matter. There were her old dress and old shoes tumbling and rolling after her down the street, for she had forgotten that she could leave them only the length of one hundred and one pussy-cats' tails behind! Oh, dear! there was nothing for it but to go back and pick them up, while all the children laughed and hooted.

She stuffed the things on top of her lovely doll, and hurried away as fast as she could. The children ran jeering along, too, until she was ready to cry with mortification, and called out: "I just wish I had a dog to frighten you away!" The next minute a big bulldog rushed so fiercely at the children that away they ran, screaming; and Sally walked out of the village, with her nose in the air, wheeling the carriage, while Trusty, the dog, followed behind.

Just the same, those old things of hers spoiled everything. "Oh, how I wish I had a bag!" said Sally, who was so in the habit of saying "I wish," that it slipped out before she knew it. Of course the bag would n't squeeze into the doll-carriage with "Dora, dear" and the basket, so Sally had to carry it.

On they tramped, and those new, thin shoes with the high heels began to hurt.

"If only I had an easier pair!" wished Sally, and then, of course, she had to pack the others in the bag. Sally and Trusty were both pretty hungry by this time. They sat down by a brook and spread out all the food that was left in the basket, for a feast. "I do wish we had some cushions to sit on," said Sally, before she thought, for she already had about as much as she could carry.

When they started, Sally packed the plates, knives, and forks in the basket, put "Dora, dear" on one cushion, tucked the other under her arm, carried the bag, besides pushing the doll-carriage. Oh, she was so tired! But she forgot about it when they passed a field in which there were a mother pig and a lot of baby pigs. They were squealing and playing with each other in the funniest way. One little black one was so cute that Sally said: "Oh, I do wish I had you!"—and then stopped suddenly; but it was too late, for Piggy was running toward her as fast as his little legs could carry him. Trusty saw him coming and growled. He did n't like pigs anyway, so after him he went! Now, neither he nor Piggy could run farther than one hundred and one pussy-cats' tails away from Sally, so around and around her they went, dodging, barking, and squealing. Sally darted this way and that after Trusty, to catch him before he could hurt Piggy, while the bag, the doll-carriage, and the cushions came wheeling and bumping behind.

Sally caught Trusty by the leg just as he was diving after Piggy and upset them all; then she sat up laughing and cried: "I wish for a muzzle. Now you must wear it, Trusty, until you learn to leave Piggy alone." After this she picked up "Dora, dear," put her with the cushion in the carriage, took the other cushion and the bag, and started on again, Piggy frisking in front, and a very woebegone dog trotting behind.

Presently they passed some children driving the cunningest Shetland pony, in a cart. "Oh," said tired little Sally, "I wish I had one just like it!" and behold! tied to the very next tree was a small black pony with a white star on his forehead, as like the other as two peas. "Why did n't I wish for it before?" exclaimed Sally. "Well, now I can have as many things as I want, for I won't have to carry them. I wish I had a brown bear, a baby doll, a red balloon, a pair of roller-skates, and a gold watch and chain!"

Even with a large pony-cart, it was a tight squeeze for them all to get in; but they managed it somehow, and drove on as merry as crickets. Sally took the muzzle off of Trusty, who kept one eye on Piggy, but left him alone.

As they were driving along, Sally spied some lovely blue flowers growing down by the brook, and out she jumped to pick them. She was halfway down the bank when she heard the greatest clattering behind; and there was Pony trotting after her, spilling out toys, dishes, and cushions; finally Piggy, with a loud squeal, rolled off as they went over a particularly big bump.

"Whoa!" shouted Sally. "Oh, dear, I forgot all about those one hundred and one pussy-cats' tails! Pony will upset the whole cart in a minute!" And she scrambled back as quickly as possible. After picking up "Dora, dear," the doll-carriage, the bag, the basket, the knives, forks, and dishes, two cushions, a bear, the baby doll, the roller-skates, and tying up Piggy's head in her handkerchief, as he had bumped it, Sally decided that she would not get out again for a whole field full of flowers! The red balloon floated overhead just one hundred and one pussy-cats' tails away—too far for Sally to catch it.

After a long time they came to another village, where Sally persuaded some good people to take her and all her friends in for the night. She had to wish for a collar and chain for Trusty, and one for Piggy, as the pig-pen was really too dirty for him to sleep in. Then Pony needed a halter, and she needed clothes. Of course all of these things had to be

pilling out tops dishes and cushions

packed into the pony-cart when they started the next morning.

Sally wished for a purseful of money and gave most of it to the kind people with whom she had stayed, but when it came flying out of their pockets the moment she had driven one hundred and one pussy-cats' tails away, they were very angry, and ran after her, shouting:

"Put her in prison!" "She's a witch!" "Catch her!"

Poor Sally tried to explain, but it only made matters worse; and they were dragging her to the lock-up, when Sally sobbed:

"I just wish I had a dragon to scare you all!"

Mercy, what a roaring and bellowing there was, as, out of a cellar, appeared the head of the most awful-looking beast! The people fled in every direction to hide, while even Sally, Trusty, and Piggy tried to creep under the cart; but Pony was dancing so in his fright that it was impossible, and Sally had to run to his head instead, to hold him. But he turned out to be a very friendly dragon after all.

"Oh, dear! what shall I do?" sobbed Sally. "I'm so frightened! And now, I suppose, that dragon will follow me everywhere—and only one hundred and one pussy-cats' tails away! Oh, why did I ever wish for such a thing? He does n't look really so very cross, though. Perhaps he is good and kind, and is sorry to have people so afraid of him! I'll speak to him. Oh, what a loud voice! It *is* pretty scary, but maybe I'll get used to it; and he seems to be very pleasant. I think I had better lead Pony until he sees that the dragon won't hurt him."

Everywhere they went, people ran away and hid the moment that they caught sight of the terrible beast. By night-time Sally was in despair.

"I shall have to wish for a house of my own," she groaned, "and then I never shall be able to go anywhere, for I can't have a house following me! Well, I don't care; there is no fun in traveling when every one is afraid of me and runs away! I might just as well stay in this lovely place, with woods to play in, and a river to row on. I will wish for a beautiful house. Oh, and stables, too, for Pony and Dragon, with room for plenty of cows and chickens."

Sally had a happy time for the next few days, in wishing for a house and ordering all the pretty things that she could think of. One room was full of dolls—big dolls, little dolls; pretty dolls and rag dolls; boy dolls, girl dolls, and even little baby dolls; so that there were no chairs to sit on, and hardly room to walk in, there were so many trunks to hold their clothes. One room held toys of every descrip-

One room was full of dolls

tion, while in others were flowers and birds. Then she had pussy-cats, yellow pussies, white pussies, gray pussies, and black pussies who frisked and frolicked around her, while Trusty kept a suspicious eye on them all.

Sally now had to be up at sunrise, to feed the animals, sweep and dust the house, dress the dolls, play with her many toys, and, in short, carry out her promise to "use" her things.

As the house was just one hundred and one pussy-cats' tails across, Dragon did not have to follow Sally inside, which was lucky, for none of the doors was large enough to let him through. When Sally came out, Dragon would gambol around, and then take her for a ride, Sally slipping and sliding on the shiny scales.

For a few days Sally was quite contented, then she began to think how much she would like to have some little friend to play with, also to help her play with the many toys. One day, as she was walking by the river with the pussies, Piggy, Pony, Trusty, and Dragon, while the birds flew overhead, and the house slipped downhill a little, so as not to be left more than one hundred and one pussy-cats' tails behind, she had just said: "I wish I had a friend of my very own," when she saw a ragged child hiding behind a tree, too frightened even to speak. And, although Sally told her that the dragon was very kind and would n't think of hurting her, she refused to come out until Sally showed her the dolly, and promised to let her have one just like it, if she would only come up to the house. Gertrude could n't resist the doll, and she and another little girl, even more ragged still, whom they passed, went with Sally to her home, where they had a beautiful time playing all the afternoon. Sally was so happy in dressing her new friends in some of her pretty clothes, and in giving them dolls, toys, and even a yellow kitten to little ragged Tatters, that she had forgotten all about that selfish wish of hers to keep and use everything herself. Her disappointment was so great when Tatters started off happily with her beautiful presents, only to have them go flying back the moment that she was the one hundred and one pussy-cats'

tails away, that Sally sat down and wept. Tatters had promised to come back the next day and bring some other children who had no toys of their own, but this only made her feel more ashamed of herself, for what would they think of a child who had so much, yet was too selfish to share?

Sally had already begun to find that it was work, not pleasure, to have so many things; and now she really commenced to hate the sight of them, when she thought of all the other children who had none, yet with whom she might not share. Well, Gertrude could have anything that she wanted, but, oh, dear, how would she like always having to follow her not more than one hundred and one pussy-cats' tails away? However, when Tatters came the next day, bringing three others, they had a grand time, playing with the wonderful toys, racing Trusty and Piggy around Sally, and also having a ride on Dragon's back; but when they went home, and the littlest began to cry because he had to leave behind a beautiful brown bear, Sally wept, too.

The next day was still worse. When it came time to say good-by, Sally ran and hid her head on the Dragon's scales, and cried her heart out over her past selfishness. The little girl felt so badly, and was so much in earnest, that the dragon promised to help, for—what do you think?—the dragon was really the wise fairy, who had turned herself into the dragon that she might see what Sally did with her wishes!

She told the little girl how glad she was that she had found out that it did not make one happy to have everything one could want, unless one could share with others. The fairy promised to take back the wish gift, but Sally might do as she liked with what she already had.

It was a very bright, contented little girl who drove Pony over the next day to the good people who had cared for her when she had nothing, and brought them to live with her, as well as Gertrude and the other little child, whose name never again was Tatters.

They all lived together happily ever afterward, giving pleasure and help to all who were in need.

Taking Dolly out for an airing

Trouble in the Doll's House

By Last Year's Christmas Dolly

Oh, dear! I'm in such trouble I don't know what to say!
I heard somebody talking of a Christmas doll to-day!
I'm quite upset about it, for if Santa Claus should bring
Another doll to our house, 't would be a dreadful thing!
I'm certain no one wants her, and I don't see any need,
For I am just a Christmas doll myself—I am indeed!

Perhaps you don't believe it, but I know it cannot be
A year since I was hanging on a lovely Christmas tree,
And I'm sure I'm still a treasure for any little girl—
Though my nose is somewhat battered and my hair is out of curl;
My broken arm's been mended, and the eye that's left, you know,
Is just as blue and smiling as it was a year ago!

If another doll should come here, all beautifully dressed,
And my mama should love her a little bit the best,
My heart would just be broken, for little May and I
Have been such happy playmates in the year that's just gone by!
And I'm very sure no stranger, however fine and new,
Could love my little mother as dearly as I do.

No wonder I'm unhappy! It's dreadful to be told,
"You look forlorn and shabby, and are getting very old,"
When you feel so brisk and lively you know it can't be true!
Oh, dear! I wish that some one would make me something new,
And fix me up a little, so nobody would say
A Christmas doll was needed for dearest little May!

So if you meet with Santa, do tell him, please, for me,
That I and little mother are as happy as can be;
That I'm just as good to play with as any doll you know,
And not a minute older than I was a year ago;
Tell him *not* to bring a dolly, whatever he may do,
For whoever says we want one, *I* say it is n't true!

The Dolls' Complaint

by N.P. Babcock

"h! certainly, open the door:
We have n't the least privacy;
Dear me!
You never *do* knock
And we have n't a lock.
So you've come for a Four-o'clock-Tea,
I see.

But how do you know that we dolls
Are happy at Four-o'clock-Teas
Like these?
(Oh! you're hurting my back,
For I've had an attack
Of acute fol-de-rols.
How you squeeze!
Don't, please.)

"SO Miss Fanny is coming, is she?
And you want us to put on our *best?*
We're dressed
Twenty-six times a day:
Oh! *you* call it play?
What *we* want, it must be confessed,
Is rest."

The Dolls' Baby-Show

By B. M. B.

It all began at a missionary-meeting.

"Do you want to make fifty children perfectly happy?" asked Sister Eliza, as we sat there together, we two girls and the sweet, self-denying woman with the peace in her face.

"Of course we do—but how?" was our exclamation, "what do you mean?" And what she meant, by making fifty children perfectly happy, and how she thought that we could do this good thing, and how, when we heard about it, we determined to do it, and how we did it, and how the dolls' baby-show came about, and what it really was, and what followed this novel baby-show,—is just what we propose to tell to those who care about making children happy and who choose to read our story.

It is n't a pleasant thing to have no father and no mother and no home by one's self; but to live, fifty children, all together, in a great, bare barn of a house, every one with the same gray dress and the same white apron, and not a dolly among them all! Yet this was what Tabitha did, and forty-nine other Tabithas, and Janes, and Elizas, and Carries, Nellys, and Mary Anns, along with her. Poor little Tabitha! She had nobody to love her. When her father and mother died, there was nothing for the neighbors to do but to send her to the orphan-asylum of the county, and this was where she was, not many miles from New York itself. There was a great long room, with columns down the middle; no carpet on the floor; nothing pretty on the walls; twenty-six cold-looking beds straight along the sides,—and this was all the home poor little Tabitha had. Some of the other children were sick and dreadful, and she had n't very good times playing with them. How she would have liked to have a doll! Sometimes she got an old newspaper and twisted it up, or sometimes she made believe with a pillow-case; but if she could only have a real, live doll! A real, live doll!

But there was one bright day every week, and that was the day when Sister Eliza came. She always brought a bright face,—just like sunshine, after they had n't been out for a week, Tabitha thought,—and pleasant words, and goodies. Candy? Bless you, no! These poor, little gray ducklings never saw a peppermint stick. But she brought always a little paper of sweet crackers, just enough for two bites all

around, and that was pudding, and pie, and candy, and marmalade to them for a whole week. And one day, the very day before Christmas, she came with her brightness and her crackers, and—something else! Something, she said, that a kind lady had given her, and that they should know all about on Christmas-day. The children wondered what it could be,—more crackers? a Christmas-cake? perhaps only shoes and stockings,—everybody sent them shoes and stockings, shoes with the toes out, and stockings with the heels darned, so that they hurt. They talked about nothing else. Tabitha stayed awake almost all the night thinking it over, and then dreamed about it till she woke up Christmas morning.

"'Liza," said she, to her little bed-neighbor, before she had said "Merry Christmas!" even, "'Liza, what do you think I dweamed about last night? Oh, I dweamed—oh, it wath such a nice dweam! I dweamed that Sister Sunshine's bundle (that's what the children called her) that she would n't let us

Sister Eliza's visit

know anythin' about, wath a funny little square box, an' she left it in the closet, an' then I woke up in the middle of the night an' Santa Clauth he came down the register and he opened the closet door, an' the little box it grew and it grew, an' by and by it wath a big, *big*, BIG baby house, an' out came a big doll, an' then a littler doll, and then heaps of littler dolls, and their heads were all made of sweet crackers, and they kept dancing about all 'round in the air with a funny kind o' light about their heads, and one of them came bobbing up to me and says, 'Eat me up!' an' I bit off its head, an' I was so sorry, an' I bit my tongue, too; and I woke up an'—oh-h-h, my goodness! There is a dolly!"

Sure enough there was a dolly! Not fifty dolls, indeed, but one! A big, funny, rag dolly, tied to the post in the middle of the room, and "Merry Christmas!" written over it. Tabitha's cry had roused up all the other forty-nine children from the twenty-six white beds, and in an instant they had all jumped out—all but the two little sick ones in beds by themselves who could n't get up at all—and were dancing round the post in their nightgowns, trying to get a hug at the 'most suffocated doll. Such a noise they made, and such a quarrel they began to get into,—yes, a quarrel even on Christmas morning,—that the matron came running in, and actually took the dolly away. The poor disappointed faces! But after breakfast they were to have the doll again, and each child, the matron said, should have it five minutes for her very own. The children who came next actually stood in line waiting their turns, and by the time each of them had given the poor doll fifty hugs and thirty kisses apiece, it was so worn to pieces that it did not seem as though it could live through the night, the matron said. In the midst of it, in came Sister Sunshine herself, and such a welcome as she had. Presently little Tabitha crept up to her and told her her dream.

"I fink it's weal nice to dweam," said Tabitha, "when you can't have things weally an' twuly; an' when I waked up and saw that dear dolly, I thought my dweam had weally come twue. Only it does take so long to go wound, and I only had it such a little bit of a minute to myself."

"Dear little souls," said Sister Eliza to herself, "next Christmas you shall have a dolly each to yourself." And this was how she was to make fifty children "*per*-fectly happy."

Meanwhile, the dolly lived in the orphan asylum with the fifty children. She was almost bigger than the smallest child, and the matron always called her "Fifty-one," so that this got to be her name. By and by one of the little sick children died, on Easter day, and when summer came two new children were brought in; but dolly stayed "Fifty-one." One doll to fifty children! Fifty dolls to one child would not be so very remarkable,—the every-day doll, and grandmother's doll, and the doll Aunt Lottie brought from Paris, and the boy doll she was married to, and the rag-baby, and all the paper dolls that are its lineal descendants! This one dolly had a hard time of it. She had so much hugging that it gave her the chromatics, which is a curious doll disease, when they get very black and blue and dirty-like, particularly in the face, and the feet begin to drop off, and the stuffing (if it's a stuffed doll) comes out. Her best friend would n't have recognized her; but she lived a whole year, and to these poor little children, who had no "folks" of their own, she was papa, mamma, and brother and sister, all together. They actually remembered her in their prayers, and one queer little girl made a rhyme, which they said after "Now I lay me:"

"And till the birds wake up the sun,
Dear Lord, take care of Fifty-one!"

At the Doll's Baby Show

Taking care of Number Fifty-One

Every time that Sister Eliza saw the doll, it put her in mind of her promise. That was how we came into the story. She asked us if we could n't get our friends to give us fifty dolls,—old ones the girls did not want; and we thought we could, and said we would. But we had forgotten a very important matter,—that nobody ever saw, or heard of, or dreamt of a single, solitary doll, brainless or headless, banged or stuffingless, without arms or without feet, that its little mother did not cling to as "her own dear child." So we began to take up contributions for new dollies, when a generous friend sent us—as a Christmas gift for the poor—the dollies themselves, fifty and to spare, packed like sardines in boxes of six, and all of them twins. So alike, indeed, that you could only tell them apart by their boots, which were pink, and green, and blue, and black, and almost any color you can think of.

And now the dolls began to start on their travels, for we had engaged all our friends as doll-dressmakers, and the dressmakers lived pretty much all over the country. The dolls went by cars, they went by boat, they went by pocket. One found her way to Staten Island, where there was a little girl who wanted to dress at least one, and she came back as though she had been to Paris and had her dress made by the man dressmaker, Worth,—a real Miss Flora McFlimsey. Presently the door-bell began to ring at all sorts of hours, and they all came trooping, one after another, "back to mamma's, home again!" Now you could tell them apart easily: here was a French *bonne*, with her white cap and white apron; here a black-hooded nun; here a little boy in a Scottish suit; here two sailor laddies; another dressed just like Sister Eliza herself; and still another in the gray gown of the asylum children they were all to visit. If those dolls could only have told the stories of their travels, what a book they would make!

So the dolls were all home again, waiting for Christmas morning. You could n't go anywhere in the house but a new doll would seem to pop out. And then everybody said we must have a baby-show. We wanted to give the fifty children some candy, too, and make their cold, bare room pretty, for once, with Christmas-greens, and now the dolls themselves should earn the money to buy their mammas candy. Then came the show!

"Walk in, ladies and gentlemen, only ten cents admission, to see the prize baby, and the biggest baby in the world, and the smallest baby in the world, and everyone the best baby in the world,— ten cents admission, fifty babies, five for a cent,— walk in, ladies and gentlemen," said the manageress, a Mrs. Jarley with doll-babies instead of wax-works, to those who gave their tickets at our parlor door. And such a show of babies! Shawls and sashes, hung around the walls, served as screens and decorations, and ranged around were not only the fifty dollies themselves, but lots of other dollies who had been sent in as prize babies. As they could n't tell their own names, placards did it for them. Here were "other people's children," mischievous as "Budge and Toddie," but quiet as mice. Over them was the little girl who was "born with a silver spoon in her mouth," dressed as fine as a fiddle, and next to her the one "born with no spoon at all," in sober homespun. "The convalescent" sat up in her tiny bed, looking as pretty as a pink. Opposite to her was "a child of the dark ages," a dreadful rag-baby thing, made of a pillow and a black mask, with curls of carpenters' shavings. And in the back-room were the talking midgets,—"no extra charge,"—for the two boys had covered a table with a sheet, and dressed up their hands as doll-babies, which stood on the table, while they hid themselves underneath, and asked conundrums, and answered questions from the audience.

The baby-show was a success; we counted the money after each new-comer bought a ticket, and the last time of counting we had eight dollars and

"The children stood in line waiting their turns."

forty cents. This bought us fifty fine large cornucopias, and candy to fill them all, and a great bundle of Christmas-greens. What fun we had buying the candy, and filling the horns! And when Christmas-eve at last came, the fifty dolls said good-by, marched out of the house into an expressman's carriage, and so rode off to the asylum.

Fifty dolls had never been seen there before, and their arrival created a grand excitement. But they were kept quiet from the children till Christmas morning, and on Christmas morning they woke up to find the great room dressed with greens, the Star in the East at one end and at the other the Cross, and festoons of greenery all between, and a dolly and candy for each one. Tabitha's dream had come true. Her bed-neighbor, 'Liza, was no longer there; they had found for her a home in the great, far West, where kind people would take care of her until she grew up to be a little serving-maid,—to milk the cows and help about the house. But little Tabitha told her dream to 'Lisbeth, who had taken 'Liza's

place, and hugged and squeezed her dolly, "her very own all the whole time." And so each of the fifty dolls found a new mamma and each of fifty children was made "*per*-fectly happy." Only most of them ate their candy so all at once, that the doctor had to come next day, and give them each a dreadful dose of medicine.

Sister Eliza and we two girls came later in the day,—and did we laugh or did we cry? Both, I think. The children were most of them not pretty and not bright,—not very merry, even,—and we could not but think of the prettier, and brighter, and happier children we knew. One little, sick child with red, weak eyes hugged her dolly tight, as though she could n't have so good a time very long.

"Well, you've got your dolly at last; you're always hugging up some bundle or other," said the nurse.

The days are dull for these poor things, they have not much to brighten them; we were very glad we had made the Star in the East shine once into their lives with Christmas brightness.

A Doll's Wedding

By Lucy Larcom

Says Ivanhoe to Mimi:
 "It is our wedding-day;
And will you promise, dearest,
 Your husband to obey?"

And this is Mimi's answer:
 "With all my heart, my dear;
If you will never cause me
 To drop a single tear;

"If you will ask me nothing
 But what I want to do,
I'll be a sweet, obedient,
 Delightful wife to you."

Says Mr. Fenwick, giving
 His brown mustache a twist:
"I shall command you, madam,
 To do whate'er I list!"

Miss Mimi answers, frowning,
 His very soul to freeze:
"Then, sir, I shall obey you
 Only just when I please!"

Says Ivanhoe to Mimi:
 "Let us to this agree,—
I will not speak one word to you,
 If you'll not speak to me;

"Then we shall never quarrel,
 But through our dolly-life
I'll be a model husband,
 And you a model wife!"

And now all men and women
 Who make them wedding-calls,
Look on, and almost envy
 The bliss of these two dolls.

They seem so very smiling,—
 So graceful, kind, and bright!
And gaze upon each other
 Quite speechless with delight.

Never one cross word saying,
 They stand up side by side,
Patterns of good behavior
 To every groom and bride.

Sweethearts, it is far better,—
 This truth they plainly teach,—
The solid gold of silence,
 Than the small change of speech!

A Nightmare

By Anna May Cooper

There was once a little girlie,
  And she had an awful dream;
It really was so awful,
  That she woke up with a scream!

She dreamed that all her dollies came
  And climbed upon the bed—
There must have been a score or more
  In groups upon the spread.

There was one-eyed "Arabella,"
  And headless "Lucy Ann,"
And a most distressing cripple
  Whose name was "Peter Pan."

There was "Maud," and proud "Belinda";
  There was "Evelina Grace";
Each with an arm or leg off,
  And a scratched and battered face.

They held a consultation
  While she shivered there in bed;

Then up spake Arabella,
  And this is what she said:

"You have been a cruel mother!
  I say it to your shame!
We none of us can love you,
  And you have been to blame.

"You've pulled our arms and legs off!
  You've scalped us every one!
You've often scratched our faces,
  And thought that it was fun.

"Belinda's full of needles!
  You've stuck pins in Emmy Lou!
And now we have decided
  To do the same to you!"

It was then the little girlie
  Awakened with a scream;
And oh, but she was thankful
  To find it was a dream!

The True Story of a Doll

By Rebecca Harding Davis

It is a single little doll, laid away by itself in a box— a cheap china doll, such as you buy for a few cents, but dressed in a gay slip, with lace; the sewing on the dress very bad indeed—in some places the stitches long and gaping. I want to tell the readers of St. Nicholas the story of the doll and the sewing on it.

A year ago, a young girl, one of the teachers in a school in a great city, bade good-bye to the children and went home. The children laughed a great deal, and the story went about how that Miss Nelly was going to be married soon, and was going home to learn to keep house.

Nelly was one of the merriest girls in the world. In school or at home, everybody tried to sit next to her, to hear her laugh. Nobody was ever so friendly or so full of life, they said. But she was not strong; and when she went home, instead of learning to keep house, she grew thinner and weaker day by day, while the doctors stood helplessly looking on. The marriage was put off again and again. At last she could not leave her room. Yet still people tried to

come close to her; the laugh was always ready on her lips, and the big blue eyes grew more friendly with each fading day. The valley of the shadow of death was sunnier to her than life is to most people. She held the hands of all her friends as she went through it, and the best Friend of all was close beside her.

It began to be noticed, however, that she was anxious to sew or knit all the time, to make something for little children—soft, white little shirts, or baby's socks. It may be that the thought of a little child which never should rest on her own bosom was the tenderest memory in the world she was leaving. In the city where she lived there is a hospital for sick children, in which there are many "memorial beds" given as legacies by dying women, or in remembrance of them by their friends. Nelly had no money to endow a memorial bed, but her thoughts were busy with the sick babies.

"I will dress a box of dolls," she said, "so that each can have one on Christmas morning."

"Taking Turns"—Only one baby carriage
to three dolls.

They gave her the doll, and scraps of silk and lace, and she worked faithfully at it with her trembling fingers.

"I will have them ready," she would say.

But it seemed as if she would not have even one ready, she was forced so often to lay it down. One September night she was awake all night, and by dawn made them wash and dress her and give her her work-box and scissors.

By noon the doll was dressed, and she laid it down, smiling.

An hour or two later, they told her that the end was near. She kissed them all good-bye. Her face was that of one who goes upon a pleasant journey; and, holding her mother's hand, she closed her eyes and went away.

There is the little doll, alone in its box. I thought if each little girl who reads this story in St. Nicholas would dress a doll and send it to a poor child in some asylum or hospital on Christmas morning, that Nelly would surely know of it, and be glad that she and her loving fancy had not been forgotten.

The Conscientious Corregio Carothers

By Malcolm Douglas

Corregio Carothers was a man of much renown;
The dolls he made and painted were the talk of all the town;
In a room half shop, half study, he would gayly work away,
Completing, by his diligence, one dozen dolls a day.

If it chanced to be fine weather, every Monday he would go
With a number to the toyman's, where he'd lay them in a row;
And some would be so beautiful that one could scarce refrain
From kissing them; while others would be very, very plain!

"Corregio, Corregio," the toyman oft would cry,
"Oh, why do you persist in making dolls no one will buy?
In my second-story wareroom I have hundreds stored away;
And, if each had a pretty face, they'd not be there to-day!"

"My work is conscientious, sir," he proudly would explain;
"As dolls are mimic people, some of them must needs be plain.
I can not, I assure you, give good looks to every doll,
Since beauty is a priceless gift that does not come to all!"

The Dolls' Convention

By George Cooper

Say, have you been to the Dolls' Convention?
No! then at once it is my intention
A few of the startling facts to mention,
That kept all Dolldom in fierce contention;—
These are the notes of a special reporter,
Taken in short-hand,—they could n't be shorter.

Some of the handsomest dolls in the city
Answered the call of the "working committee."
Was n't it fun when the toddlekins met!
O, but they came in a terrible pet!
Dolls in merino, and moire-antique,
Dolls that were dumb, and dolls that could speak,
And dolls that could only just manage to squeak;
Single dolls, married dolls, all sorts and ages,
Fluttered like birds that had just left their cages.
One "stuck-up" doll, by her servant attended,
Made the remark that the weather was splendid;
This being said with her nose to the sky,
No one felt anxious to make a reply.
Two crying dolls, whose eyes were still red,
For fear of disturbance were sent up to bed.

Up rose a dolly—some said double-jointed—
And moved that a Speaker at once be appointed.
After a general squabble and flutter,—
Ten, all at once, trying something to utter,—
One little lady with long flaxen hair,
Amid great excitement, was led to the chair.
Hand on her spencer, she spoke of the honor
Which those who were present had thus cast upon her,
And so on at random; the very same capers
Of speech you have read in the daily papers.
Every one present then had opportunity
To say "what was what," with the utmost impunity.

A Dangerous
Dolly

·J·E·Travis·

Speech of a member;—her face was of wax;
By her wardrobe, she paid a superb income-tax.
She said, she had suffered with grief and vexation,
To see the dismay "boys" had brought on the nation;
They seemed to delight in their grim dissipation;
There was n't a day, and there was n't a night,
That her eyes did n't open and shut with affright;
For, not contented with snipping her toes off,
A tyrant in short-clothes had melted her nose off;
Though she tried hard to put a good face on the matter,
Grief had melted her down,—she had been *so much* fatter.

A lady from Paris was next on the floor,
Her train was some twenty-five inches or more.
She said that abroad she found nothing to vex her,
Or ruffle her mind; no boys to perplex her;
They honored the delicate creatures of Dolldom
Whose grace and deportment and beauty appalled 'em;
But since her return she daily expected
To call the police in to keep her protected.
She never had dared to put half her bows on her
For fear some sly rogue would tear off the clothes on her.
The bellows kept heaving just here where her corset is,
To find throughout "boyland" such frightful atrocities.

Another got up who appeared sadly mussed.
She said she was only a poor doll of dust,
But recently she had received such a shaking,
Her bones even then were most fearfully aching;—
A doll plump with sawdust held out rare inducements
To boys who were fond of "cutting" amusements.

A China doll said that her heart was 'most broken
To hear the complaints which her sisters had spoken;—
That, as for herself, she had a small daughter,—
She wished these remarks to be heard by reporter;—
She once laid her offspring to sleep in its cradle,
When down came a fiend with a poker or ladle,
And struck at her darling, so hard it was odd he
Had not cut her "sugar-plums" head from its body.
She thought they were shocking, these barbarous ways,—
And China dolls, too, being so hard to raise!

A rag doll remarked that her case was still harder:
Her home was a shelf in the kitchen or larder;
She had n't been blessed with the lot of some dolls
Who were tricked out with laces and such fol-de-rols;
She was trampled and sat on from Monday till Monday,
Her dress never changed, not even on Sunday;
Not to speak of small frights that were scarce worth repeating,
When the rats held a "ratification meeting."

A fine walking doll caught the eye of the Speaker.
She said that her voice always went for the weaker;
She'd vote for the total destruction of all boys;
She shuddered in sight of fat, lean, short, and tall boys,
Especially, too, at the whole race of small boys.
They pinched her arm in the door, with a slam;
They dipped her legs in the raspberry jam;
She wondered how, she assured her beholders,
She kept her head sewed on her shoulders.

A paper doll rose, but was soon called to order,
They had n't a moment, they said, to afford her.

This was the least of their grave resolutions;
"To banish forever those base 'institutions,'
The 'boys,' who are known as our natural foes:
They'd better take care how they tread on our toes!
They even deny us the rights of a cat,
And now we'll endure them no longer,—that's flat!"

Tattle and tea soon followed in turn,
Then somebody moved that the meeting "adjourn."

"If you don't go away right now, I'll call the cat!"

Dressing Mary Ann

1. She came to me one Christmas day,
   In paper, with a card to say:

2. *"From Santa Claus and Uncle John,"*—
   And not a stitch the child had on!

3. "I'll dress you; never mind!" said I,
   "And brush your hair; now, don't you cry."

4. First, I made her little hose,
   And shaped them nicely at the toes.

5. Then I bought a pair of shoes,—
   A lovely "dolly's number twos."

6. Next I made a petticoat;
   And put a chain around her throat.

7. Then, when she shivered, I made haste,
   And cut her out an underwaist.

8. Next I made a pretty dress,
   It took me 'most a week, I guess.

9. And then I named her Mary Ann,
   And gave the dear a paper fan.

10. Next I made a velvet sacque
    That fitted nicely in the back,

11. Then I trimmed a lovely hat,—
    Oh, how sweet she looked in *that!*

12. And dear, my sakes, that was n't all,
    I bought her next a parasol!

She looked so grand when she was dressed
You really never would have guessed
How very plain she seemed to be
The day when first she came to me.

Borrowing a Grandmother

By Helen Angell Goodwin

"We sha' n't have much of a Fanksdivin 'is year," said Sophie to her doll. "You know, Hitty, how we all went to dranma's last year, and now she's dead and buried up in 'e dround, and we sha' n't see her any more, ever and ever, amen!"

Hitty looked up into the little mother's face, with eyes open very wide, but she did not answer a word. Perhaps she was too sorry to talk, and perhaps she was n't a talking doll; at any rate, she kept still.

"Last year," resumed Sophie, "we wode 'way out into 'e country, froo big woods wivout any leaves 'cept pine-leaves, and along by a deep wiver, and 'en we came to dranma's house, and Uncle Ned came out to 'e date and carried me in on his s'oulder, and dranma took off my fings and dave me some brown bread and cheese 'at she made all herself; but I did n't see her, 'cause folks make cheese in 'e summer, and 'at was Fanksdivin time. I went out to see Uncle Ned milk 'e cow, and had some dood warm milk to drink, and mamma put on my nightie and put me to bed in such a funny bed, not a bit like ours at home 'at you can roll over and over in and not muss 'em up a bit; but it was a feaver bed,—live geese feavers, dranma said,—and I fought 'ey would cover me all up, I sank down in so. In 'e morning, Uncle Ned built a fire in 'e dreat bid oven; and when it dot all burned down to coals, dranma poked 'em wiv a dreat long shovel, so heavy I could n't lift it; and by and by she shoveled an scraped 'em all out into 'e fireplace; and 'en she put in 'e chicken-pie to bake, and a big turkey wiv stuffing, and a pudding wiv lots o' waisins in it, and shut 'e door. 'En everybody 'cept mamma and me went off to church, and after 'at we had dinner.

"You'd ought to been 'ere, Hitty, to see it; but you was n't made den, so course you could n't. There was all 'at was in 'e oven, and bread and cheese, and cake and cranberry-sauce, and apple-pie and mince-pie, and punkin-pie and custard—no, 'ere was n't any custard, for 'e cat dot at it, and in 'e evening we had walnuts—"

Just here, little "Lady Talkative," as papa often called her, was interrupted by the voice of her mother from the kitchen, where she and Aunt Ruth staid most of the time lately, getting ready for Sophie's uncles and aunts and cousins, who were invited for Thanksgiving.

In spite of the motherly feelings supposed to be strong in the breasts of little girls, poor Hitty landed, head first, in the plaything box, as Sophie sprang up to answer her mother's summons.

"Sophie, I want you to go over to Mrs. Green's and borrow a nutmeg for me. Go quickly as you can. I don't believe in borrowing," she added to Aunt Ruth, "but two of mine proved poor ones, and the cake cannot wait."

By this time, Sophie's sack was on and her bonnet tied. She was an active little creature, very bright for a child of her age, and it was her delight to be of use in domestic affairs.

"Now, what is your errand, Sophie?"

"Please, Mrs. Dreen," began the child, in accordance with previous instructions, "my mamma would be much 'bliged if you will lend her a nutmeg."

"That will do. Now run."

The little feet trotted as fast as they could across the two yards and in at the side gate of Mrs. Green's; but the busy brain went so much faster than the flying feet, that the child blundered in her errand.

"Please, Mrs. Dreen, my mamma wants to bo'ow a dranma for Fanksdivin."

Mrs. Green's eyes opened so wide, Sophie thought she looked like Hitty, and wondered if they were " 'lations".

"What did your mother send for?"

"A dran—No, 'at's what I want mine own self. Oh dear! I fordot what she does want, and she's in an awful hurry."

"What is she doing?"

"Making cake, and it can't wait, she said so. I know what it is, but I can't fink."

"Was it fresh eggs?"

"No, ma'am."

"Some kind of spice?"

"No, ma'am."

"What is it like?"

"Like a walnut, and you drate it wiv a drater."

"Oh, a nutmeg!"

"A nutmeg—'at's it ezactly. Funny I couldn't wemember"—and the blue eyes brightened behind the gathering tears like the sunlit sky through a rift in a rain-cloud.

Three minutes later, Sophie picked up her long-suffering doll, and entertained her with an account of the affair sufficiently minute to satisfy a New York reporter, ending by asking Hitty's opinion.

"Oh, Hitty, was n't it funny to tell Mrs. Dreen mamma wanted to bo'ow a dranma? I dest wish I could, don't you? I want one, more 'n anyfing. Don't you s'pose I could? I'll ask Uncle Ned. He knows 'most everyfing."

Uncle Ned was in his room writing when he heard little hurrying footsteps on the stair, followed by three little raps at the door. He pushed back the ink-stand, stuck his pen up over his ear, and called out:

"Come in, Pussy-cat. Push hard; the door is not fastened."

"I'm sorry to 'sturb you, Uncle Ned," began the small lady while she climbed up into his lap and threw Hitty on the table, "but you must escuse me, 'cause I dot a very 'portant twestion."

"Let us have it, little one."

"Can anybody bo'ow a dranma?"

"Borrow a grandma! That's a new idea!"

"You should n't ought to laugh at me, Uncle Ned, for I want one weal bad for Fanksdivin."

The tears came into Uncle Ned's eyes, for he was the youngest son of the grandmother Sophie mourned, and the pain of loss had not had time to soften. He held her quite still for a little, and then said, softly:

"A sad Thanksgiving we shall have this year, my pet, and the only way to make it a little less sorrowful will be to try and make others happy. That was always grandma's way. I rather like your idea after all. Your own dear grandmother is beyond the tokens of love and gratitude we fain would set before her, and why should we not make some other child's grandmother happy to-morrow? Whose shall it be?"

"Let me see. Fanny Turner's one. Her dranma lives in a splendid drate house, and she's dot lots o' money and servants and everyfing she wants. I dess we don't want her. Mrs. Allen—'at's two; but she's dot lots o' dranchildren wivout us. Oh my! you could n't count 'em. If 'ey should all come at once, 'ey'd fill her little teenty tawnty house wonning over full. Not any woom for we folks, 'nless 't was in 'e door-yard."

Sophie stopped and thought a moment.

"Oh, I know!" she exclaimed at last, the funny gravity of the small features chased away by a sudden smile which lit up all the dimples. "Mamie Hall! she's dest 'e one. She lives all alone wiv her dranma down by 'e bridge. 'Ey 're dweadful poor, and Mrs. Hall works for 'e rich folks and leaves Mamie all alone a'most every day; but she's dood, and Mamie's dood too, and her house is big enough, only I dess we better carry somefing to eat, for may be she has n't dot much baked."

"Always looking out for your stomach," laughed Uncle Ned. "We will go and ask mamma about it."

On the afternoon of that same day, Mamie Hall sat by the window, wishing some one would come, for she was very lonesome. Her grandmother went early to help a neighbor, and charged her not to leave the house till her return, as she expected some persons to pay her some money, and they might call when no one was in, and the money was needed at once. She got along very well till her knitting-work was done and her story-book read through, and then she sat by the window and watched the people passing. Hark! Somebody surely rapped. Mamie answered the summons, and was delighted to see her little friend Sophie, who said she could stay till night, and then Uncle Ned would come for her again.

"Oh, I'm so glad!" exclaimed Mamie. "Come right in and take off your things."

Uncle Ned stepped inside to charge the children to be careful about the fire—a charge which Mamie rather resented, being eight years old and accustomed to responsibility.

"I brought my doll," said Sophie, proceeding to take off her things too.

"That's right. I'll get Lady Jane, and we will have a first-rate time playing keep house. What is your child's name?"

"Sophronia Mehitable Feodosia Caroline," said Sophie, slowly, and speaking every syllable with precision.

"What a long name!" laughed Mamie. "Do you have to call her all that every time you speak to her?"

"Oh, no! I call her Hitty for short, and if she's cross I call her Hit. Her first name is for me, and 'e next for Aunt Mehitable, and Feodosia was my dranma's name, and Caroline, my cousin, dave her to me."

"I am afraid she wont want to play with a rag-doll," sighed the small

"It's 'diculous to see 'em together!"

hostess as she drew Lady Jane from the rude cradle where she usually slept, her little mother being too busy generally to attend to her.

"Oh, no!" cried Sophie. "I teach Hitty 'at when she's dood she's no better 'an a wag-doll 'at behaves herself, and when she's naughty she's worser, 'cause she's had better 'vantages."

"But she's all dressed up in silk and jewelry, and Lady Jane has only a calico slip and a white apron," said Mamie, just to see what her mite of a visitor would answer.

" 'At don't make 'e leastest diffunce in 'e world. All Hit's fine fings were dived to her. She is n't pwoud a bit. If she was I'd spank her. I s'ould n't for anyfing like her to be like Biddy Marty's doll that lives in the brick grocery—so *awful* big and pwould. It's 'diculous to see 'em together. Your child's zactly the right size. And, dear me, how clean she does keep herself! I dess she don't play in 'e dirt like my Hit."

"Oh, she is older, and has learned better. But what ails your daughter's nose? The skin seems to be off."

" 'At's where she bumped it 'is morning. She fell wight into my playfing box." And then, instead of telling how she threw her there herself, the small fibber remarked: "She is dest bedinning to do alone, and she dets lots o' bumps."

Hitty took all the implied blame very coolly, for she neither blushed nor winked.

"What made you think to come and see me, little Sophie? I have been wishing you would ever since the good times we had the day my grandma worked for your mamma."

"I fought of it long ado, and teased and teased, but mamma would n't let me, till she had intwired about you to see if you was dood. I knew it all 'e time, but she said she must ask some one who had known you longer. She lets me play wiv anybody 'at's dood," added Sophie, with startling frankness, "no matter if 'ey live in little bits o' houses, and have to wear calico dresses to church. But I came now to bo'ow somefin. You'll lend it to me, wont you now?"

"Yes, indeed, anything I *can* lend. But what can I possibly have that you have not?" glancing inquiringly at her small stock of playthings.

Sophie leaned forward with her fat forefinger lifted in a ludicrously solemn gesture.

"Mamie, you've dot a dranma, and mine is all dead and buried up in 'e dround."

"Yes, I have got a grandma, and the best one in the world too, but what has she to do with it? You surely cannot want to borrow her!" and Mamie laughed at the very thought.

"Yes, I do," persisted Sophie, with the utmost gravity. "You can't have Fanksdivin wivout a dranma, more 'n you can Christmas wivout Santa Claus. You need n't fink I'm dreedy. I'll lend you all my 'lations to pay,—papa and mamma, and Aunt Wuth and Uncle Ned, and all 'e cousins 'at are coming.

Mamie declines to lend her grandmother

And here's a letter," she continued, tugging at a tiny pocket until she produced a little three-cornered note directed to Mrs. Hall.

"I don't really know what to make of it," said Mamie, "but when grandma reads the note, she will find out, I guess."

So she crowded the corner of it carefully under the edge of the clock for safe keeping, and the playing went on. With riding out and visiting, caring for Lady Jane's fever and Hitty's wounded nose, as well as eating apples and doughnuts, the afternoon flew swiftly by. They were surprised when Mrs. Hall came in. Mamie instantly gave her the note, which she read with a smile and a tremor of lip.

"What is it?" asked Mamie.

"An invitation for us to spend Thanksgiving with Sophie and her friends. She feels so badly about her grandmother, she wants to borrow me! Will you lend me, Mamie, just for that one day?"

"No, indeed," replied Mamie, decidedly. "I should look well lending all the relative I have in the world to a girl who has got a houseful of cousins," and she threw her arms about the old lady.

"She can be yours dest the same, Mamie," pleaded Sophie. "Do, Mamie, let me call her so for just one day."

"Oh, you may call her so always, if that is all; but I must keep her too. I'll not lend her at all, but I'll give you half of her to keep for your very own."

"Oh, will you? will you?" cried Sophie, dancing with delight, never noticing that she held Hitty by one foot, to the imminent danger of the rest of her china body.

"You'd better keep the whole of me, and give her, at the same time, the whole," said grandma. "I shall love you none the less for taking this dear little Sophie right into my heart of hearts."

And so it was. The morrow was a very happy day. Sophie introduced Mamie as her new sister, and she was heartily welcomed by all the cousins, big and little. After dinner, the "new grandma," as all called her, told them wonderful stories about the times when she was young, and Sophie would not part with her till she promised to spend the Christmas holidays with them.

But before the Christmas holidays, the "new grandma" died. It was sudden. She was sick only a week. Sophie's friends cared for her tenderly; and just before the end, her father took the last care from the dying woman's heart by promising to care for Mamie as if she were his own.

So Mamie and Sophie are adopted sisters now, and though they are grown-up ladies they never forget how the good God provided for the fatherless through Sophie's childish whim.

Lucindy Listens

By Esther A. Harding

Come, sit by me, Lucindy,
    And hear what I would do,
Were you my little mother,
    And I a doll like you.

If you a lovely secret
    Should whisper in my ear,
I would not keep on staring
    As if I did not hear.

And when you sang, Lucindy,
    Your sweetest lullabies,
And said, "The dear is sleeping,"
    I'd *try* to close my eyes.

Or, s'pose that in the twilight,
    We two were taking tea,
I would *pretend* to eat, dear,
    The bread you held for me.

In fact, my dear Lucindy,
    I'd give my brightest curl,
Were you less like a dolly,
    More like a little girl.

Cynthia Ann

By Eleanore Myers Jewett

Cynthia Ann is my oldest child,
　　She's not the least bit pretty.
She's made of rag and her clothes are worn,
　　But she's sweet and good and witty.

My other children—five in all—
　　Are made of bisque or china,
Clara Louise and Michael John
　　And Prue and May and Dinah.

But Cynthia Ann is really best,
　　She's so serene and steady;
When unexpected things occur,
　　It's Cynthia Ann that's ready.
Just listen to this! One summer night,—

The moon was full and round and bright,—
　　Into the nursery softly gliding,
A fairy came on a moonbeam riding.
　　She twinkled with light; her folded wings
Were the loveliest, softest,
　　gossamer things!

She looked about, and she said: "Dear me!
What a curious household this must be!
Dolls all rumpled, the doll-house bare,
With upset furniture here and there!
A tea-set broken and blocks about,
And a calico cat with its eye put out!
This is n't the place for fairy or elf—
I'll fly away from it fast, myself!"

But just as she turned to ride away,
The midnight chimes began to play,
And ere they'd got to the stroke of five,
The dolls and animals came alive.
(They always do in the dead of night
Whenever the moon is round and bright.)

Now Clara Louise and Dinah stood
As stiff as if they'd been made of wood;
And Michael John and Prue and May
Just stared and hadn't a word to say.
(You'd think they'd never been brought up right,
And I've taught them manners with all my might!)
But Cynthia Ann, she saw at a glance
The awkward side of each circumstance.
She said to the fairy: "How do you do?
You've come to call? That is dear of you!

"Excuse disorder—one moment, please.
Come, children, clear away all of these!"
And in just a minute the room began
To look as neat as a nursery can—
The blocks in order, the chairs set right,
The children's dresses all pressed and white.

Before the fairy could say, "Dear me!"
Cynthia Ann was pouring tea,
While the calico kitten sat close by
With a neat white bandage over its eye!

When the fairy rose at the end to go,
She said: "My dears, I've enjoyed it so!

Such a lovely house! Such a cozy call!
Drop in at Fairyland, one and all—
I'm always at home by five each day."
Then she summoned her moonbeam and rode
    away.

Perhaps you wonder how I know
What happened there that night?
Next morning in the nursery all
Was orderly and bright;
Each toy was in its proper place,
The children trim and neat—
I loved them all, but Cynthia Ann
Was twice as good and sweet.

I knew these things had come to pass
While I was tucked in bed,
For Cynthia Ann, she told me all
And this is what she said:
"I did my very best, you know;
'T was just because I loved you so!"

France, 1430   Nuremberg, ca. 1520   Burgundy, ca. 1490   France, ca. 1420

A Fashion Parade

When those of us who live in the larger cities read in the papers that a fashion parade is to be held, we see in imagination a slow-moving line of people, engaged for the occasion, dressed in the latest styles and passing and repassing before a crowd of spectators gathered to see what are the latest decrees of Dame Fashion.

A similar parade, but much more interesting to young folk, is one to be found in the Metropolitan Museum, in New York City (in the basement of Wing H, to be exact), where the spectators form the slow-moving line, passing around three glass cases in which are displayed some forty daintily modeled figures, scarcely more than a foot high, dressed in

exquisitely made costumes of the styles worn from far back in 1400 down to 1874.

A gay little company they are, marching down through the centuries, attired in brocaded silk and lace and satin, each one the very pink of the fashion of her day.

Since our pictures were taken, the little Burgundian lady, with her wonderful pearl-laced headgear, has assumed a new pose there on her glass shelf,—I wonder if it was her own idea,—for now she stands with her full skirt partly lifted and held in her left hand, showing a green satin petticoat and a pair of scarlet velvet shoes of astonishing length and tapering to a sharp point.

England, 1536   Germany, ca. 1520   France, 1605   France, ca. 1590

France, 1646

France, 1725

England, 1649

France, 1740

France, 1755

France, 1775

France, 1780

France, 1795

France, 1819

LEFT BEHIND AND FALLEN IN STRANGE COMPANY.

Prue's Dolls

By Mary N. Prescott

There was once a little girl who did not own a doll—who never had owned one. Just think, what a condition for a modern child! At the same time, there were six or eight dolls that she called her own, that were hers to all intents and purposes, except that she had never held them in her arms, nor undressed them and tucked them into bed—the tasks so precious to little girls. Some of the dolls which Prue called her own were magnificent creatures, with cheeks as rosy as the dawn, with long curling wigs, and eyelids that fell bewitchingly over bright eyes; dolls with trained dresses and overskirts, with necklaces and earrings and fans—perfect dolls of the period; and there were others, little tots of things in china, which Prue longed to put into swaddling clothes and rock in the hollow of her hand.

You will laugh, perhaps, to know that she really played dolls with these, and had a name and history for each, though her only acquaintance with them was through the windows of the various toy-shops in the place where she lived.

Prue was a little chore-girl in a boarding-house; her business was to scour knives, wash dishes, answer the bell, and run of errands in hot or sloppy weather. She slept in a little dark closet, where she never saw the sun rise, though she was up early enough, indeed. She had her bread and butter and clothes for her services, and probably that was quite

as much as she earned; naturally, there was nothing about dolls, and the things in which little folks delight, in the agreement. Nevertheless, Prue's real life was passed with her treasures, though the window-panes between herself and them sometimes distorted their lovely features. She never dreamed of complaining, however. Every spare moment was devoted to them, no matter what the weather. Sometimes she was on the spot before the shop-keeper had taken down his blinds, and I regret to say that she often met with a rebuke for lingering on her errands.

Sometimes she would speak about her dolls to her few companions.

"And who gave *you* a doll?" they would ask.

"Nobody. I got them my own self. I found them; nobody else has ever played with them before."

"Let's see 'em!" demanded her listeners.

And then she would lead her playmates to the toy-shops and point out her favorites, and generously offer them the rest, and tell them that her Curlylocks was always looking out the window, because she had a husband at sea. One little girl got angry at what she believed to be a trick of Prue's to impose upon her.

"They are n't yours one bit," she cried out; "they all belong to the man inside, and it's just like stealing to play with other folks' dolls. So now!"

"No, it can't be stealing," Prue answered, thoughtfully. "I never touched one of them; I never took one away."

"But you would if you could!" said the other. "You covet 'em, and that's wicked,—the commandment says so."

"No," persisted Prue, "I would n't take one if I could—I don't believe I would! I have n't got any place to keep it in but my closet, and that's too dark; and she'd get smutches and grease spots down in the kitchen. I guess I'd great deal rather have 'em stay here."

"I don't believe it!" answered the other.

Prue did not forget this conversation; it made a deep impression on her mind, and gave her a sense of uneasiness. Every time that she paid a visit to her doll-world, she repeated:

"I would n't take them if I could—would I?"

And then she told Curlylocks all about it, and how the cook scolded when she broke the handle off a cup, and sent her to bed without a candle, and how she spilled the pitcher of yeast; and Curlylocks comforted her with her perpetual smile, and sympathy seemed to shine out of her two beady eyes, like glow-worms in the dark. One of Prue's dolls was always going out to parties and balls, where they had frosted cake and fiddle-music; that was n't at all remarkable, because she was a walking-doll. There was a smaller one in pantalets, with a satchel, who went to school, but who never got beyond "twice twelve" and words of two syllables, her progress being limited by Prue's acquirements. All her dolls behaved like the people she knew. They were ferruled at school and spelled above each other, and played truant; they quarreled and made-up like other children; they went shopping, and caught the measles. Whatever Prue had known, or heard of, or read about, was enacted in her doll-world. The children were naughty, and it was the cook who scolded; they had visits from Santa Claus and fairy godmothers; they were sent to bed when it was dark under the table, or they were allowed to sit up half-an-hour after tea, if they would n't ask questions; they sat for their photographs, and they took pleasure in all the things which had been denied to Prue herself. Sometimes she dreamed that they all came trooping up the garret stairs into her dark closet, and, instead of being dark any longer, the walls and ceiling grew transparent, and sunbeams searched it till it was warm as summer. Whenever she felt unhappy, she had only to take a run to the nearest shop-window and say "good morning" to her friends, and their rosy contentment seemed catch-

ing, and their unfailing smiles warmed her small heart. When she had been a little naughty, she confided her sins to them, because the cook and the chambermaid failed to receive her confidences with kindness so real, and one always feels that a fault confessed is half-forgiven.

One day, a great happiness and a great misfortune happened to Prue. She was in the thick of a chat with Curlylocks, when the shopkeeper deliberately took the beauty from the window, rolled her up in brown paper and gave her to a strange child who toddled out of the store and dropped her on the pavement outside. Prue sprang to her rescue. Curlylocks was going to leave her for ever and ever, but she should have the happiness of embracing her—of holding her in her own arms one instant! But Prue hugged Curlylocks so affectionately, with the doll's cheek against her own, and the tears standing in her eyes, that the strange child began to whimper, thinking she had lost her new treasure, which brought the shopkeeper out to her help, who hastily accused poor Prue of wishing to take what did n't belong to her.

"I was only kissing her good-by," was Prue's defense. "I meant to give her right back; it only seemed a minute. I never would have taken her for my own."

"You would if you could," said the man, repeating the very words that had stung Prue once already.

She ran home to her dishes and duster, with the tears frozen in her eyes, asking herself if it was indeed true that she would have kept Curlylocks if she could, hardly daring to look into her own heart for an answer, wondering if it was really stealing *a little* to play with other people's dolls without leave. And with some dim idea in her child's mind, for which she had no words, that she ought to get over caring for the dolls that were n't her own, if, as everybody said, she would take them if she could, she bravely bade them all good-by one morning, since folks were n't likely to "take" the things they did n't care for any longer. After that, Prue always looked the other way when she passed her favorite trysts, hoping that her dolls did n't mind it so much as she did.

But, one day, when she could bear her solitude no longer, she borrowed needle and thread of the cook and fashioned herself a rag-baby, stuffed it with sawdust and dressed it in her own clothes,—which fitted loosely, to be sure,—and cradled it in her own bed; and if it was not as handsome as Curlylocks, Prue's closet was too dark to reveal the truth. You know there are curious fishes that have no eyes, because they live in dark caves where eyes are useless; and perhaps for the same reason Prue's rag-baby was without them; but though it was blind and had only a few stitches in the place of a nose, yet it was a great comfort to Prue. It was something to love, something that never answered her ill-humoredly, that never looked at Prue but with a smile on its face,—or so Prue fancied. It was something upon which she could lavish her best; if Duster, the chambermaid, gave her a cast-off ribbon, she hastened to adorn her rag-baby with the treasure. A bunch of dead violets which had been thrown out of the window, Prue picked up and laid as a votive offering upon her baby's bosom. She sang it asleep before she closed her own eyes, and waked in the morning with the blissful consciousness of possession. When things crossed her downstairs, and the cook scolded and the housekeeper threatened, she would steal up to her rag-baby and be consoled. They held long talks together about what would happen when Prue grew up, and the places they would go to see,—only Prue did all the talking herself, and the baby listened. She was the best listener in the world, and that was just what Prue needed.

One day, Duster discovered the rag-baby, and had a good laugh over it behind Prue's back; and taking pity, she good-naturedly popped it into the rag-bag, and put in its place a first cousin of Curlylocks which she bought from her own savings. But when Prue waked next morning and found her child gone, not even the crockery eyes and flaxen tresses and rosebud mouth of Curlylocks' first-cousin could make up for the rag-baby's familiar and beloved ugliness; and Prue raised such a pitiful hue and cry that Duster was obliged to fish it out of the rag-bag.

"Whatever you can see in such a bundle of sawdust passes me," cried the provoked maid.

"Oh, Duster," answered Prue, hugging her darling, "it is *such* a comfort to have her again."

But Curlylocks' first-cousin was by no means to be despised. Prue could not help admiring her beauty. In fact the little lady smiled so sweetly and constantly upon Prue's best baby that soon Prue began to take a pride in her, and, as Duster often said, "it really did one's heart good to see the three together."

Chorus: "*Should old acquaintance be forgot?*"

The Lament of the Outgrown Doll

by *Julia Schayer*

I.

Oh, listen well
While a tale I tell
Of a poor, unfortunate dolly,
Who was born in France
And given by chance
To a sweet little girl named Polly.

II.

A wee little girl
With hair all a-curl,
And dimpled cheeks and
    shoulders;
When I and she
Took an airing, we
Were the joy of all beholders!

III.

Day after day,
As time passed away,
We'd nothing to do but keep
    jolly;
But it could not last,
For she grew so fast,
This dear little girl named
    Polly!

IV.

First she was seven,
Eight, nine, ten, eleven,
And then she was four
    times three!
She out-grew her crib,
Her apron and bib,
And now—she has out-
    grown Me!

V.

Forgotten, forlorn,
From night till morn
I'm left in the play-room corner;
From morn till night
In the same sad plight,
Like a pie-less Little Jack Horner!

VI.

And Polly, she
At school must be,
Or else the piano strumming,
While I sit here
Growing old and queer,
Vainly expecting her coming.

VII.

With a frozen stare
At the walls I glare,
My mind to the question giving;
If the life of a dolly
Out-grown by Polly
Be really worth the living!

Two Little Travelers

By Louisa May Alcott

The first of these true histories is about Annie Percival, a very dear and lovely child, whose journey interested many other children, and is still remembered with gratitude by those whom she visited on a far-off island.

Annie was six when she sailed away to Fayal with her mother, grandmamma, and "little Aunt Ruth," as she called the young aunty who was still a school-girl. Very cunning was Annie's outfit, and her little trunk was a pretty as well as a curious sight, for everything was so small and complete it looked as if a doll was setting off for Europe. Such a wee dressing-case, with bits of combs and brushes for the curly head; such a cozy scarlet wrapper for the small woman to wear in her berth, with slippers to match when she trotted from state-room to state-room; such piles of tiny garments laid nicely in, and the owner's initials on the outside of the trunk; not to mention the key on a ribbon in her pocket as grown-up as you please.

I think the sight of that earnest, sunshiny face must have been very pleasant to all on board, no matter how sea-sick they might be, and the sound of the cheery little voice as sweet as the chirp of a bird, especially when she sung the funny song about the "Owl and the pussy cat, in the pea-green boat," for she had charming ways, and was always making quaint, wise or loving remarks.

Well, "they sailed and they sailed," and came at last to Fayal, where everything was so new and strange that Annie's big brown eyes could hardly spare time to sleep, so busy were they looking about. The donkeys amused her very much, so did the queer language and ways of the Portuguese people round her, especially the very droll names given to the hens of a young friend. The biddies seemed to speak the same dialect as at home, but evidently they understood Spanish also, and knew their own names, so it was fun to go and call Rio, Pico, Cappy, Clarissa, Whorpie, and poor Simonene whose breast-bone grew out so that she could not eat and had to be killed.

But the thing which made the deepest impression on Annie was a visit to a charity school at the old convent of San Antonio. It was kept by some kind ladies, and twenty-five girls were taught and cared for in the big bare place, that looked rather gloomy and forlorn to people from happy Boston, where charitable institutions are on a noble scale, as everybody knows.

Annie watched all that went on with intelligent interest, and when they were shown into the play-room she was much amazed and afflicted to find that the children had nothing to play with but a heap of rags, out of which they made queer dolls with raveled twine for hair, faces rudely drawn on the cloth, and funny boots on the shapeless legs. No other toys appeared, but the girls sat on the floor of the great stone room,—for there was no furniture,—playing contentedly with their poor dolls, and smiling and nodding at "the little Americana," who gravely regarded this sad spectacle, wondering how they could get on without china and waxen babies, tea sets, and pretty chairs and tables to keep house with.

The girls thought that she envied them their dolls, and presently one came shyly up to offer two of their best, leaving the teacher to explain in English their wish to be polite to their distinguished guest. Like the little gentlewoman she was, Annie graciously accepted the ugly bits of rag with answering nods and smiles, and carried them away with her as carefully as if they were of great beauty and value.

But when she was at home she expressed much concern and distress at the destitute condition of the children. Nothing but rags to play with seemed a peculiarly touching state of poverty to her childish mind, and being a generous creature she yearned to give of her abundance to "all the poor orphans who did n't have any nice dollies." She had several pets of her own, but not enough to go round even if she sacrificed them, so kind grandmamma, who had been doing things of this sort all her life, relieved the child's perplexity by promising to send twenty-five fine dolls to Fayal as soon as the party returned to Boston, where these necessaries of child-life are cheap and plenty.

Thus comforted, Annie felt that she could enjoy her dear Horta and Chica Pico Fatiera, particular darlings rechristened since her arrival. A bundle of gay bits of silk, cloth, and flannel, and a present of money for books, were sent out to the convent by the ladies. A treat of little cheeses for the girls to eat with their dry bread was added, much to Annie's satisfaction, and helped to keep alive her interest in the school of San Antonio.

After many pleasant adventures during the six months spent in the city, our party came sailing home again all the better for the trip, and Annie so full of tales to tell that it was a never-failing source of amusement to hear her hold forth to her younger brother in her pretty way "splaining and 'scribing all about it."

Grandmamma's promise was faithfully kept, and Annie brooded blissfully over the twenty-five dolls till they were dressed, packed and sent away to Fayal. A letter of thanks soon came back from the teacher, telling how surprised and delighted the girls were, and how they talked of Annie as if she were a sort of fairy princess who in return for two poor rag-babies sent a miraculous shower of splendid china ladies with gay gowns and smiling faces.

This childish charity was made memorable to all who knew of it by the fact that three months after she came home from that happy voyage Annie took the one from which there is no return. For this journey there was needed no preparations but a little white gown, a coverlet of flowers, and the casket where the treasure of many hearts was tenderly laid away. All alone, but not afraid, little Annie crossed the unknown sea that rolls between our world and the Islands of the Blest, to be welcomed there, I am sure, by spirits as innocent as her own, leaving behind her a very precious memory of her budding virtues and the relics of a short, sweet life.

Every one mourned for her, and all her small treasures were so carefully kept that they still exist. Poor Horta, in the pincushion arm-chair, seems waiting patiently for the little mamma to come again; the two rag-dolls lie side by side in grandma's scrap-book, since there is now no happy voice to wake them into life; and far away in the convent of San Antonio the orphans carefully keep their pretty gifts in memory of the sweet giver. To them she is a saint now, not a fairy princess; for when they heard of her death they asked if they might pray for the soul of the dear little American, and the teacher said, "Pray rather for the poor mother who has lost so much." So the grateful orphans prayed and the mother was comforted, for now another little daughter lies in her arms and kisses away the lonely pain at her heart.

* * *

The second small traveler I want to tell about lived in the same city as the first, and her name was Maggie Woods. Her father was an Englishman who came to America to try his fortune, but did not find it; for when Maggie was three months old, the great Chicago fire destroyed their home; soon after, the mother died; then the father was drowned, and Maggie was left all alone in a strange country.

She had a good aunt in England, however, who took great pains to discover the child after the death of the parents, and sent for her to come home and be cared for. It was no easy matter to get a five-years' child across the Atlantic, for the aunt could not come to fetch her, and no one whom she knew was going over. But Maggie had found friends in Chicago; the American consul at Manchester was interested in the case, and every one was glad to help the forlorn baby, who was too young to understand the pathos of her story.

After letters had gone to and fro, it was decided to send to child the England in charge of the captain of a steamer, trusting to the kindness of all fellow-travelers to help her on her way.

The friends in Chicago bestirred themselves to get her ready, and then it was that Annie's mother found that she could do something which would have delighted her darling, had she been here to know of it. Laid tenderly away were many small garments belonging to the other little pilgrim, whose journeying was so soon ended; and from among all these precious things Mrs. Percival carefully chose a comfortable outfit for that cold March voyage.

When all was ready, Maggie's small effects were packed in a light basket, so that she could carry it herself if need be. A card briefly telling the story was fastened on the corner, and a similar paper recommending her to the protection of all kind people was sewed to the bosom of her frock. Then, not in the least realizing what lay before her, the child was consigned to the conductor of the train to be forwarded to persons in New York who would see her safely on board the steamer.

I should dearly like to have seen the little maid and the big basket as they set out on that long trip as tranquilly as if for a day's visit; and it is a comfort to know that before the train started the persons who took her there had interested a motherly lady in the young traveler, who promised to watch over her while their ways were the same.

All went well, and Maggie was safely delivered to the New York friends, who forwarded her to the steamer, well supplied with toys and comforts for the voyage, and placed in charge of captain and stewardess. She sailed on the third of March, and on the twelfth landed at Liverpool after a pleasant trip, during which she was the pet of all on board.

The aunt welcomed her joyfully, and the same day the child reached her new home, the Commercial Inn, Compstall, after a journey of over four thousand miles. The consul and owners of the steamer wanted to see the adventurous young lady who had come so far alone, and neighbors and strangers made quite a lion of her, for all kindly hearts were interested, and the protective charity which had guided and guarded her in two hemispheres and across the wide sea, made all men fathers, all women mothers to the little one till she was safe.

So ends the journey of my second small traveler, and when I think of her safe and happy in a good home, I always fancy that (if such things may be) in the land which is lovelier than even beautiful old England, Maggie's mother watches over little Annie.

Parasols

This morning in the wood I found
    A lot of lovely parasols—
Such darling red and yellow ones,
    And just the size to suit my dolls.

I gathered, oh! such heaps and heaps,
    And meant to take them home with me,
When Nursey came, and broke them all,
    And was as scared as scared could be!

She said that they would poison me,
    And they would make me very dead
If I should eat them, though they looked
    So very pretty—pink and red.

And now there is n't any left—
    Not even one for my best doll.
How very stupid Nursey is!—
    As if I 'd eat a parasol!

Unselfish Betty: "Well, Nursie, it's a comfort
that Dolly doesn't have to take it too!"

Jemima Brown

By Laura E. Richards

Bring her here, my little Alice—
  Poor Jemima Brown!
Make the little cradle ready,
  Softly lay her down.
Once she lived in ease and comfort,
  Slept on couch of down;
Now upon the floor she's lying—
  Poor Jemima Brown!

Once she was a lovely dolly,
  Rosy-cheeked and fair,
With her eyes of brightest azure,
  And her golden hair.
Now, alas! no hair's remaining
  On her poor old crown;
And the crown itself is broken—
  Poor Jemima Brown!

Once her legs were smooth and comely,
  And her nose was straight;
And that arm, now hanging lonely,
  Had, methinks, a mate.

Ah, she was as finely dressed as
  Any doll in town.
Now she's old, forlorn and ragged—
  Poor Jemima Brown!

Yet be kind to her, my Alice!
  'T is no fault of hers
If her willful little mistress
  Other dolls prefers.
Did she pull her pretty hair out?
  Did she break her crown?
Did she tear her arms and legs off?
  Poor Jemima Brown!

Little hands that did the mischief,
  You must do your best
Now to give the poor old dolly
  Comfortable rest.
So we'll make the cradle ready,
  And we'll lay her down;
And we'll ask papa to mend her—
  Poor Jemima Brown!

A Year with Dolly

By Eudora S. Bumstead

My darling Dolly is one week old;—
   Her forehead is fair and creamy,
Her cheeks are pink and her hair is gold,
   And her eyes are dark and dreamy.
She's lovely and sweet as she can be;
   She's Santa Claus' own little daughter,
But she came to me on the Christmas Tree:—
   How glad I am that he brought her!

I never am lonely since she came,
   And the only trouble with me is
That I haven't been able to find a name
   One half as pretty as she is.
Mama's in favor of "Isabel";
   And papa says "Betsy or Polly!"
And I've thought and thought and maybe—well,
   I guess I shall call her Dolly.

My Dolly went to ride in a sleigh,
    And I was the horse to draw her;
She tumbled out—I was running away—
    And O there was nobody saw her;
But I found her at last in a bank of snow,
    All so smiling and rosy,
Just as patient and good, you know,
    As if it were warm and cozy.

I took her in and put her to bed—
    I was sure she must be freezing;
I rubbed her feet and I rubbed her head
    For fear it would set her sneezing.
Now she will soon be well, no doubt,
    But I've made a resolution
To take more care when she goes out
    Of my Dolly's constitution.

I keep my Dolly so warm and nice
    This cloudy, stormy weather.
My Dolly and I are quiet as mice
    Whenever we play together.
And yet we have the pleasantest play—
    Would you like to ask "What is it?"
Why, over and over, every day,
    My Dolly and I "go visit.

Sometimes on "Towser" we like to call,
    Or travel to see the Kitty;
'Tis Grandpa's farm just out in the hall,
    And the parlor is Boston City;
'Tis mama's house in the corner there,
    And then, when the lamps are lighted,
My papa's at home in his easy chair,
    And Dolly and I are invited.

April

Taurus

We went for a promenade today,
    My Dolly and I together;
The sun came out and, I'm sorry to say,
    We were April-fooled by the weather;
For while we walked to the end of the lane
    The clouds were quietly slipping
Over the sky, and they poured the rain
    Until we were cold and dripping.

Mama was ready to change my clothes
    And set poor Dolly a-drying;
But the drops ran down her cheeks and nose
    Till it seemed as if she were crying;
And her feet were wet, and her hair was down
    And blown in every direction;
And it nearly ruined her nicest gown
    nd her delicate wax complexion.

Under the trees, in the loveliest place,
    Where the shadow and sun were playing,
Fanny and Lida and Lottie and Grace
    And Dolly and I went maying;
But the flowers were lost or hidden away
    So safe we could scarce find any—
So we made the Dolly Queen of the May
  ' Cause she wouldn't need so many.

We gathered moss for a throne of green,
    And with violets blue we crowned her;
We played that she was a Fairy Queen,
    And gaily we danced around her.
A robin sang to us overhead,
    A squirrel capered and chattered;—
Then a little gray mouse popped out of his bed,
    And O how we jumped and scattered!

The air was warm and the clouds were few,
　　The birds were chirping and hopping;
And everything was pretty and new
　　When Dolly and I went shopping.
Our money-bank was yellow and sweet
　　With its dandelion dollars,
So we hurried away to Garden Street
　　To look for some cuffs and collars.

For a cap I bought her a great red rose,
　　I'm certain it gave her pleasure
And for lady-slippers to fit her toes
　　I was careful to leave her measure;
And I told the spiders to spin some lace
　　As strong as other folks make it,
And to sew the beads of dew in place,
　　And then we'd be glad to take it.

July

LEO

My Dolly went to the Fourth of July—
    I never should have allowed her—
We both were careless, Dolly and I,
    And come too close to the powder.
I don't know how it happened, myself—
    'Twas something about the fuses—
But Dolly and I were laid on the shelf
    With blisters and bumps and bruises.

I wasn't hurt very much, you know,
    Tho' mama declared it shocked her;
My troubles were cured, long, long ago
    Without once calling the doctor.
But Dolly will never again be fair
    Where the horrid powder shot her,
And it frizzled and singed her golden hair
    Till she's balder than Uncle Potter.

We slipped thro' the gate this afternoon
  When Bridget forgot to latch it;
A cricket fiddled a queer little tune,
  And we hurried along to catch it.
I wish we'd stayed in the yard and played,
  For we've wandered and turned and crossed
Up and down all over the town,
  Till Dolly is 'fraid we're lost.

I wish I'd minded mama just right,
  And thought of her smiles and kisses,
For if we were forced to spend the night
  In any such place as this is,
My Dolly would die—and so should I—
  But the only plan I see
Is just to stay till they come this way
  And find my Dolly and me.

September

LIBRA

My Dolly has been so quiet and sad
   That nothing appeared to rouse her;
So I thought perhaps it would make her glad
   To give her a ride on Towser.
I pushed him off the step in the sun—
   He looked so lazy and idle—
For a saddle I fastened my apron on,
   And my ribbon sash for a bridle.

Then Dolly sat on his back to ride,
   And he neither growled nor grumbled;
I held her hand and walked by her side
   Till I suddenly tripped and tumbled!
Poor Dolly fell with a dreadful crash—
   For of course I couldn't hold her—
One arm and one leg went all to smash,
   And a great crack came in her shoulder.

The sky is blue and the weather is fair,
   But Dolly is sick and ailing;
In spite of all my trouble and care,
   I can see that her health is failing.
The weather is fair and the sky is blue,
   And there's naught to trouble or fret her,
But, spite of all I can say and do,
   She's worse in the place of better.

SCORPIO

I've given her baths both hot and cold,
   I've regulated her diet,
And every remedy, new or old,
   I've hastened at once to try it.
So many errands for her I've run;
   I've tended and trotted and rocked her;
If she does not improve with all I've done,
   I really must send for the Doctor.

The Doctor came, and he said 'twas plain
   That Dolly's trouble was chronic;
And he thought a ride on a rail-road train
   Would suit her best for a tonic.
So I wrapped her up with the greatest care
   And put on her Sunday bonnet;
And the engine, that was the rocking-chair
   With Engineer Harry upon it.

I gave my Dolly all she would need
   And propped her up with a pillow;
She was flying along at lightning speed
   In her palace car of willow;
But all at once she fell on the track;—
   O! 'twas a dreadful ending!
The engine rocker went over her back,
   And I'm 'fraid she's past all mending.

December

CAPRICORNVS

♑

Doctor Mama knows what to do
  When girls and dollies are troubled;
With needle and thread and a bottle of glue
  My Dolly's strength she has doubled.
But she never can make her new and bright;
  I'm almost ashamed to show her.—
If Santa Claus could see her to-night
  I don't suppose he would know her.

Mama has said if I learn to be
  A careful, kind little mother,
He surely will notice the change in me,
  And *maybe* he'll bring me another;
But, dear little Dolly, you need not care
  Nor be jealous one bit if I get her,
For tho' you may never be quite so fair,
  I'll only love you the better.

Racketty-Packetty House

As told by Queen Crosspatch

By Frances Hodgson Burnett

Now this is the story about the doll family I liked and the doll family I didn't. When you read it you are to remember something I am going to tell you. This is it: If you think dolls never do anything you don't see them do, you are very much mistaken. When people are not looking at them they can do anything they choose. They can dance and sing and play on the piano and have all sorts of fun. But they can only move about and talk when people turn their backs and are not looking. If anyone looks, they just stop. Fairies know this and of course Fairies visit in all the dolls' houses where the dolls are agreeable. They will not associate, though, with dolls who are not nice. They never call or leave their cards at a dolls' house where the dolls are proud or bad tempered. They are very particular. If you are conceited or ill-tempered yourself, you will never know a fairy as long as you live.

QUEEN CROSSPATCH

Racketty-Packetty House was in a corner of Cynthia's nursery. And it was not in the best corner either. It was in the corner behind the door, and that was not at all a fashionable neighborhood. Racketty-Packetty House had been pushed there to be out of the way when Tidy Castle was brought in, on Cynthia's birthday. As soon as she saw Tidy Castle, Cynthia did not care for Racketty-Packetty House and indeed was quite ashamed of it. She thought the corner behind the door quite good enough for such a shabby old dolls' house, when there was the beautiful big new one built like a castle and furnished with the most elegant chairs and tables and carpets and curtains and ornaments and pictures and beds and baths and lamps and book-cases, and with a knocker on the front door, and a stable with a pony cart in it at the back. The minute she saw it she called out:

"Oh! What a beautiful doll castle! What shall we do with that untidy old Racketty-Packetty House now? It is too shabby and old-fashioned to stand near it."

In fact, that was the way in which the old dolls' house got its name. It had always been called, "The Dolls' House," before, but after that it was pushed into the unfashionable neighborhood behind the door and ever afterwards—when it was spoken of at all—it was just called Racketty-Packetty House, and nothing else.

Of course Tidy Castle was grand, and Tidy Castle was new and had all the modern improvements in it, and Racketty-Packetty House was as old-fashioned as it could be. It had belonged to Cynthia's Grandmamma and had been made in the days when Queen Victoria was a little girl, and when there were no electric lights even in Princesses' dolls' houses. Cynthia's Grandmamma had kept it very neat because she had been a good housekeeper even when she was seven years old. But Cynthia was not a good housekeeper and she did not re-cover the furniture when it got dingy, or re-paper the walls, or mend the carpets and bedclothes, and she never thought of such a thing as making new clothes for the doll family, so that of course their early Victorian frocks and capes and bonnets grew in time to be too shabby for words. You see, when Queen Victoria was a little girl, dolls wore queer frocks and long pantalets and boy dolls wore funny frilled trousers and coats which it would almost make you laugh to look at.

But the Racketty-Packetty House family had known better days. I and my Fairies had known them when they were quite new and had been a birthday present just as Tidy Castle was when Cynthia turned eight years old, and there was as much fuss about them when their house arrived as Cynthia made when she saw Tidy Castle.

Cynthia's Grandmamma had danced about and

clapped her hands with delight, and she had scrambled down upon her knees and taken the dolls out one by one and thought their clothes beautiful. And she had given each one of them a grand name.

"This one shall be Amelia." she said. "And this one is Charlotte, and this is Victoria Leopoldina, and this one Aurelia Matilda, and this one Leontine, and this one Clotilda, and these boys shall be Augustus and Rowland and Vincent and Charles Edward Stuart."

For a long time they led a very gay and fashionable life. They had parties and balls and were presented at Court and went to Royal Christenings and Weddings and were married themselves and had families and scarlet fever and whooping cough and funerals and every luxury. But that was long, long ago, and now all was changed. Their house had grown shabbier and shabbier, and their clothes had grown simply awful; and Aurelia Matilda and Victoria Leopoldina had been broken to bits and thrown into the dustbin, and Leontine—who had really been the beauty of the family—had been dragged out on the hearth rug one night and had had nearly all her paint licked off and a leg chewed up by a Newfoundland puppy, so that she was a sight to behold. As for the boys, Rowland and Vincent had quite disappeared, and Charlotte and Amelia always believed they had run away to seek their fortunes, because things were in such a state at home. So the only ones who were left were

Market-Day at Racketty-Packetty House

Clotilda and Amelia and Charlotte and poor Leontine and Augustus and Charles Edward Stuart. Even they had their names changed.

After Leontine had had her paint licked off so that her head had white bald spots on it and she had scarcely any features, a boy cousin of Cynthia's had put a bright red spot on each cheek and painted her a turned-up nose and round saucer blue eyes and a comical mouth. He and Cynthia had called her "Ridiklis" instead of Leontine, and she had been called that ever since. All the dolls were jointed Dutch dolls, so it was easy to paint any kind of features on them and stick out their arms and legs in any way you liked, and Leontine did look funny after Cynthia's cousin had finished. She certainly was not a beauty but her turned-up nose and her round eyes and funny mouth always seemed to be laughing so she really was the most good-natured-looking creature you ever saw.

Charlotte and Amelia, Cynthia had called Meg and Peg, and Clotilda she called Kilmanskeg, and Augustus she called Gustibus, and Charles Edward Stuart was nothing but Peter Piper. So that was the end of their grand names.

The truth was, they went through all sorts of things, and if they had not been such a jolly lot of dolls they might have had fits and appendicitis and died of grief. But not a bit of it. If you will believe it, they got fun out of everything. They used to just scream with laughter over the new names, and they laughed so much over them that they got quite fond of them. When Meg's pink silk flounces were torn she pinned them up and didn't mind in the least, and when Peg's lace mantilla was played with by a kitten and brought back to her in rags and tags, she just put a few stitches in it and put it on again; and when Peter Piper lost almost the whole leg of one of his trousers he just laughed and said it made it easier for him to kick about and turn somersaults and he wished the other leg would tear off too.

You never saw a family have such fun. They could make up stories and pretend things and invent games out of nothing. And my Fairies were so fond of them that I couldn't keep them away from the dolls' house. They would go and have fun with Meg and Peg and Kilmanskeg and Gustibus and Peter Piper, even when I had work for them to do in Fairyland. But there, I was so fond of that shabby, disrespectable family myself that I never would scold much about them, and I often went to see them. That is how I know so much about them. They were so fond of each other and so good-natured and

Leontine (who was afterward called "Ridiklis")

always in such spirits that everybody who knew them was fond of them. They were so fond of each other and so good-natured and always in such spirits that everybody who knew them was fond of them. And it was really only Cynthia who didn't know them and thought them only a lot of old disreputable-looking Dutch dolls—and Dutch dolls were quite out of fashion. The truth was that Cynthia was not a particularly nice little girl, and did not care much for anything unless it was quite new. But the kitten who had torn the lace mantilla got to know the family and simply loved them all, and the Newfoundland puppy was so sorry about Leontine's paint and her left leg, that he could never do enough to make up. He wanted to marry Leontine as soon as he grew old enough to wear a collar, but Leontine said she would never desert her family; because now that she wasn't the beauty any more she became the useful one, and did all the kitchen work, and sat up and made poultices and beef tea when any of the rest were ill. And the Newfoundland puppy saw she was right, for the whole family simply adored Ridiklis and could not possibly have done without her. Meg and Peg and Kilmanskeg could have married any minute if they had liked. There were two cock sparrows and a gentleman mouse, who proposed to them over and over again. They all three said they did not want fashionable wives but cheerful dispositions and a happy home. But Meg and Peg were like Ridiklis and could not bear to

leave their families—besides not wanting to live in nests, and hatch eggs—and Kilmanskeg said she would die of a broken heart if she could not be with Ridiklis, and Ridiklis did not like cheese and crumbs and mousy things, so they could never live together in a mouse hole. But neither the gentleman mouse nor the sparrows were offended because the news was broken to them so sweetly and they went on visiting just as before. Everything was as shabby and disrespectable and as gay and happy as it could be until Tidy Castle was brought into the nursery and then the whole family had rather a fright.

It happened in this way:

When the dolls' house was lifted by the nurse and carried into the corner behind the door, of course it was rather an exciting and shaky thing for Meg and Peg and Kilmanskeg and Gustibus and Peter Piper (Ridiklis was out shopping). The furniture tumbled about and everybody had to hold on to anything they could catch hold of. As it was, Kilmanskeg slid under a table and Peter Piper sat down in the coal-box, but notwithstanding all this, they did not lose their tempers and when the nurse sat their house down on the floor with a bump, they all got up and began to laugh. Then they ran and peeped out of the windows and then they ran back and laughed again.

"Well," said Peter Piper, "we have been called Meg and Peg and Kilmanskeg and Gustibus and Peter

"She did all the kitchen work."

Piper instead of our grand names, and now we live in a place called Racketty-Packetty House. Who cares! Let's join hands and have a dance."

And they joined hands and danced round and round and kicked up their heels, and their rags and tatters flew about and they laughed until they fell down, one on top of the other.

It was just at this minute that Ridiklis came back. The nurse had found her under a chair and stuck her in through a window. She sat on the drawing-room sofa which had holes in its covering and the stuffing coming out, and her one whole leg stuck out straight in front of her, and her bonnet and shawl were on one side and her basket was on her left arm full of things she had got cheap at market. She was out of breath and rather pale through being lifted up and swished through the air so suddenly, but her saucer eyes and her funny mouth looked as cheerful as ever.

"Good gracious, if you knew what I have just heard!" she said. They all scrambled up and called out together.

"Hello! What is it?"

"The nurse said the most awful thing," she answered them. "When Cynthia asked what she should do with this old Racketty-Packetty House, she said, 'Oh! I'll put it behind the door for the present and then it shall be carried down-stairs and burned. It's too disgraceful to be kept in any decent nursery.' "

"Oh!" cried out Peter Piper.

"Oh!" said Gustibus.

"Oh! Oh! Oh!" said Meg and Peg and Kilmanskeg. "Will they burn our dear old shabby house? Do you think they will?" And actually tears began to run down their cheeks.

Peter Piper sat down on the floor all at once with his hands stuffed in his pockets.

"I don't care how shabby it is," he said. "It's a jolly nice old place and it's the only house we've ever had."

"I never want to have any other," said Meg. "They shan't burn our dear old house."

Gustibus leaned against the wall with his hands stuffed in his pockets.

"I wouldn't move if I was made King of England," he said. "Buckingham Palace wouldn't be half as nice."

"We've had such fun here," said Peg. And Kilmanskeg shook her head from side to side and wiped her eyes on her ragged pocket handkerchief. There is no knowing what would have happened to

"They did not want fashionable wives, but cheerful dispositions and happy homes."

them if Peter Piper hadn't cheered up as he always did.

"I say," he said, "do you hear that noise?" They all listened and heard a rumbling. Peter Piper ran to the window and looked out and then ran back grinning.

"It's the nurse rolling up the arm-chair before the house to hide it, so that it won't disgrace the castle. Hooray! Hooray! If they don't see us they will forget all about us and we shall not be burned up at all. Our nice old Racketty-Packetty House will be left alone and we can enjoy ourselves more than ever—because we shan't be bothered with Cynthia—Hello! Let's all join hands and have a dance."

So they all joined hands and danced round in a ring again and they were all so relieved that they laughed and laughed until they all tumbled down in a heap just as they had done before, and rolled about giggling and squealing. It certainly seemed as if they were quite safe for some time at least. The big easy chair hid them and both the nurse and Cynthia seemed to forget that there was such a thing as a Racketty-Packetty House in the neighborhood. Cynthia was so delighted with Tidy Castle that she played with nothing else for days and days. And instead of being jealous of their grand neighbors the Racketty-Packetty House people began to get all sorts of fun out of watching them from their own windows. Several of their windows were broken and some had rags and paper stuffed into the broken panes, but Meg and Peg and Peter Piper would go and peep out of one, and Gustibus and Kilmanskeg would peep out of another, and Ridiklis could scarcely get her dishes washed and her potatoes pared because she could see the castle kitchen from her scullery window. It was *so* exciting!

The Castle dolls were grand beyond words, and they were all lords and ladies. These were their names. There was Lady Gwendolen Vere de Vere. She was haughty and had dark eyes and hair and carried her head thrown back and her nose in the air. There was Lady Muriel Vere de Vere, and she was cold and lovely and indifferent and looked down the bridge of her delicate nose. And there was Lady Doris, who had fluffy golden hair and laughed mockingly at everybody. And there was Lord Hubert and Lord Rupert and Lord Francis, who were all handsome enough to make you feel as if you could faint. And there was their mother, the Duchess of Tidyshire; and of course there were all sorts of maids and footmen and cooks and scullery maids and even gardeners.

"We never thought of living to see such grand society," said Peter Piper to his brother and sisters. "It's quite a kind of blessing."

"It's almost like being grand ourselves, just to be able to watch them," said Meg and Peg and Kilmanskeg, squeezing together and flattening their noses against the attic windows.

They could see bits of the sumptuous white and gold drawing-room with the Duchess sitting reading near the fire, her golden glasses upon her nose, and Lady Gwendolen playing haughtily upon the harp, and Lady Muriel coldly listening to her. Lady Doris was having her golden hair dressed by her maid in her bedroom and Lord Hubert was reading the newspaper with a high-bred air, while Lord Francis was writing letters to noblemen of his acquaintance, and Lord Rupert was—in an aristocratic manner—glancing over his love letters from ladies of title.

Kilmanskeg and Peter Piper just pinched each other with glee and squealed with delight.

"Isn't it fun," said Peter Piper. "I say; aren't they awful swells! But Lord Francis can't kick about in his trousers as I can in mine, and neither can the others. I'd like to see them try to do this,"—and he turned three somersaults in the middle of the room and stood on his head on the biggest hole in the carpet—and wiggled his legs and twiggled his toes at them until they shouted so with laughing that Ridiklis ran in with a saucepan in her hand and perspiration on her forehead, because she was cooking turnips, which was all they had for dinner.

"You mustn't laugh so loud," she cried out. "If we make so much noise the Tidy Castle people will begin to complain of this being a low neighborhood and they might insist on moving away."

"Oh! scrump!" said Peter Piper, who sometimes invented doll slang—though there wasn't really a bit of harm in him. "I wouldn't have them move away for anything. They are meat and drink to me."

"They are going to have a dinner of ten courses," sighed Ridiklis, "I can see them cooking it from my scullery window. And I have nothing but turnips to give you."

"Who cares!" said Peter Piper, "Let's have ten courses of turnips and pretend each course is exactly like the one they are having at the Castle."

"I like turnips almost better than anything—almost—perhaps not quite," said Gustibus. "I can eat ten courses of turnips like a shot."

"Let's go and find out what their courses are," said Meg and Peg and Kilmanskeg, "and then we will write a menu on a piece of pink tissue paper."

And if you'll believe it, that was what they did. They divided their turnips into ten courses and they called the first one "Hors d'oeuvres," and the last one "Ices," with a French name, and Peter Piper

"Two cock sparrows and
a gentleman mouse proposed to them."

kept jumping up from the table and pretending he was a footman and flourishing about in his flapping rags of trousers and announcing the names of the dishes in such a grand way that they laughed till they nearly died, and said they never had had such a splendid dinner in their lives, and that they would rather live behind the door and watch the Tidy Castle people than be the Tidy Castle people themselves.

And then of course they all joined hands and danced round and round and kicked up their heels for joy, because they always did that whenever there was the least excuse for it—and quite often when there wasn't any at all, just because it was such good exercise and worked off their high spirits so that they could settle down for a while.

This was the way things went on day after day. They almost lived at their windows. They watched the Tidy Castle family get up and be dressed by their maids and valets in different clothes almost every day. They saw them drive out in their carriages, and have parties, and go to balls. They all nearly had brain fever with delight the day they watched Lady Gwendolen and Lady Muriel and Lady Doris, dressed in their Court trains and feathers, going to be presented at the first Drawing-Room.

After the lovely creatures had gone the whole family sat down in a circle round the Racketty-Packetty House library fire, and Ridiklis read aloud to them about Drawing-Rooms, out of a scrap of the Lady's Pictorial she had found, and after that they had a Court Drawing-Room of their own, and they made tissue paper trains and glass bead crowns for diamond tiaras, and sometimes Gustibus pretended to be the Royal family, and the others were presented to him and kissed his hand, and then the others took turns and he was presented. And suddenly the most delightful thing occurred to Peter Piper. He thought it would be rather nice to make them all into lords and ladies and he did it by touching them on the shoulder with the drawing-room poker which he straightened because it was so crooked that it was almost bent double. It is not exactly the way such things are done at Court, but Peter Piper thought it would do—and at any rate it was great fun. So he made them all kneel down in a row and he touched each on the shoulder with the poker and said:

"Rise up, Lady Meg and Lady Peg and Lady Kilmanskeg and Lady Ridiklis of Racketty-Packetty House—and also the Right Honorable Lord

"Peter Piper kept jumping up from the table pretending he was a footman."

Gustibus Rags!" And they all jumped up at once and made bows and curtsied to each other. But they made Peter Piper into a Duke, and he was called the Duke of Tags. He knelt down on the big hole in the carpet and each one of them gave him a little thump on the shoulder with the poker, because it took more thumps to make a Duke than a common or garden Lord.

The day after this another much more exciting thing took place. The nurse was in a bad temper and when she was tidying the nursery she pushed the easy chair aside and saw Racketty-Packetty House.

"Oh!" she said, "there is that Racketty-Packetty old thing still. I had forgotten it. It must be carried downstairs and burned. I will go and tell one of the footmen to come for it."

Meg and Peg and Kilmanskeg were in their attic and they all rushed out in such a hurry to get downstairs that they rolled all the way down the staircase, and Peter Piper and Gustibus had to dart out of the drawing-room and pick them up, Ridiklis came staggering up from the kitchen quite out of breath.

"Oh! Our house is going to be burned! Our house is going to be burned!" cried Meg and Peg clutching their brothers.

"Let us go and throw ourselves out of the window!" cried Kilmanskeg.

"I don't see how they can have the heart to burn a person's home!" said Ridiklis, wiping her eyes with her kitchen duster.

Peter Piper was rather pale, but he was extremely brave and remembered that he was the head of the family.

"Now, Lady Meg and Lady Peg and Lady Kilmanskeg," he said, "let us all keep cool."

"We shan't keep cool when they set our house on fire," said Gustibus. Peter Piper just snapped his fingers.

"Pooh!" he said. "We are only made of wood and it won't hurt a bit. We shall just snap and crack and go off almost like fireworks and then we shall be ashes and fly away into the air and see all sorts of things. Perhaps it may be more fun than anything we have done since we were given to Cynthia's grandmother."

"But our nice old house! Our nice old Racketty-Packetty House," said Ridiklis. "I do so love it. The kitchen is so convenient—even though the oven won't bake any more."

And things looked most serious because the Nurse really was beginning to push the armchair away. But it would not move and I will tell you why. One of my Fairies, who had come down the chimney when they were talking, had called me and I had come in a second with a whole army of my Workers, and though the Nurse couldn't see them, they were all holding the chair tight down on the carpet so that it would not stir.

And I—Queen Crosspatch—myself—flew downstairs and made the footman remember that minute that a box had come for Cynthia and that he must take it upstairs to her nursery. If I had not been on the spot he would have forgotten it until it was too late. But just in the very nick of time up he came, and Cynthia sprang up as soon as she saw him.

"Oh!" she cried out, "it must be the doll who broke her little leg and was sent to the hospital. It must be Lady Patsy!"

And she opened the box which the footman gave her, and gave a little scream of joy, for there lay Lady Patsy (her whole name was Patricia) in a lace-frilled night-gown, with her lovely leg in bandages, and a pair of tiny crutches and a trained nurse by her side

That was how I saved them that time. There was such excitement over Lady Patsy and her little crutches and her nurse that nothing else was thought of and my Fairies pushed the arm-chair back and Racketty-Packetty House was hidden and forgotten once more.

"And I—Queen Crosspatch—myself—flew downstairs and made the footman remember."

The whole Racketty-Packetty family gave a great gasp of joy and sat down in a ring all at once, on the floor, mopping their foreheads with anything they could get hold of. Peter Piper used an antimacassar.

"Oh! we are obliged to you, Queen B-bell-Patch," he panted out, "But these alarms of fire are upsetting."

"You leave them to me," I said, "and I'll attend to them. Tip!" I commanded the Fairy nearest me. "You will have to stay about here and be ready to give the alarm when anything threatens to happen." And I flew away, feeling I had done a good morning's work. Well, that was the beginning of a great many things and many of them were connected with Lady Patsy; and but for me there might have been unpleasantness.

Of course the Racketty-Packetty dolls forgot about their fright directly, and began to enjoy themselves again as usual. That was their way. They never sat up all night with Trouble, Peter Piper used to say. And I told him they were quite right. If you make a fuss over trouble and put it to bed and nurse it and give it beef tea and gruel, you can never get rid of it.

Their great delight now was Lady Patsy. They thought she was prettier than any of the other Tidy Castle dolls. She neither turned her nose up, nor looked down the bridge of it, nor laughed mockingly. She had dimples in the corners of her mouth and long curly lashes and her nose was saucy and her eyes were bright and full of laughs.

"She's the clever one of the family," said Peter Piper. "I am sure of that."

She was treated as an invalid at first, of course,

and kept in her room; but they could see her sitting up in her frilled nightgown. After a few days she was carried to a soft chair by the window and there she used to sit and look out; and the Racketty-Packetty House dolls crowded round their window and adored her.

After a few days, they noticed that Peter Piper was often missing and one morning Ridiklis went up into the attic and found him sitting at a window all by himself and staring and staring.

"Oh! Duke," she said (you see they always tried to remember each others' titles). "Dear me, Duke, what are you doing here?"

"I am looking at her," he answered. "I'm in love. I fell in love with her the minute Cynthia took her out of her box. I am going to marry her."

"But she's a lady of high degree," said Ridiklis, quite alarmed.

"That's why she'll have me," said Peter Piper in his most cheerful manner. "Ladies of high degree always marry the good-looking ones in rags and tatters. If I had a whole suit of clothes on, she wouldn't look at me. I'm very good-looking, you know,"

The courtyard of Tidy Castle

and he turned round and winked at Ridiklis in such a delightful saucy way that she suddenly felt as if he *was* very good-looking, though she had not thought of it before.

"Hello," he said all at once. "I've just thought of something to attract her attention. Where's the ball of string?"

Cynthia's kitten had made them a present of a ball of string which had been most useful. Ridiklis ran and got it, and all the others came running upstairs to see what Peter Piper was going to do. They all were delighted to hear he had fallen in love with the lovely, funny Lady Patsy. They found him standing in the middle of the attic unrolling the ball of string.

"What are you going to do, Duke?" they all shouted.

"Just you watch," he said, and he began to make the string into a rope ladder—as fast as lightning. When he had finished it, he fastened one end of it to a beam and swung the other end out of the window.

"From her window," Peter Piper said, "Lady Patsy can see Racketty-Packetty House and I'll tell you something. She's always looking at it. She watches us as much as we watch her, and I have seen her giggling and giggling when we were having fun. Yesterday when I chased Lady Meg and Lady Peg and Lady Kilmanskeg round and round the front of the house and turned somersaults every five steps, she laughed until she had to stuff her handkerchief into her mouth. When we joined hands and danced and laughed until we fell in heaps I thought she was going to have a kind of rosy-dimpled, lovely little fit, she giggled so. If I run down the side of the house on this rope ladder it will attract her attention and then I shall begin to do things."

He ran down the ladder and that very minute they saw Lady Patsy at her window give a start and leap forward to look. They all crowded round their window and chuckled and chuckled as they watched him.

He turned three stately somersaults and stood on his feet and made a cheerful bow. The Racketty-Packettys saw Lady Patsy begin to giggle that minute. Then he took an antimacassar out of his pocket and fastened it round the edge of his torn trousers leg, as if it were lace trimming, and began to walk about like a Duke—with his arms folded on his chest and his ragged old hat cocked on one side over his ear. Then the Racketty-Packettys saw Lady Patsy begin to laugh. Then Peter Piper stood on his head and kissed his hand and Lady Patsy covered her face and rocked backwards and forwards in her chair laughing and laughing.

"They made Peter Piper the Duke of Tags."

Then he struck an attitude with his tattered leg put forward gracefully and he pretended he had a guitar and he sang—right up at her window.

From Racketty-Packetty House I come,
It stands, dear Lady, in a slum,
A low, low slum behind the door
The stout arm-chair is placed before,
(Just take a look at it, my Lady).

The house itself is a perfect sight,
And everybody's dressed like a perfect fright,
But no one cares a single jot
And each one giggles over his lot,
(And as for me, I'm in love with you).

I can't make up another verse,
And if I did it would be worse,
But I could stand and sing all day,
If I could think of things to say,
(But the fact is I just wanted to make you
look at me).

And then he danced such a lively jig that his rags and tags flew about him, and then he made another bow and kissed his hand again and ran up the ladder like a flash and jumped into the attic.

After that Lady Patsy sat at her window all the time and would not let the trained nurse put her to bed at all; and Lady Gwendolen and Lady Muriel and Lady Doris could not understand it. Once Lady Gwendolen said haughtily and disdainfully and scornfully and scathingly:

"If you sit there so much, those low Racketty-Packetty House people will think you are looking at them."

"I am," said Lady Patsy, showing all her dimples at once. "They are such fun!"

And Lady Gwendolen swooned haughtily away, and the trained nurse could scarcely restore her.

When the castle dolls drove out or walked in their garden, the instant they caught sight of one of the Racketty-Packettys they turned up their noses and sniffed aloud, and several times the Duchess said she would remove because the neighborhood was absolutely low. They all scorned the Racketty-Packettys—they just *scorned* them.

One moonlight night Lady Patsy was sitting at her window and she heard a whistle in the garden. When she peeped out carefully, there stood Peter Piper waving his ragged cap at her, and he had his rope ladder under his arm.

"Hello," he whispered as loud as he could. "Could you catch a bit of rope if I threw it up to you?"

"Yes," she whispered back.

"Then catch this," he whispered again and he threw up the end of a string and she caught it the first throw. It was fastened to the rope ladder.

"Now pull," he said.

She pulled and pulled until the rope ladder reached her window and then she fastened that to a hook under the sill and the first thing that happened—just like lightning—was that Peter Piper ran up the ladder and leaned over her window ledge.

"Will you marry me?" he said. "I haven't anything to give you to eat and I am as ragged as a scarecrow, but will you?"

She clapped her little hands.

"I eat very little," she said. "And I would do without anything at all, if I could live in your funny old shabby house."

"It is a ridiculous, tumble-down old barn, isn't it?" he said. "But every one of us is as nice as we can be. We are perfect Turkish Delights. It's laughing that does it. Would you like to come down the ladder and see what a jolly, shabby old hole the place is?"

"Oh! do take me," said Lady Patsy.

So he helped her down the ladder and took her under the arm-chair and into Racketty-Packetty House and Meg and Peg and Kilmanskeg and

"Peter Piper ran
up the ladder"

Ridiklis and Gustibus all crowded round her and gave little screams of joy at the sight of her.

They were afraid to kiss her at first, even though she was engaged to Peter Piper. She was so pretty and her frock had so much lace on it that they were afraid their old rags might spoil her. But she did not care about her lace and flew at them and kissed and hugged them every one.

"I have so wanted to come here," she said. "It's so dull at the Castle I had to break my leg just to get a change. The Duchess sits reading near the fire with her gold eye-glasses on her nose and Lady Gwendolen plays haughtily on the harp and Lady Muriel coldly listens to her, and Lady Doris is always laughing mockingly, and Lord Hubert reads the newspaper with a high-bred air, and Lord Francis writes letters to noblemen of his acquaintance, and Lord Rupert glances over his love letters from ladies of title, in an aristocratic manner—until I could *scream*. Just to see you dears dancing about in your rags and tags and laughing and inventing games as if you didn't mind anything, is such a relief."

She nearly laughed her little curly head off when they all went round the house with her, and Peter Piper showed her the holes in the carpet and the stuffing coming out of the sofas, and the feathers

out of the beds, and the legs tumbling off the chairs. She had never seen anything like it before.

"At the Castle, nothing is funny at all," she said. "And nothing ever sticks out or hangs down or tumbles off. It is so plain and new."

"But I think we ought to tell her, Duke," Ridiklis said. "We may have our house burned over our heads any day." She really stopped laughing for a whole minute when she heard that, but she was rather like Peter Piper in disposition and she said almost immediately:

"Oh! they'll never do it. They've forgotten you." And Peter Piper said:

"Don't let's think of it. Let's all join hands and dance round and round and kick up our heels and laugh as hard as ever we can."

And they did—and Lady Patsy laughed harder than any one else. After that she was always stealing away from Tidy Castle and coming in and having fun. Sometimes she stayed all night and slept with Meg and Peg and everybody invented new games and stories and they really never went to bed until daylight. But the Castle dolls grew more and more scornful every day, and tossed their heads higher and higher and sniffed louder and louder until it sounded as if they all had influenza. They never lost an opportunity of saying disdainful things and once the Duchess wrote a letter to Cynthia, saying that

"The Duchess sits reading near the fire"

she insisted on removing to a decent neighborhood. She laid the letter in her desk but the gentleman mouse came in the night and carried it away. So Cynthia never saw it and I don't believe she could have read it if she had seen it because the Duchess wrote very badly—even for a doll.

And then what do you suppose happened? One morning Cynthia began to play that all the Tidy Castle dolls had scarlet fever. She said it had broken out in the night and she undressed them all and put them into bed and gave them medicine. She could not find Lady Patsy, so *she* escaped the contagion. The truth was that Lady Patsy had stayed all night at Racketty-Packetty House, where they were giving an imitation Court Ball with Peter Piper in a tin crown, and shavings for supper—because they had nothing else, and in fact the gentleman mouse had brought the shavings from his nest as a present.

Cynthia played nearly all day and the Duchess and Lady Gwendolen and Lady Muriel and Lady Doris and Lord Hubert and Lord Francis and Lord Rupert got worse and worse.

By evening they were all raging in delirium and Lord Francis and Lady Gwendolen had strong mustard plasters on their chests. And right in the middle of their agony Cynthia suddenly got up and went away and left them to their fate—just as if it didn't matter in the least. Well in the middle of the night Meg and Peg and Lady Patsy wakened all at once.

"Do you hear a noise?" said Meg, lifting her head from her ragged old pillow.

"Yes, I do," said Peg, sitting up and holding her ragged old blanket up to her chin.

Lady Patsy jumped up with feathers sticking up all over her hair, because they had come out of the holes in the ragged old bed. She ran to the window and listened.

"Oh! Meg and Peg!" she cried out. "It comes from the Castle. Cynthia has left them all raving in delirium and they are all shouting and groaning and screaming."

Meg and Peg jumped up too.

"Let's go and call Kilmanskeg and Ridiklis and Gustibus and Peter Piper," they said, and they rushed to the staircase and met Kilmanskeg and Ridiklis and Gustibus and Peter Piper coming scrambling up panting because the noise had wakened them as well.

They were all over at Tidy Castle in a minute. They just tumbled over each other to get there—the kind-hearted things. The servants were every one fast asleep, though the noise was awful. The loudest groans came from Lady Gwendolen and Lord Francis because their mustard plasters were blistering them frightfully.

Ridiklis took charge, because she was the one who knew most about illness. She sent Gustibus to waken the servants and then ordered hot water and cold water, and ice, and brandy, and poultices, and shook the trained Nurse for not attending to her business—and took off the mustard plasters and gave gruel and broth and cough syrup and castor oil and ipecacuanha, and every one of the Racketty-Packettys massaged, and soothed, and patted, and put wet cloths on heads, until the fever was gone and the Castle dolls all lay back on their pillows pale and weak, but smiling faintly at every Racketty-Packetty they saw, instead of turning up their noses and tossing their heads and sniffing loudly, and just *scorning* them.

Lady Gwendolen spoke first and instead of being haughty and disdainful, she was as humble as a new-born kitten.

"Oh! you dear, shabby, disrespectable, darling things!" she said. "Never, never will I scorn you again. Never, never!"

"That's right!" said Peter Piper in his cheerful, rather slangy way. "You take my tip—never you scorn any one again. It's a mistake. Just you watch

"Ridiklis took charge because she knew most about illness."

me stand on my head. It'll cheer you up."

And he turned six somersaults—just like lightning—and stood on his head and wiggled his ragged legs at them until suddenly they heard a snort from one of the beds and it was Lord Hubert beginning to laugh and then Lord Francis laughed and then Lord Hubert shouted, and then Lady Doris squealed, and Lady Muriel screamed, and Lady Gwendolen and the Duchess rolled over and over in their beds, laughing as if they would have fits.

"Oh! you delightful, funny, shabby old loves!" Lady Gwendolen kept saying. "To think that we scorned you."

"They'll be all right after this," said Peter Piper. "There's nothing cures scarlet fever like cheering up. Let's all join hands and dance round and round once for them before we go back to bed. It'll throw them into a nice light perspiration and they'll drop off and sleep like tops." And they did it, and before they had finished, the whole lot of them were perspiring gently and snoring as softly as lambs.

When they went back to Racketty-Packetty House they talked a good deal about Cynthia and wondered and wondered why she had left her scarlet fever patients so suddenly. And at last Ridiklis made up her mind to tell them something she had heard.

"The Duchess told me," she said, rather slowly because it was bad news—"The Duchess said that Cynthia went away because her Mama had sent for her—and her Mama had sent for her to tell her that a little girl Princess is coming to see her to-morrow. Cynthia's Mama used to be a maid of honor to the Queen and that's why the little girl Princess is coming. The Duchess said—" and here Ridiklis spoke very slowly indeed,— "that the Nurse was so excited she said she did not know whether she stood on her head or her heels, and she must tidy up the nursery and have that Racketty-Packetty old dolls' house carried down stairs and burned, early to-morrow morning. That's what the Duchess *said*—"

Meg and Peg and Kilmanskeg clutched at their hearts and gasped and Gustibus groaned and Lady Patsy caught Peter Piper by the arm to keep from falling. Peter Piper gulped—and then he had a sudden cheerful thought.

"Perhaps she was raving in delirium," he said.

"No, she wasn't," said Ridiklis, shaking her head, "I had just given her hot water and cold, and gruel, and broth, and castor oil, and ipecacuanha and put ice almost all over her. She was as sensible as any of us. To-morrow morning we shall not have a house

"She put her ragged old apron over her face and cried."

over our heads," and she put her ragged old apron over her face and cried.

"If she wasn't raving in delirium," said Peter Piper, "we shall not have any heads. You had better go back to the Castle to-night, Patsy. Racketty-Packetty House is no place for you."

Then Lady Patsy drew herself up so straight that she nearly fell over backwards.

"I—will—*never*—leave you!" she said, and Peter Piper couldn't make her.

You can just imagine what a doleful night it was. They went all over the house together and looked at every hole in the carpet and every piece of stuffing sticking out of the dear old shabby sofas, and every broken window and chair-leg and table and ragged blanket—and the tears ran down their faces for the first time in their lives. About six o'clock in the morning Peter Piper made a last effort.

"Let's all join hands in a circle," he said quite faintly, "and dance round and round once more."

But it was no use. When they joined hands they could not dance, and when they found they could not dance they all tumbled down in a heap and cried instead of laughing and Lady Patsy lay with her arms round Peter Piper's neck.

Now here is where I come in again—Queen Crosspatch, who is telling you this story. I always come in just at the nick of time when people like the Racketty-Packettys are in trouble. I walked in at seven o'clock.

"Get up off the floor," I said to them all and they got up and stared at me. They actually thought I did not know what had happened.

"A little girl Princess is coming this morning," said Peter Piper, "and our house is going to be burned over our heads. This is the end of Racketty-Packetty House."

"No, it isn't!" I said. "You leave this to me. I told the Princess to come here, though she doesn't know it in the least."

A whole army of my Working Fairies began to swarm in at the Nursery window. The Nurse was working very hard to put things in order and she had not sense enough to see Fairies at all. So she did not see mine, though there were hundreds of them. As soon as she made one corner tidy, they ran after her and made it untidy. They held her back by her dress and hung and swung on her apron until she could scarcely move and kept wondering why she was so slow. She could not make the Nursery tidy and she was so flurried she forgot all about Racketty-Packetty House again—especially as my Working Fairies pushed the arm-chair close up to it so that it was quite hidden. And there it was when the little girl Princess came with her Ladies in Waiting. My fairies had only just allowed the Nurse to finish the Nursery.

Meg and Peg and Kilmanskeg and Ridiklis and Gustibus and Peter Piper and Lady Patsy were huddled up together looking out of one window. They could not bear to be parted. I sat on the arm of the big chair and ordered my Working Fairies to stand ready to obey me the instant I spoke.

The Princess was a nice child and was very polite to Cynthia when she showed her all her dolls, and last but not least, Tidy Castle itself. She looked at all the rooms and the furniture and said polite and admiring things about each of them. But Cynthia realized that she was not so much interested in it as she had thought she would be. The fact was that the Princess had so many grand dolls' houses in her palace that Tidy Castle did not surprise her at all. It was just when Cynthia was finding this out that I gave the order to my Working Fairies.

"Push the arm-chair away," I commanded; "very slowly, so that no one will know it is being moved."

So they moved it away—very, very slowly—and no one saw that it had stirred. But the next minute the little girl Princess gave a delightful start.

"Oh! What is that!" she cried out, hurrying towards the unfashionable neighborhood behind the door.

Cynthia blushed all over and the Nurse actually turned pale. The Racketty-Packettys tumbled down in a heap beneath their window and began to tremble and quake.

"It is only a shabby old dolls' house, your Highness," Cynthia stammered out. "It belonged to my Grandmamma, and it ought not to be in the Nursery. I thought you had had it burned, Nurse!

"Burned!" the little girl Princess cried out in the most shocked way.

"Why if it was mine, I wouldn't have it burned for worlds! Oh! please push the chair away and let me look at it. There are no dolls' houses like it anywhere in these days." And when the arm-chair was pushed aside she scrambled down on to her knees just as if she was not a little girl Princess at all.

"Oh! Oh! Oh!" she said. "How funny and dear! What a darling old dolls' house. It is shabby and wants mending, of course, but it is almost exactly like one my Grandmamma had—she kept it among her treasures and only let me look at it as a great, great treat."

Cynthia gave a gasp, for the little girl Princess's Grandmamma had been the Queen and people had knelt down and kissed her hand and had been obliged to go out of the room backwards before her.

The little girl Princess was simply filled with joy. She picked up Meg and Peg and Kilmanskeg and Gustibus and Peter Piper as if they had been really a Queen's dolls.

"Oh! the darling dears," she said. "Look at their nice, queer faces and their funny clothes. Just—just like Grandmamma's dollies' clothes. Only these poor things do so want new ones. Oh! how I should like to dress them again just as they used to be dressed, and have the house all made just as it used to be when it was new."

"That old Racketty-Packetty House," said Cynthia, losing her breath.

"If it were mine I should make it just like Grandmamma's and I should love it more than any dolls' house I have. I never—never—never—saw anything as nice and laughing and good-natured as these dolls' faces. They look as if they had been having fun ever since they were born. Oh! if you were to burn them and their home I—I could never forgive you!"

"I never—never—will,—your Highness," stammered Cynthia, quite overwhelmed. Suddenly she started forward.

"You are going to come and live with me!"

"Why, there is the lost doll!" she cried out. "There is Lady Patsy. How did she get into Racketty-Packetty House?"

"Perhaps she went there to see them because they were so poor and shabby," said the little girl Princess. "Perhaps she likes this one," and she pointed to Peter Piper. "Do you know when I picked him up their arms were about each other. Please let her stay with him. Oh!" she cried out the next instant and jumped a little. "I felt as if the boy one kicked his leg."

And it was actually true, because Peter Piper could not help it and he had kicked out his ragged leg for joy. He had to be very careful not to kick any more when he heard what happened next.

As the Princess liked Racketty-Packetty House so much, Cynthia gave it to her for a present—and the Princess was really happy—and before she went away she made a little speech to the whole Racketty-Packetty family, whom she had set all in a row in the ragged old, dear old, shabby old drawing-room where they had had so much fun.

"You are going to come and live with me, funny, good-natured loves," she said. "And you shall all be dressed beautifully again and your house shall be mended and papered and painted and made as lovely as ever it was. And I am going to like you better than all my other dolls' houses—just as Grand-mamma said she liked hers."

And then she was gone.

And every bit of it came true. Racketty-Packetty House was carried to a splendid Nursery in a Palace, and Meg and Peg and Kilmanskeg and Ridiklis and Gustibus and Peter Piper were made so gorgeous that if they had not been so nice they would have grown proud. But they didn't. They only grew jollier and jollier and Peter Piper married Lady Patsy, and Ridiklis's left leg was mended and she was painted into a beauty again—but she always remained the useful one. And the dolls in the other dolls' houses used to make deep curtsies when a Racketty-Packetty House doll passed them, and Peter Piper could scarcely stand it because it always made him want to stand on his head and laugh—and so when they were curtsied at—because they were related to the Royal Dolls' House—they used to run into their drawing-room and fall into fits of giggles, and they could only stop them by all joining hands together in a ring and dancing round and round and kicking up their heels and laughing until they tumbled down in a heap.

What do you think of that for a story! And doesn't it prove to you what a valuable Friend a Fairy is—particularly a Queen one?

"Ridilkis's left leg was mended and she was painted into a beauty again."

Perfect Mary Jane

By Nahda Frazee-Wheeler

Now listen, my dears, and I will tell
  A story strange, but true,
Of a dear little girl with golden hair
  And eyes like the sky so blue.

This little girl's name was Mary Jane—
  A common name no doubt;
But Mary Jane was no common child,
  For I never saw her pout.

Her lips were always smiling,
  And I never heard her sigh;
Although she fell and bumped her head,
  She did n't even cry.

She never was rude to her mother,
  Or said, "Well, I don't care!"
She always held her head quite still
  When nursie combed her hair.

She never played mean tricks on others,
  Or joined in any folly.
Who was this child? You 'd like to know?
  Why—"Mary Jane" 's my dolly!

The Dead Doll

by Margaret Vandegrift

You need n't be trying to comfort me—I tell you my dolly is dead!
There's no use in saying she is n't, with a crack like that in her head.
It's just like you said it would n't hurt much to have my tooth out, that day;
And then, when the man 'most pulled my head off, you had n't a word to say.

And I guess you must think I'm a baby, when you say you can mend it with glue!
As if I did n't know better than that! Why, just suppose it was you?
You might make her *look* all mended—but what do I care for looks?
Why, glue's for chairs and tables, and toys, and the backs of books!

My dolly! my own little daughter! Oh, but it's the awfulest crack!
It just makes me sick to think of the sound when her poor head went whack
Against that horrible brass thing that holds up the little shelf.
Now, Nursey, what makes you remind me? I know that I did it myself!

I think you must be crazy—you'll get her another head!
What good would forty heads do her? I tell you my dolly is dead!
And to think I had n't quite finished her elegant new Spring hat!
And I took a sweet ribbon of hers last night to tie on that horrid cat!

When my mamma gave me that ribbon—I was playing out in the yard—
She said to me, most expressly, "Here's a ribbon for Hildegarde."
And I went and put it on Tabby, and Hildegarde saw me do it;
But I said to myself, "Oh, never mind, I don't believe she knew it!"

But I know that she knew it now, and I just believe, I do,
That her poor little heart was broken, and so her head broke too.
Oh, my baby! my little baby! I wish *my* head had been hit!
For I've hit it over and over, and it has n't cracked a bit.

But since the darling *is* dead, she'll want to be buried, of course;
We will take my little wagon, Nurse, and you shall be the horse;
And I'll walk behind and cry; and we'll put her in this, you see—
This dear little box—and we'll bury her then under the maple-tree.

And papa will make me a tombstone, like the one he made for my bird;
And he'll put what I tell him on it—yes, every single word!
I shall say: "Here lies Hildegarde, a beautiful doll, who is dead;
She died of a broken heart, and a dreadful crack in her head."

How I Play
with My
Dollies

Playing going to th Fancier's to buy a new Pug.

Playing Going to the Zoo.

Playing Going to th Flower-Market.

Playing Going to th Seashore.

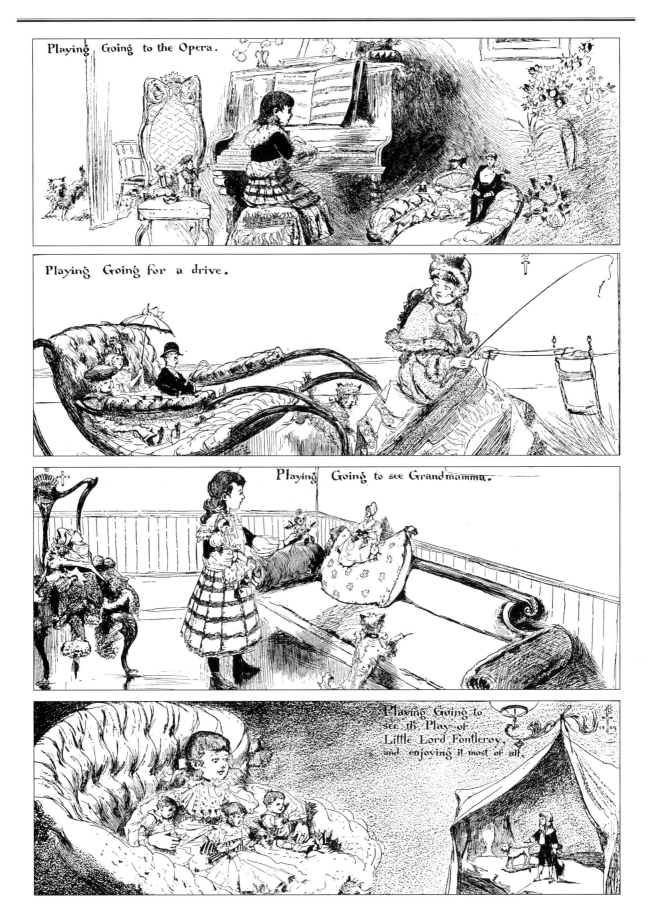

The Pine-Stick Doll

By Mary L. B. Branch

One morning when sister Sue and Bunny Miller and I reached the old gray school-house, and ran up on the grassy bank, where we girls always gathered to wait for the teacher, we saw a new scholar standing a little apart from the rest, with a slate and spelling-book in her hand.

Nobody knew her, and so nobody spoke to her; but one of the girls whispered to us that she *guessed* her folks lived in the little old tumble-down house over by the woods, for she heard her father say, the night before, that a man named Beck had moved in there, and that he had four or five children. Bunny and I felt very curious, so we slipped around where we could get a good look at the stranger. She was n't pretty,—so much was certain at the first glance; the freckles almost ran together on her face, they were so thick; her lips were shut tight, and there was a queer look about her light gray eyes. Her dress showed where the tucks had been let down, but still it was too short; her hands were brown as the sun could make them, and so were her bare feet. Bunny and I smoothed down our clean check aprons with our hands, and confided to each other our belief that we should not like her.

When the teacher came, she called us all in at once. We hung up our sun-bonnets and dinner-pails in the entry, and pressed into the schoolroom. Bunny and I sat on the little girls' bench, because we were not old enough to have desks, but Sue had a desk and was in the first class.

We were all looking to see what seat the new scholar would have. The teacher called her to her side, and asked what her name was.

"Nan Beck," said the girl, readily enough.

"I have not seen you before," remarked Miss Bowen. "Where do you live?"

"In the old house by the woods."

Miss Bowen was surprised, for she knew, as well as the rest of us, how long the old house had been tenantless and forsaken; so she made a few more inquiries, and found that the family had been emigrants to the far West, but, meeting with continued bad luck, had undertaken to retrace their course. On their way back through our country, the deserted house on the edge of the woods had caught the father's eye, and finding that there was good fishing in the river, and a quarry not far off where he could get work, he had decided at once to "locate."

Our teacher spoke kindly to Nan Beck, when she had heard her story, and, on discovering that she was eleven years old and a good speller, placed her in the first-class, and gave her a desk among the large girls. I saw Dely Moore draw her beautiful calico dress out of the way, when Nan sat down by her, and Sarah King on the other side looked very grave and sober.

At recess the girls played "catch," and Nan joined in the game. She proved to be the fleetest runner of them all, but the rest seemed to have tacitly made up their minds to dislike her, and after a little while she left them, and came to the side of the wall, where the smallest children were playing house. She offered to be "mother," but we shrank away from her, and little fat dimpled Rosie Moore whispered to Bunny:

"I'm real 'fraid she's a wild girl!"

And so on every side poor Nan's first overtures were repulsed. When noon came, we took our pails and scattered in all directions to eat our luncheon. we had a fashion of going in pairs; each girl had some particular friend with whom she would wander off, their arms around each other's waist, and their voices lowered confidentially. These friendships were of uncertain duration, but full of devotion while they lasted. Bunny had been my friend all the term, and Sue went with Sarah King.

Nan looked longingly at these little groups and pleasant intimacies, but she was not invited to join any of them, so she withdrew under some bushes and ate her dinner all by herself.

So it went on from day to day, and there was not a girl to be found who took a fancy to Nan Beck. It was not because she was poor, for Dilly Brown was even poorer, but we all made a pet of merry, rosy-faced Dilly. It was not because she was ignorant, for she learned as fast as any of us. It must have been her looks and manners that repelled us. Her tangled hair and tawny face, her constrained, awkward ways, her utter lack of the pleasant traits that characterized our favorites,—all these things made us shy of the stranger.

As the days grew warmer, the girls left off running

races and playing tag, and, gathering all the stones they could find by the road-side, built little enclosures on the bank beside the wall, and in these played house with their rag-babies. Not one of us owned a "store-doll," and only two or three had even seen one, but we hugged our rag-babies to our hearts, and made their dresses long to hide their lack of feet. My sister Sue had twelve, and one, the most beautiful, had an artificial pink rose sewed on the top of her head, and was always in full-dress.

One recess, Nan Beck came among our houses, holding up something in her hand for us all to see. It was a doll cut out of a pine stick, with a round head and a pretty face, not one feature omitted, and it had hands and feet. There was a general chorus of admiration, and we all crowded around the fortunate Nan.

"Oh, Nan, how pretty! Nan, where *did* you get it?" echoed on every side, and there were not wanting a few bold enough to beg,—"O, *do* give it to *me*, Nan!"

"My brother whittled it out for me last night," said Nan, turning her treasure so as to display it to the best advantage.

"I'll give you any two of my rag-babies you like for it," said Sarah King, very graciously.

"So will I! So will I!" cried one after another in sharp competition.

"I'll tell you what," said Nan, with a sort of awkward resoluteness, "I aint agoing to swap it; I'm agoing to give it away; I'm agoing to give it to the first girl that will agree to be my friend, and go with me all the rest of the term."

A silence fell on us, and the girls looked at each other. There was not one but wanted the wooden doll. It was so much prettier than anything we had, and could be dressed so beautifully. I could not help thinking what a nice dress I could make for it of a piece of pink delaine in my box at home. But to go with Nan all the time, and be her friend; to lock arms with her, and whisper secrets to her, and stand up for her at all times and places—who could do that? I turned around and hugged my darling Bunny. No. I could not give up Bunny to buy the doll!

The girls glanced at each other uneasily. Dely Moore stood biting the corner of her white apron, and Sarah King looked vexed and undecided. Not one could make up her mind to the conditions. Nan waited, looking homelier than ever, with a dull red flush of mortification spreading over her face. Suddenly she turned as if to go.

"Stop, Nan!" exclaimed my sister Sue, her shrewd black eyes sparkling with sudden determination; "I'll go with you, I'll be your friend!"

"Well, if I ever! Sue Butler, you need n't ever try to go with *me* again!" said Sarah King, hotly, as Nan stopped in glad surprise, and waited half timidly for Sue to join her.

"Ho, I don't believe they'll be friends more than two days," said Dely Moore, tossing her curly head.

"I don't see why not," remarked another girl, derisively. "Birds of a feather flock together—you know."

Sue laughed over her shoulder at them all. She had the wooden doll, and that was enough. Faithful to her bargain, she invited Nan into her own little enclosure, and there played house with her till recess was over.

When noon came the girls all watched to see what Sue would do. Bunny and I betook ourselves to our pet corner in a shady angle of the wall, and peeped out as we nibbled our seed-cake.

Presently along came Sue and Nan arm in arm, and Sue said:

"Where shall we go to eat our dinner, Nan?"

"I wish you would come and see my place in among the bushes," said Nan, eagerly; "it's a real nice place, and nobody ever found it but me."

"I should n't wonder if they both hid in a rat-hole nest," was Sarah King's spiteful remark, when she saw Nan lifting up the overhanging bushes, and Sue stooping carefully and following her in under them. But when, a moment after, we all heard Sue exclaiming, "Why, how nice! how beautiful! I never did see such soft, pretty moss, and it's just like an arbor, is n't it?"—the girls began to wonder what there was in there, and I know they all wanted to see.

"Let's go in there too," I whispered to Bunny; "we can, 'cause Sue is my sister." So we crept under the bushes after them, and found ourselves in a regular fairy bower, with moss three inches deep for a carpet, and a long, low stone for a seat. Overhead two or three young trees interwove their leaves and twigs and shaded us from the sun's heat, and in one of the trees there was a bird's nest. Bunny and I thought we had never seen anything so nice in our lives, and Nan's face beamed all over, she was so glad of company. We put all our dinners together, and had a little picnic on the moss, which was great fun. The girls tried to tease Bunny and me when we came out, but we had had such a good time we did n't care.

That evening, in the big kitchen at home, Sue

"There was a general chorus of admiration."

dressed the doll. I gave her my pink delaine for a dress, and she made a little white ruffled apron, just as cunning as it could be, and a little bonnet too. I told mother all about the bargain, how Sue had promised to go with Nan, and mother said she was glad of it.

Next morning Sue took the doll to school, and it looked so handsome, the girls had not a word to say. When Nan came, she brought a whole pocketful of sassafras root which her brothers had dug for her, and with a very bright face gave it all to Sue, and then they strolled off together arm in arm. The sassafras root made a great impression on the rest of us, for we all loved it dearly, but it was so hard to dig, we never had much at a time.

The days slipped by, and Sue was true to her bargain. I don't suppose she would ever have thought of being friends with Nan Beck, if it had not been for the doll; but Sue was a shrewd little business woman, an honest one too, and always carried out whatever she undertook. She found it pleasanter than she expected in this case, and by degrees quite a number of the girls fell into the habit of hanging about with Bunny and me when Nan had sassafras and checker-berries to give away, or when sitting under some tree she told us stories of her wild, pioneering life in the West; or when, lithe as a panther, she climbed young saplings till she bent them to the ground, so that we could take hold in turn and swing gayly through the air.

In fact, the school soon formed itself into two parties,—one friendly to Nan and ready to follow wherever her adventurous spirit led, and the other, headed by Sarah King and Dely Moore, standing aloof, and exchanging meaning glances and sarcastic whispers whenever they happened to be near us.

"There go the *Nannies!*" said Sarah contemptuously one day, as we ran past her with Nan down to the brook. "I'd be ashamed to be a tom-boy," added Dely, holding back her little sister Rosie, who looked longingly after us.

Meanwhile Sue's friendship was taking a practical shape. She did not want her chosen companion laughed at, so she gave Nan some hints from time to time, which the latter eagerly received; the tangled hair was trimmed and neatly combed, the old dress was pieced down and made long enough, and one day after Sue had been holding a long consultation with mother, Nan appeared in a pretty plaid apron, which we thought made her look as nice as any of us.

But still Sarah King and her party were not to be won over, and one day when Nan went above them all to the head of the spelling-class, they became so teasing and irritating at recess, that they finally made her cry, in spite of her stout little heart. Sue swept an indignant glance around, and drew her away out of sight of her foes.

I shall always remember that day; we had no school in the afternoon, for it was Saturday, and Sue and I trudged home along the dusty road at noon, much roused in spirit over Sarah King's enmity to Nan. We told the whole story to mother, who, with her wise, gentle words, finally calmed us, and to divert our minds sent us out into the garden to gather the raspberries for jam. I remember just how the bushes looked, loaded down with the red and purple berries, and how warm and sultry it was, and how we scratched our hands reaching after the highest clusters. We had picked nearly four quarts, when we realized that it had suddenly become cool and dark though so early in the afternoon. Great black clouds had overcast the sky, and even while we looked large drops fell on our faces.

"Run in, girls, run in quick!" cried mother at the door; "there is going to be a hard thunder-storm!"

We had hardly time to reach the house before the rain was pouring down and beating against the windows, and the thunder came rolling up nearer and nearer. According to my usual custom in thunderstorms, I drew a little cricket up into a corner, and sat there with my face to the wall, and my fingers in my ears. But Sue played with her doll unconcernedly, and began a new suit of clothes for it. After an hour or so the storm passed off, and just as the sun was breaking out and shining in the great rain-drops that hung everywhere, there came a loud knocking at the door. Before we could open it, in rushed Tom Moore, asking wildly if we had seen Rosie. When he found we had not, he fairly cried, big boy as he was.

"She is lost, then! little Rosie's lost!" he said, despairingly. "I've been to all the neighbors looking for her, and nobody has seen her since dinner!"

Mother caught up her bonnet, and hurried over to Mrs. Moore's at once. Sue and I followed her, too frightened to speak. We found Dely crying and sobbing as if her heart would break, and Mrs. Moore was blowing the horn to call home her husband and the men at work in the far-off barn. The neighbors were gathering about, to sympathize and wonder. One had seen little Rosie with her sunbonnet on, wandering past her house before one o'clock, and that was the last that could be learned of her.

"I'll drive up and down the road three or four miles each way," said my father, "and make inquiries. You boys here had better go over the fields, and look in all the barns."

Just as he was ready to start, one of the women exclaimed that she saw something like a speck coming down the distant hill, and might it not be Rosie?

"No," said father, looking attentively that way for a few moments, "it is a little old woman almost bent double."

My sister Sue could see farther and quicker than any one I ever knew, and now, shading her eyes, she scanned the figure coming down the hill.

"It's Nan Beck!" she cried excitedly. "She is bringing something in her arms, and I think it is Rosie!"

Father and Mr. Moore sprang into the wagon and drove that way with all speed. Whoever it was, we saw them carefully lift her in, and then they drove speedily back again. Sure enough, it *was* Nan, with little Rosie clasped tight in her arms. They had both been drenched with the rain, and Rosie's face was pale and tear-stained, while her little legs were covered with black mud up to her dimpled knees. Mrs. Moore caught her frantically in her arms.

"Change her clothes right off," said a practical old aunt, "or she'll catch her death of cold. And give her some hot catnip tea."

While this was going on Nan told her story. Before the storm came on, she had gone over to the swamp to dig sweet-flag. When it began to rain, she sheltered herself in a hollow tree. In a lull of the storm, she thought she heard a child crying; and becoming sure that it was so, she left the tree and wound her way along the edge of the swamp, till at last she came in sight of Rosie, standing in a treacherous bog, holding fast to the rushes with a scared face, and crying piteously. Nan waded out to her through the mud, brought her to solid ground, and then started at once with the child in her arms to take her home.

Every face was pale, and every heart was thrilled, at Nan's simple recital, for all realized what peril little Rosie had been in. It would have been impossible for such a child to make her way alone out of that dangerous swamp. When her mother asked her why she ran away, she said it was "to find sweet-flag and vi'lets, and to find Nan, because Dely would not *never* let her play with her at school."

"O, Nan, Nan, how I have treated you!" said Dely, remorsefully, "but I'll always be your friend now forever and ever!"

This was Nan's final triumph. She became the heroine of all the neighborhood, and when Dely and Rosie joined her adherents, there was not a girl in the school who would hold out against her, not even Sarah King. She became leader in all our lessons and our games, and could choose any girl she pleased to be her friend and to "go with her."

But I think she never liked any one quite so well as my sister Sue, and of all the little ones she petted Rosie and Bunny and me the most.

The child-days are all gone now, and much that happened in them has faded out of my memory, but I never forget brave little Nan who wanted to be loved, and who bought her first friend with a pine-stick doll.

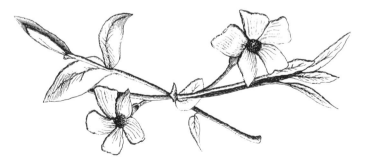

Mary's little lamb: "Baa! That doll's hair is *wool!*"

Maisy's Christmas

By C. T.

"I wonder," cried Maisy, small and fair,
　On Christmas eve, as the night shut down,
"How Santa Claus can go everywhere
　And find all the stockings in every town!"

She skipped from the window lofty and wide,
　And questioning stood at her mother's knee
In the beautiful light of the fireside,—
　"Mamma, does he ever forget?" asked she.

"A poor child is begging out there in the storm,
　So cold, Mamma, and so pale and thin!
Can't we have her here to get dry and warm?
　And may I tell Bessie to bring her in?"

Astonished, the shivering beggar was brought,
　And thankfully stood in the fire-light's glow
While Maisy gazed at her, deep in thought.—
　"Do you hang up your stocking? I'd like to
　know!"

"My stocking? I have n't a stocking," she said.
　"Oh, dear, kind people, please give to me
For starving Mother a piece of bread;
　Too weak to rise from her bed is she."

They gave her stockings, clothes, food and wine,
　With fuel to burn and candles to cheer,
And sent her home in a carriage fine
　Quite dumb and breathless with joy and fear.

"Mamma, Mamma," cried Maisy, small,
　When the child had gone in her dream of bliss,
"She never has hung up a stocking at all!
　She does n't know, even, who Santa Claus is!"

Then she kneeled on the hearth-stone, "O Santa
　Claus dear,"
　She cried, with her pretty head all in a whirl,
"You need n't bring anything beautiful here;
　Please take all my things to that poor little girl!"

87

And Santa Claus heard what she said, and she hung
   No stocking at all by the fire that night.
But up in the morning rejoicing she sprung,
   Herself like the sunshine, so cheerful and bright.

Not a trace of a present by bed or by fire!
   The good saint had taken her quite at
     her word;
And Maisy sweet, having had her desire,
   Set up her old playthings, as blithe as
     a bird.

She played till 't was time to the church to go;
   Then in satin and velvet and fur and plume,
The mother and daughter tripped over the snow,
   With red lips smiling and cheeks abloom.

And after the service was over, and out
   The people poured from the portal wide;
Her playmates round Maisy pressed about,—
   And "What did you get in your stocking?"
     they cried.

Then answered our Maisy sweet and small,
   While her color grew to a deeper red,
"What did *you* get? *I* got nothing at all!"
   "Nothing! She must have been naughty!" they said.

That moment, a beautiful sound in the air!
   The blast of a horn, so clear and loud
That it caused all the people to start and stare!—
   And a horseman dashed swift past the waiting crowd.

     And up to Maisy where she stood,
       A little apart from the rest, he spurred;
     Dismounted as quickly as ever he could,
       And bowed to the ground ere he uttered a word.

     Such a splendid messenger, plumed and curled,
       Booted and spurred, with a sword so grand!
     There never was such a surprise in the world;
       And what do you think he held in his hand

     Tied up with ribbons?—Such trinkets and toys,
       (Oh, the snow-birds fluttered to hear the news!)
     A music-box, and no end of joys,
       And the dearest dolly, with pointed shoes!

     "Good Santa Claus sent me," he said, and he smiled,
       "To bring you some presents and wish you delight;
     He did what you asked for the poor little child,
       But it made him too late for your stocking last night!"

CUDDLE DOWN, DOLLY

By Kate Douglas Wiggin

They sent me to bed, dear, so dreadfully early,
I had n't a moment to talk to my girlie;
But while Nurse is getting her dinner, down-stairs,
I'll rock you a little and hear you your prayers.

Not comfor'ble, dolly?—or why do you fidget?
You're hurting my shoulder, you troublesome midget!
Perhaps it's that hole that you told me about.
Why, darling, your sawdust is trick-ker-ling out!

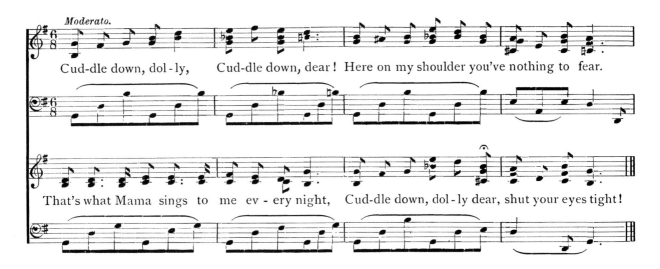

Moderato.

Cud-dle down, dol-ly, Cud-dle down, dear! Here on my shoulder you've nothing to fear.

That's what Mama sings to me ev-er-y night, Cud-dle down, dol-ly dear, shut your eyes tight!

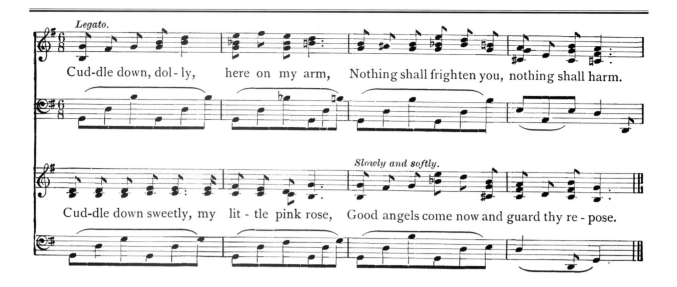

Cud-dle down, dol-ly, here on my arm, Nothing shall frighten you, nothing shall harm.

Slowly and softly.

Cud-dle down sweetly, my lit-tle pink rose, Good angels come now and guard thy re-pose.

We'll call the good doctor in, right straight away;
That can't be neglected a single more day;
I'll wet my new hankchif and tie it round tight,
'T will keep you from suffering pains in the night.

I hope you've been good, little dolly, to-day,
Not cross to your nursie, nor rude in your play;
Nor dabbled your feet in those puddles of water
The way you did yesterday, bad little daughter!
Oh, dear! I'm so sleepy—can't hold up my head,
I'll sing one more verse, then I'll creep into bed.

"Hush, everybody! I've just managed
to get *one* of them asleep!"

90

A Warning to Mothers

By Elsie Hill

I could not find, the other day, my little sister Claire.
I peeped into the nursery to see if she was there,
And found instead her eldest doll—Matilda Maud by
  name;
So down we sat together then, to wait until she came.

Matilda Maud is beautiful; her cheeks are smooth and fair.
You'd never think, to look at her, she had a hidden care.
I wonder if I only dreamed I heard her murmur: "Oh,
Just what my mother means by it I really do not know!

"'My dearest child,' she's sure to cry a dozen times a day,
'Your hair is simply shocking! I must brush the snarls
  away;
No matter if it hurts you, since 't is for your *good*, my
  dear!'
So she pulls it out in handfuls, while I never shed a tear.

"But early in the morning, if you're passing by the door,
And you hear a greater scrimmage than you ever heard
  before,—
'Oh, you *jerk* so! Oh, you *hurt* so! Oh, it's more than I can
  bear!'—
Why, that's the way my mother does when people curl *her*
  hair!

"'Wise children work as well as play,' my mother oft
will state.
She puts the pencil in my hand, and holds it firm
and straight;
She sets the copy carefully, and tries her best to
teach,
'*Consistency a jewel is*,' and, '*Practise what you
preach!*

"So is n't it the *oddest* thing that I should hear her
sigh
(Her forehead all snarled up with frowns, a tear in
either eye):
'If I had just to read and spell, I'd *like* to study then;
Arithmetic is far too hard for little girls of ten!'

"For Sundays I've a velvet gown that's warm as warm
can be;
For other days the muslin one my mother made for
me.
No matter what the weather is, she'll shake her head
and say,
"T is vain, my dear, to wish to wear your best frock

"And yet this very afternoon (I was n't dressed at
all,
But lying on the window-seat just wrapped up in
a shawl)
I heard my little mother's voice, in tones of deep
distress:
'*I cannot go to Betty Brown's and wear my old
blue dress!*'

"Then, when we're at our supper I am sure *I*
　　never make
Complaints about my bread and milk, that's
　　'nicer far than cake.'
If you hear a dreadful teasing,—oh, you need
　　n't look at *me*,—
It's just my *mother* begging for a cup of 'truly
　　tea'!

"And sometimes I'm in bed at six, and sometimes half-
　　past two!
'Matilda Maud,' my mother says, 'I know what's best for
　　you!'
So when it's late and striking eight, and Nurse is at the
　　door,
It is n't *I* who always cry, 'Just fifteen minutes more!'"

I started up; a gay voice called; a step was on the
　　stair.
Matilda Maud—that injured child—sat speechless
　　in her chair.
I wonder if I only *dreamed* I heard her whisper:
　　"Well,
Just what my mother means by it I really *cannot*
　　tell!"

Mrs. Slipperkin's Family

By Clara G. Dolliver

Mrs. Slipperkin is eight years old; just eight, too, although, when she is asked, she takes pains to say that she will be nine her next birthday. It is a harmless delusion of Mrs. Slipperkin's, that such a statement makes her seem considerably older, while it has the advantage of being strictly true.

Mr. Slipperkin is said to be traveling in Europe, and his wife sometimes receives small letters bearing a foreign post-mark, which she says are from her husband. But, on examining these letters closely, we are of the opinion that the only part which has seen the post-office is the stamp; and we have frequently remarked to Mrs. Slipperkin that her husband writes a hand resembling her own in a most surprising degree; we think, but do not say, that the letters are *fat*, and the t's and i's neglected.

She lives with her dear friend,—her sister, in fact, though she does not usually call her so,—Mrs. Coppertip, in our attic.

This latter lady is six,—I beg her pardon, will be seven her next birthday,—and she also has a husband traveling in foreign lands. Mr. Coppertip, however, does not attend to his family as he should, for his wife has received but one letter from him, and that was written on a piece of an old writing-book, in a hand strongly resembling Mrs. Slipperkin's and *not* written in her best style.

Mrs. Coppertip is one of the gentlest of human beings. She has little, soft hands, which are often cold and kind on aching heads; she has gentle brown eyes, and soft brown hair, very nice to brush, and very easy to care for. I believe she loves everybody, and I am quite sure that everybody loves her, because I know they cannot help it.

Mrs. Slipperkin's eyes are likewise brown, but they have more snap in them than Mrs. Coppertip's. Her hair, too, is brown, and very pretty, being full of snarly curls, which she loves, but which are quite dreadful to brush. I know she does n't love everybody, for she goes to school, and I have heard her say that she "hates" Laura Brown, and "despises" Amelia Lake, and "can't endure" somebody else; and so we judge from this that Laura and Amelia and somebody else, do not love Mrs. Slipperkin, either.

Mrs. Coppertip has three children, all of whom have been extremely unfortunate.

One has lost an arm, another both legs, and the youngest, shocking to say, once lost her head, which was afterwards found, and is now very insecurely fastened on with white wax.

In spite of their misfortunes, they are very still and well-behaved, and their mother loves them dearly. She does not believe in dressing them too finely; she does not think it is good for children to be so much interested in fashion; and then, besides,—this is between ourselves,—she is not much of a sewer, and really finds it impossible to put many stitches in their dresses; so they are made of calico, and all the embroidery is done with the scissors.

When her youngest child, Evelina, was baptized, she attempted a little more, and actually hemmed the skirt of her dress all around; but every stitch was marked by a drop of blood, where the cruel, sharp needle pricked the patient little finger, and I counted three great big stains on it, cause by the fall of three great big tears.

The Slipperkin children, on the contrary, are always decked out in the finest of clothes.

I cannot positively state that Mrs. Slipperkin is fond of sewing, for we have to quote the old saying, "A stitch in time, saves nine," a great many times in the course of a year. But, though she can endure rents in her own dresses with perfect calmness, yet she must dress her children well, or be wretched.

If the sewing will not bear inspection, I can affirm positively that the long stitches are all on the under side.

She says, with great pride, "My children have n't got one calico dress to their names,—so!"

"How many children have you, Mrs. Slipperkin?" said a particular friend of hers to her one day.

"Three, and a baby," was the answer; but why the baby, poor innocent! is not called a child, I have been unable to discover.

The only difference I can perceive between it and the remainder of the family, is that it wears long clothes; and as it has lost both legs, I always supposed that long clothes were a necessity.

Mrs. Slipperkin has a brother, Joe, a big boy, who wears cowhide boots, which make a perfectly fearful noise; and he has no conception of the sort of thing a headache is, never having had one himself.

The two ladies wanted Joe to take the house next to them in the attic, adopt a family, which they offered to give him "for nothing," and call himself Mr. St. Clair, whose wife had recently died.

But Joe said it was "girls' play," and he would n't try it after the first day. Then he took the plaster-of-Paris children, poor infants! and fed them to his chickens.

Some of the boys heard of his new name, and he was greeted with a perfect yell the next morning, when he went into the school-yard. At first he did not know what they were saying, but when he realized that they were calling him Mr. St. Clair, he laid about him with his fists to the right and left, though without any signal success. He received seven notes that day, addressed, in large crooked, boys' letters, "Mr. Joe St. Clair," and the next day the number increased to twelve; and then having stood it as long as he could, Joe thought it quite time that something was done.

So, during the geography class, he printed on a piece of paper the word ATTENTION! in the largest letters he could make, not at all sparing the ink.

Then, at recess-time, when there was a little lull in tag-playing, he mounted a high bench, and pinned this paper across his breast.

At first there was lots of laughing, and considerable hooting of Mr. St. Clair, but as Joe did not move, the boys stopped and listened to what he had to say. His address was not long, neither was it marked by any flowers of speech, but it was delivered in an easy manner, and was very decisive.

"See here, fellers," he said, "you've been a-sending a whole pack of notes to me, and a-hollering Mr. St. Clair, and all that. Now, I wont do a mean thing without first warning; but, after this recess, I'll put every note I get with that on it, on the teacher's desk, and you'll get a lickin' for writing notes in school. And every feller that hollers after me is a coward, if he wont haul off his jacket and fight me. I'll fight every one of you,—one feller at a time,—and lick you too; you bet."

Upon that, Joe descended from the rostrum, and was no longer troubled.

One day Mrs. Slipperkin came bounding home from school, in the very best of spirits. She threw her books on a chair, and her shawl on the floor, and her hat on top of it, and cut a pigeon-wing right then and there, at the imminent risk of her hat-crown.

"Rose, Rose!" said her mother.

"O, you, Mrs. Slipperkin!" moaned the aunt, who has the headache.

Mrs. Slipperkin

"What is it, Wosey?" said Mrs. Coppertip, who does n't go to school. "If she did, she'd speak plain," as Mrs. Slipperkin says.

"Rose" stopped after awhile; not from any particular consideration for anybody, but because she was entirely out of breath.

"You know Flora!? she asked.

"No, I don't!" said Mrs. Coppertip.

"Have n't the pleasure," moaned the aunt with the headache.

"Flora who?" said Joe. "The great race-horse?"

"Race-horse!" said Mrs. Slipperkin, indignantly, "I *do* think!"

"Do, by all means," said the exasperating Joe. "Who is she, anyhow?

"You know that new girl, who sits in front of me, with those pretty curls."

"Yes," said Joe.

"Well, that's the one; her name is Flora Lane, and she's got two dolls, and a blue silk dress, and she's coming to see me Saturday afternoon,—her mother says she can,—and she's going to wear her blue silk dress, and bring her dolls; and she's awful pretty. Is n't she, Joe? And she's my most particular friend; and O, ma! can't we have some lemonade and cookies?"

All this was in one breath.

"Whew!" said Joe, "can't girls talk, though?"

"Dear, dear; hear that child," said the aunt with the headache; "how she runs on, to be sure."

"*Can* we, ma?"

"Yes, I guess so," said the mother.

"*Is n't* she pretty, though, Joe?"

"Ho, huh!" said Joe. "Pretty! her curls look like molasses candy."

"She's my most particular friend," said Mrs. Slipperkin, drawing herself up with dignity.

"Well, aint molasses candy nice?" said Joe.

"Ide," said the offended lady, "you *must* make

Mrs. Coppertip

your children some new silk dresses. I'm going to make each of mine a brand new dress for the occasion."

"O, dear!" said Mrs. Coppertip (thinking of her pricked fingers), with dismay in her voice, "I really don't see how I can."

"Ma'll help you; won't you, ma? And aunty, too; wont you, aunty, now?"

Mrs. Coppertip, who would never have asked, looked with soft, appealing eyes, and so both "ma" and "aunty" said "yes," instantly.

Saturday came at last, as all days do come, no matter how long the time seems; Flora came, too, in her blue silk dress, and an enormous sash tied in a bow, so excruciatingly fashionable and immense, that Rose and Ida winked their eyes hard, and tried not to look astonished. She brought her doll,—nearly as big as herself,—and also arrayed in the height of fashion.

"I thought you had two little china ones, like ours," said Mrs. Slipperkin, in a subdued voice.

"O, I don't make any account of *those*," said Flora, in an extremely "grand" way, "but I put them in my pocket." So she pulled them out, and Mrs. Slipperkin was rejoiced to see that they did not look half so pretty as Ida's, to say nothing of her own.

"What are their names?" she asked.

"Miranda and Eloisa."

"Mine are Lillie, Minnie, Nellie, and Carrie," said Mrs. Slipperkin, "and Ide's are named Dora, Belle, and Evelina. Ide, she's Mrs. Coppertip, and I'm Mrs. Slipperkin; now, what'll you be?"

"I'll be Madame Labelle," said Flora; "my mother knows a lady named that, and I think ti's pretty; don't you?"

"Yes," said Rose. "Now, let's take our lemonade and cookies down by the brook, and have a pic-nic; I know where there's a real nice, mossy place."

But the mother would not consent to the lemonade and cookies being taken where there were silk dresses, so they drank it all up before they went, and carried only the cookies. Flora put her big doll to sleep in a corner of the sofa.

They were right in the midst of a splendid time,— the children were dancing a quadrille on the moss, and the three mothers were playing jacks on Mrs. Coppertip's shawl,—when they heard Joe calling to them.

"What do you *want*?" screamed Mrs. Slipperkin.

"Come and look at my ship," called back Joe. "she's sailing beautiful!"

"Tow her up here!" called Mrs. Slipperkin, which Joe accordingly did.

"There!" is n't she lovely?" he said. "Whater yer doing?"

"Our children are having a pic-nic," said Madame Labelle, smoothing down her silk dress.

"Well, give' em a sailing-trip," said Joe. "Bring yours along, Ide."

"Oh, no!" said the cautious Mrs. Coppertip, who had her doubts as to the seaworthiness of Joe's craft, "I'm welly 'bliged I'm sure; but my children are always sea-sick on the water."

[She had heard *her* mamma say something like this.]

"Mine are not!" cried the adventurous Rose, "and if they are, they will have to learn better.

"Come, Lillie and Minnie and Nellie, you can go anyway; I don't know but what the baby is too young to be trusted out of my sight.

"Madame Labelle, wont you let your little darlings go, too?"

"Oh, certainly!" said that lady, catching her little darlings up by the heads, "if there's room."

"Well, there is n't !" said Joe. "You let yours wait until these come back."

The ship—"Alexander the Great"—swung out into the stream beautifully. Rose clapped her hands, and cried, "Oh, Ide, let yours go when these come back." Then she called out, "Don't catch more cold, Nellie, dear," when,—they could never tell whether it was a twig, or a bug, or the string, or what, but over went "Alexander the Great," soaking her sails, and sending Minnie and Lillie and Nellie, in their new dresses, to the bottom.

Mrs. Slipperkin gave one cry, half rage and half despair, and flying at Joe, pulled his hair with all her might.

"You did it on purpose, you horrid boy, you know you did," she cried.

"Oh, Wosey!" said Mrs. Coppertip, with tears in her voice, "I'll div you one of mine."

"And I'll give you both of mine," said Madame Labelle, who had been laughing, and now tried to look sorry.

"O, let go, do!" cried Joe, "I did n't mean to, Rosy; on my word, I did n't."

"You did!" sobbed Rose. "Oh, my precious children!"

"Let's drag the water," said Madame Labelle, with difficulty suppressing another laugh.

"No use," said Mrs. Slipperkin; "it's all deep mud."

Joe picked up his ship, Mrs. Coppertip the remainder of the cookies, while Mrs. Slipperkin clasped her sole remaining darling to her heart, and they wended their way homeward.

Madame Labelle soon took her departure, leaving Miranda and Eloisa to console the bereaved mother's heart, Mrs. Coppertip also insisting on giving up her beloved Dora as a comforter.

The next day, Mrs. Slipperkin "played" that the water had been dragged, and the bodies recovered, and had a grand funeral under the peach-tree. Penitent Joe contributed a wooden monument, on which were engraved—that is, cut with a penknife— the names: "NELLIE," "MINNIE," "LILLIE;" and this now marks the last resting-place of Mrs. Slipperkin's lamented family.

She puts it in its little bed

SHOPPING.

I'VE COME TO BUY A FROCK TODAY FOR MY

MATILDA JANE.

(I THINK SHE'S JUST A LOVELY DOLL, THOUGH FATHER CALLS HER PLAIN!)

IT MUST BE SOMETHING PRETTY _ A KIND OF PINK, OR BLUE ,

YES _ THAT IS REALLY *VERY* SWEET; I THINK THAT IT WILL DO.

THERE'S NOTHING MORE I WANT TODAY. (I HOPE IT'S NOT TOO DEAR!)

O YES I'LL PAY YOU FOR IT NOW; I'VE GOT THE MONEY HERE.

PLEASE WRAP IT UP IN PAPER AND PUT IT IN THE TRAIN .

COME BABY DEAR, I THINK WE MUST BE GETTING HOME AGAIN.

W. W. GIBSON.

A Dolly Dialogue

BISQUE

RUBBER

WORSTED.

BROWNIE

By Carolyn Wells

Scene: The Nursery.   *Time:* Midnight

Characters

THE BISQUE DOLL   THE RUBBER DOLL
THE RAG DOLL   THE BROWNIE DOLL
THE PAPER DOLL   THE WAX DOLL
THE CHINA DOLL   THE WORSTED DOLL

THE RUBBER DOLL: This night is very long and weary,
    Excuse me if I stretch and yawn,—
THE RAG DOLL: I must confess I'm tired too, dearie,
    And it is still some hours till dawn.
THE BISQUE DOLL: I'm rather glad of rest and quiet,
    The nights are better than the days.
THE PAPER DOLL: Yes, for the nursery's in a riot,
    And Polly tears me when she plays.
THE RUBBER DOLL: Don't say a word against our Polly,
    I won't allow it! Do you hear?
THE PAPER DOLL: I didn't! I'm her favorite dolly.
THE RAG DOLL: (To herself.) She called me that!
    How very queer!
THE BISQUE DOLL: What utter nonsense you are
        talking,
    Of course dear Polly loves me best,
    She takes me when she goes out walking,--
THE CHINA DOLL: Oh, that's because you're finely
    dressed.
THE RUBBER DOLL: Yes, wait till you're a little older,-
THE PAPER DOLL: Till Polly gets you torn and soiled!
THE RUBBER DOLL: (Sighing.) That child!

WAX

RAG

PAPER

CHINA

THE BISQUE DOLL:. I think some one should scold
 her,
  There's danger of her being spoiled.
THE RUBBER DOLL: She does n't mean to be so
 careless.
THE RAG DOLL: I don't mind how she batters *me*.
THE BISQUE DOLL: I should say not! Your head is
 hairless,
  And you're as ragged as can be.
THE WAX DOLL: My hand is smashed!
THE CHINA DOLL: My foot is broken!
THE WORSTED DOLL: I have n't seen my cap for
 days!
THE PAPER DOLL: Perhaps a word in kindness spo-
 ken
  Would make our Polly mend her ways.
THE RUBBER DOLL: Or mend her *dolls*.
THE PAPER DOLL: (Laughing.) That would be *better*.
THE WAX DOLL:. I'd like my arm put in a sling.
THE RUBBER DOLL: Let's send her a Round Robin
 letter.
THE BISQUE DOLL: A good idea!
THE RAG DOLL: The very thing!
THE WAX DOLL: But who will write it?
THE RAG DOLL: I'm not able.
THE BROWNIE DOLL: I think I am. I'm pretty smart.
THE RUBBER DOLL: Well, sit right down at this
 small table,
  Here is a pencil. Now let's start.
THE WAX DOLL: What shall we say?
THE BISQUE DOLL: Don't write too gruffly,
 I've no wish to offend the child.
THE RUBBER DOLL: Oh, no, we mustn't word it
 roughly.
THE BROWNIE DOLL: All right, I'll make it kind and
 mild.
THE BISQUE DOLL: Tell her we love her very dearly,
 And we regret to make a fuss—
THE WAX DOLL: But we'd be grateful,—state this
 clearly,—
  If she'd take better care of us.
THE BROWNIE DOLL: (Writing.) "Oh Polly dear, we
 love you madly,

But you are naughty, without doubt,—"
THE BISQUE DOLL: No, that won't do,—it sounds
 so badly.
THE RUBBER DOLL: Here, take my head and rub it
 out.
THE BROWNIE DOLL: Thank you.
THE BISQUE DOLL: Now try a new beginning.
THE BROWNIE DOLL: (Writing again.) "Our Polly
 dear, we love you much,
  Your smile is sweet, your ways are winning,
  But, oh, destruction is your touch!"
THE RAG DOLL: Tell her we love to have her pet
 us,
  We don't mind thumps and bumps and cracks.
THE WAX DOLL: Speak for yourself! She should not
 set us
  Too near the fire if we're of wax.
THE WORSTED DOLL: She must n't give us to the kit-
 ten.
THE CHINA DOLL: Nor step on us.
THE PAPER DOLL: Nor get us wet.
THE BROWNIE DOLL: Everything that you've said,
 I've written,
  And there's room on the paper yet.
THE BISQUE DOLL: Well, fill it up with greetings ten-
 der,
  Tell her our love is strong and true.
THE WORSTED DOLL: And any loving message send
 her
  That as you write, occurs to you.
THE RAG DOLL: Tell her we're glad that we're her
 dollies.—
THE RUBBER DOLL: Of all small girlies she's our
 choice.—
THE BISQUE DOLL: No smile is half so sweet as
 Polly's.
THE PAPER DOLL: No voice so merry as her voice.
THE BROWNIE DOLL: There, now it's done!
THE BISQUE DOLL: We'll light this taper,
 And sign and seal it.
THE RAG DOLL: Come, be brisk!
 My name first? "Rag." Next! "Worsted."
 "Paper." "Wax." "China."
 "Rubber." "Brownie." "Bisque."

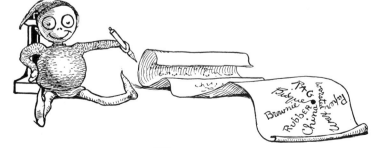

Jo-An of Ark

By George Merrick Mullet

n her room, popularly known as the Ark because of its vast array of battered animals handed down by the older Lane children, Betsy lay in "big comfy chair," reading:

"Once upon a time there lived a beautiful Queen whose every wish but one had been granted—for years she had longed and prayed for a little daughter. When, finally, a princess was born to her, her joy knew no bounds—" Betsy heaved a sigh of perfect understanding and turned adoring eyes on Josephine-Annabelle, who stood with outstretched arms on one of the white shelves which lined the walls. She understood perfectly how the Queen had felt—every pang of longing, every throb of satisfied motherhood. Had she not longed steadily for Josephine-Annabelle from the time when at the church bazaar there had been offered one of the new, jointed, wooden dolls that looked just like a "really child"? And could any one plumb the depths of her disappointment when, after choosing the most beautiful name in the world as the guess to which her twenty-five-cent ticket entitled her, she had failed to win the coveted prize? How hard she had tried to give up wishing for such an extravagance, because the "littlest" child of a government clerk whose salary has not been adjusted to meet the present-day high cost of living should never harbor such desires, especially when there are big brothers and sisters to educate! Unfortunately, the longing refused to listen to reasonable argument, and in spite of a most hopeless outlook, persisted in making a big place for itself in Betsy's "wishery." And then—would she ever forget last Christmas morning when the impossible had happened and she had found the twin sister to the bazaar doll

awaiting her, Aunts Josephine and Annabelle having played Fairy Godmothers?

"Her joy knew no bounds"—Betsy started to read again, but a flood of maternal love made her rush to get Josephine-Annabelle snuggled in her arms before she could comfortably resume her story. Betsy was a born mother; tender-hearted Little Grandmother never had to hunt up half-clad dolls for Betsy and tuck them under small covers on chilly nights, as she had had to do for Betsy's big sisters. As for Josephine-Annabelle—never princess in a fairy-tale had more tender care than she.

Brought to a realization of the bond between the Queen Mother and herself, it was but a step farther for her, as she lay petting Josephine-Annabelle after the story was finished, to enter into the feelings of her own mother. She believed she knew exactly how Muddy Dear must be feeling in these war times. First Roger, a year out of college, had joyously offered his services and had been accepted in the Officers' Reserve Corps; then Mildred, making her last year in a nurses' training school, had entered active service in the Red Cross. How brave Muddy Dear had been! She was a true patriot. Betsy decided that they were a patriotic family. Daddy was trying to skimp out payments on a Liberty bond from his inadequate salary by walking the three miles to and from his office; Muddy Dear gave of her already work-filled moments to service in the Red Cross Aid; Eleanor, a high-school senior, was knitting a humpy-looking scarf for some soldier-boy; and even happy-go-lucky Jack had donated every cent made as a Boy-Scout peach-picker to the same cause. Betsy felt that here was a record of which to be proud. There remained only herself, a blot on an otherwise stainless

escutcheon. To be sure, she had tried to knit wash-cloths, but even patient Little Grandmother had, in nervous tears, given up trying to train her limp hands for the task, hopelessly declaring that "the child seems to have no bones in her fingers."

Betsy had not minded much about the wash-cloths, although she had tried valiantly to make them, but what she really yearned to do was *something big*—something that involved a real sacrifice and would make her feel like a patriot; knitting the wash-cloths hadn't seemed to give her that feeling.

Then had come the reading in school of the President's proclamation to the school-children of the United States, requesting them to join the Junior Red Cross which had just been arranged for, and she felt that here was the thing for which she wished to work. In the two days that had passed since then all of her thoughts that had not been devoted to her lessons and Josephine-Annabelle had been spent in trying to find the *something big* which she might do for this cause that seemed designed especially for her.

Jo-An of Ark astride her spirited charger

It was while fired by such thoughts that she began stripping Josephine-Annabelle for her latest and favorite "pretend," which had been suggested by Roger's teasing remark that she ought to shorten her child's name to Jo-An—"Jo-An of Ark, by George!" Betsy's vivid imagination had seized eagerly on the suggestion, and though, out of courtesy to the aunts, the doll remained Josephine-Annabelle to the public, in the secret recesses of the Ark she was more often Jo-An. Betsy slipped the disrobed Josephine-Annabelle into a suit of mail, fashioned with the aid of some scouring-rings borrowed from the kitchen, encased her head in a helmet made from part of a tin can, and presto, she became Jo-An! Astride a spirited charger (Bill, handed down by Jack), Betsy felt that her child did credit not only to the family but to the immortal maid whose name hers parodied.

Then, with the brilliancy of a sword swiftly drawn from its scabbard, flashed upon Betsy the idea which would enable her to do her part for her country—and like a sword it pierced. The game stopped right in the middle, while Betsy alternately hugged the plan in an ecstasy of unselfish, patriotic zeal and thrust it from her with outraged mother-love. For fully half an hour the patriot and the mother fought a hand-to-hand conflict; then Betsy, mother, kissed Josephine-Annabelle with passionate renunciation, and Betsy, patriot, unflinchingly dedicated Jo-An to her country's service.

The suit of mail was replaced by the doll's purple and fine linen—dainty, hand-sewn garments, crisp and fresh as when they were made—and the jaunty hat, with long black-velvet streamers, was tenderly placed on her fluffy red-gold hair. In a small grass suitcase Betsy lingeringly packed all of the doll's "other clothes"—the little crêpe nightie, with its crochet-lace yoke and pink-ribboned boudoir-cap to match, her gingham "everydays," and even the plaited serge skirt and middy blouse with tiny embroidered emblems.

To her own toilet Betsy gave no thought. Mechanically she swished a brush over her own fiery mop; mechanically she jammed a hat upon it; then with Jo-An hugged close with one arm, the suitcase in the other hand, she started off. There were no undeveloped parts to her plan. Betsy knew exactly what had to be done; and as Jo-An was her very own, she determined to do it without consulting anyone—her heart was too full to talk it over even with Muddy Dear.

About three quarters of an hour later the secretary of Mr. Arthur Manley, with a face upon which were mixed equal portions of perplexity and amusement, announced Betsy's arrival in the offices of the National Trust Company.

"A small girl with a big doll and a suitcase wishes to speak with you."

Mr. Manley's face reflected the perplexity of his secretary's.

"With me? Are you sure?"

"She asked for you most earnestly; in fact, it seems very pressing," he motioned toward the open door. The banker turned and encountered the beseeching blue eyes of a small, red-haired maid who was standing expectantly in the anteroom. She looked very small and very appealing in the big office rooms.

"Come right in, Miss——," he hesitated.

"Betsy Lane," she murmured shakily, as she advanced to take his welcoming hand.

"What can I do for you, Miss Betsy Lane?" he smiled, motioning to a chair.

"I go to the same church as you," Betsy hardly knew how to begin, "and I took a chance on the bazaar doll."

"Oh, I see. So you are the lucky winner."

"No, I didn't guess the name a bit right; but Josephine-Annabelle is just like her, but all her hair. Aunt Josephine had her wig made specially for her out of mine that had been cut off."

"I noticed she had her mother's hair," he smiled.

"Well—I came to get you to choose a name for Josephine-Annabelle, a different one, and not tell anyone what it is, just as you did for the bazaar doll. Then I will sell the tickets, and the one who guesses the name will get her."

Mr. Manley protested, "But, Miss Betsy, disposing of doll-babies is not my regular business, you know."

Betsy's face fell. "Oh, I thought sure you would do it! You know just how it was done before; and I knew if you would choose the name and put it in a sealed envelope, that everyone would be sure it was all fair and buy my tickets."

Mr. Manley looked at her rather helplessly.

"But she looks like a perfectly good doll-baby to me; I don't see why you want to get rid of her."

"I *don't* want to get rid of her!" flared Betsy, with tragic earnestness. "I wouldn't give her up for anything but my country. Everyone in the family is doing something but me; I couldn't even knit washcloths. It seemed as if there wasn't anything in the world I could do; but Muddy Dear said there was something each person could do, and they must do it—no matter how hard it was."

"My sentiments exactly!" said Mr. Manley, with emphasis, thinking of the conversation he had just had with his only sister. "You must have a very nice mother."

"Oh, I have!" said Betsy, emphatically; "and Daddy, too," loyally.

"I'm sure of that, or such a nice mother wouldn't have had him. That is the reason I have never married—the nice ones wouldn't have me."

"You look pretty good to me," said Betsy, politely.

Mr. Manley threw back his head and laughed heartily. "Thank you, thank you!" he said; "you look pretty good to me, too, Miss Betsy. I shall have to get you to grow up for me."

"I'll be ten the twenty-eighth of November," said Betsy, encouragingly, rather attracted by the idea.

"That is fine!" He took out a small notebook, "Miss Betsy Lane, ten the twenty-eighth of November; and what is your address?"

"1999 R Street, N.W."

He wrote in the notebook: "Now, since you are my fiancé, I suppose I shall have to do whatever you ask. Let's hear all about this idea of yours."

"Well, after the President told about the Junior Red Cross, it seemed as if I just *must* do something, and all of a sudden, when I was playing with Josephine-Annabelle, I remembered about how the bazaar doll made twenty-five dollars. She didn't have 'really and truly' hair, and Josephine-Annabelle has lots more clothes, too." She squatted down beside the suitcase and spread diminutive garments upon the Oriental rug. "I've had her ever since Christmas, but you can see for yourself that she hasn't any scratches or anything on her," and she thrust the doll into his unaccustomed hands.

The banker held the doll gently, and looked with soft eyes on the child's eager face. "I would be delighted to give such an unselfish little girl some money for such a worthy object and let her keep her doll," he suggested, by way of compromise. "I'm strong for all the branches of the Red Cross, myself."

Betsy's face flushed, "Oh, no, thank you, sir; but you see that wouldn't be doing it my very own self. The Junior Red Cross was made just special for children, and the President said it was so every pupil in the United States could have a chance to serve our country."

"Excuse me; you have the right idea; I see we shall have to do it your way. Let me think." He toyed with a paper-cutter on the desk beside him. "I have it," he said at last. "I'll get Mr. Corson to act with us—you know Corson's Department Store? I'll get

Corson to put Josephine-Annabelle in one of his big windows and sell the tickets on the inside. He'll be glad to do it, I know."

Betsy was so staggered with the magnificence in store for her beloved child that she could only give a startled "Oh!" then a lump came in her throat as she realized that now everything was ready for the final sacrifice.

"I think, in view of the `really and truly' hair and her extensive trousseau, that the chances ought to sell for at least fifty cents apiece," he suggested hurriedly, seeing a shadow chase the joy from Betsy's face and guessing the cause; "don't you?" Betsy nodded.

"And there ought to be about a hundred tickets, there will be so many who will want to help this new movement. Can you figure that?"

Betsy wiggled a finger in the air, making imaginary numbers. "Fifty dollars?" she hazarded, her eyes big.

"Correct! A mighty fine donation for a slip of a kiddie, isn't it?"

Her eyes shone exultantly, and Mr. Manley looked at her thoughtfully as he pressed his chin between thumb and index finger. "I want you to take Josephine-Annabelle up to my sister's house and leave her there, so I can get her tonight; I have the very name for the baby, and I'll see that Corson gets her in the window bright and early tomorrow. I want you to visit with Mrs. Stanton a little while and talk to her—tell her all about what you are doing and why. She's home, I have just been talking to her over the 'phone, but I'll call her up and let her know you are coming. Now don't forget to tell her all about it; I'm sure she will take a ticket."

Betsy stiffened with awe as she stopped before the great house which bore the address given her by Mr. Manley, but she marched valiantly to the door and made her request for Mrs. Stanton. When that lady appeared, however, she forgot both her awe and a sudden shyness, in rapt admiration of the charming woman who seemed to know so well how to put an embarrassed little girl at her ease. The story fairly unfolded itself under such sympathetic interest, and it was such a comfort to display Josephine-Annabelle's clothes to one who so thoroughly appreciated their manifold attractions.

"Josephine-Annabelle seems just like a reall child to me," Betsy confided, "but, you see, she was the only thing I had to give, and Muddy Dear was so brave about letting Roger and Mildred go to war, I knew I ought to be willing to let Josephine-Annabelle do what she could for her country."

"Has your mother given up two children to this terrible war?"

Betsy nodded. "It almost is breaking her heart; but when Roger wanted to go, she said it would break it worse to have him stay at home and know that he was shirking a duty that some other boy would have to do for him."

Her listener started. "Muddy Dear said," continued Betsy, "that if she kept him home, every time she heard of a soldier-boy dying in battle she would feel that some other woman's son had given up his life that her boy might stay home safe."

Mrs. Stanton turned pale and put out a hand in quick protest. "I don't see how any woman who loves her son can let him go to those horrible trenches!" she said fiercely.

"Muddy Dear says a mother doesn't love her son if she would keep him from being the finest thing he can be—a patriot."

Mrs. Stanton looked at Betsy earnestly for a moment. "Did my brother tell you to talk to me?" she asked suddenly.

"Oh, yes; he said to tell you all about it—he said it twice."

Mrs. Stanton nodded comprehendingly; her eyes were soft with mist, but her lips were set in a straight, defiant line. She realized that he had sent this small patriot with a purpose—he had seen through her request this morning, that he get Edwin a berth with the railroad in Panama, and knew it had been made because such a position would afford him exemption from the draft. Of course, he with his high ideals and clear vision would have read her purpose—her lips tightened—but she did not care whether he despised her cowardice or not if he would only save her boy for her.

Betsy watched Mrs. Stanton's face uneasily, and, not knowing what else to do, precipitated the moment she had been dreading—separation from Jo-An. "I must go now," she said, hugging the doll close to her for a moment; "I hope the one who gets her will care for her most as much as I do."

Mrs. Stanton came back to Betsy's problem with a start. "Must you go, my dear? You are a brave and unselfish little maid to give up your baby for your country. I hope someone will give you another dolly just like her."

"Oh, no!" exclaimed Betsy, her eyes tragic; "I shall never want another—no one could ever take her place! Good-by," she said abruptly, resolutely keeping her face turned away from the chair where she had put Jo-An.

"Good-by, dear," her woman's intuition making her see deep into the heart of her small caller. "Remember, I shall see that Josephine-Annabelle has the best of care."

Betsy made her way home blindly and went straight to the Ark. Plunging through the door, she threw herself on the bed, sobbing hysterically, until her pillow had a big damp hollow in its center and her lips tasted salty when she put her tongue against them. Finally she sat up and shook herself angrily. "I'm ashamed of myself! Anyone would think I didn't want to serve my country—and I do, I do! I mustn't let anyone else see how I miss Jo-An, though, 'cause they mightn't understand. I must smile bravely even if I do feel bad on the inside." She went to the glass and scanned her face intently, trying on various expressions to find the one best fitted to present to the world. It was most absorbing, but when it had been decided on, it only served to remind her how many, many years she might have to wear it. She must find some way to fill in the dreary, Jo-Anless hours, and decided that she would do so by writing poems and becoming famous. Years later, when her fame had become world-wide, people would comment on her sad beauty and whisper that she had turned to writing for comfort after having given up her only child to her country.

With Betsy, action always trod upon the heels of thought. Going to a small desk that had belonged to every little Lane since Roger, she hunted up a stubby pencil, which she chewed diligently for inspiration, and evolved the following lines:

> Jo-An of Ark went bravely forth
> When she heard her country call;
> And her mother wept, for she knew full well
> That she'd never come back at all.

Betsy wept a little more, herself, and became so saturated with self-pity that she decided her grief would, no doubt, not allow her to live long after all, and she had a vividly clear picture of herself, still and cold upon her bed around which were clustered a grief-stricken family. The spirit of sadness proved so stimulating to her Muse that she was able to drip out a "farewell poem," which bore the further information, in wonderfully curly letters, that it was "Blank Verse." She read it over feelingly, in trembling tones:

> "I am going o'er the river,
> Do not mourn when I am gone.
> I am going to my Father,
> Who is Lord and God of all.

> I can hear the ripple of the waters,
> I can hear voices soft and clear,
> I can see Him coming to see me,
> A weary traveleer."

The dinner bell rang while she was reading this over for the third time, so she put the poems away in a sandalwood box that held her treasures—a baby ring and chewed gold locket—and, assuming the expression of forced cheerfulness which she must wear before the world, she bent not entirely reluctant steps toward the enticing aroma of hot rolls.

When bedtime came there was no Jo-An to undress and tuck under the covers, there remained only her empty bed and a forlorn suit of mail that she had so lately and so spiritedly worn. Betsy swallowed hard and turned her back on them and fell asleep, feeling even more forlorn than she had felt on those long-ago nights when she had first stopped sucking her thumb.

It was not until the next evening that knowledge of Betsy's sacrifice became family property. Mrs. Lane looked up from the evening paper and smiled at Betsy, who seemed to her strangely distrait.

"This will interest you, little daughter; it is about the Junior Branch of the Red Cross in which you are so interested." She read:

"One little girl 'somewhere in Washington' has made a prompt response to the President's proclamation of Wednesday, which should prove inspiring to all children. In one of the big windows of Corson's store, surrounded by Red Cross emblems and American flags, stands a large doll with a mop of real, red curls and a wonderful assortment of clothes. A large card bears this announcement:

> GUESS MY NAME AND TAKE ME HOME!
>
> I belong to a little girl who wants to raise some money of her "very own" to give to the Junior Red Cross. The person who guesses the name given to me by, and known only to, Mr. Arthur Manley, of the National Trust Company, who is acting as my guardian, will become my future owner. Guessing tickets may be bought inside at the jewelry counter at fifty cents a ticket.

"The window has been a source of great interest to the shoppers that throng F Street, and this afternoon the doll was honored by a visit from a no less exalted personage than the President himself, who looked the pleasure which had been given him by this action of an unselfish and patriotic child."

"The window has been a source of great interest to the shoppers."

Betsy clasped her hands. "Jo-An!" she screamed excitedly.

"What?" exclaimed Mrs. Lane, in surprise.

"Jo-An," repeated Betsy, "my Jo-An!" I gave her, Muddy Dear, but I never knew she'd be so famous."

Mrs. Lane held out inviting arms. "Come and tell Mother every word about it."

Betsy snuggled into the dear shelter and told her story.

"I can't tell you how proud Mother is that her little daughter has had such a lovely thought; and I know just what it means to you, sweetheart, for I know just how dearly you loved Josephine-Annabelle. I will take you down tomorrow to see her in all of her glory."

Betsy shook her head violently. "No, Muddy Dear,

I don't think I could stand it. Do you s'pose all the chances will be taken?"

"They're certain to be. I suppose in a day or so the name of the prize-winner will be announced."

When in a few days Mr. Manley's check for fifty dollars arrived, Betsy could scarcely contain her rapture—it seemed impossible that she, Betsy Lane, should have such untold wealth at her disposal. She decided promptly that the money must be donated in the name of Jo-An of Ark, "Because you know, Muddy Dear, she is the one who really earned it." And so it was acknowledged in the first list of contributions published. Betsy clipped this list from the paper and put it, with the other article, beside her poems. When the want of Jo-An pressed too hard upon her, Betsy obtained a great deal of painful pleasure in going over these mementos.

As the time for her birthday drew near, Betsy tried to shame away her longing for the absent one by sternly reminding herself that ten was too old for dolls. This assurance, however, seemed to lack conviction, so she tried to comfort herself with the thought that, even though she could not help missing her baby, at least she did it without a shadow of regret that she had made the sacrifice.

The birthday dawned a sparkling, perfect autumn day, and there flooded through her small person that wonderful feeling of delightfully unexpected things just about to happen that one can feel at ten, and thereabouts. Under her breakfast plate were ten new dimes, and beside it the story of Joan of Arc, with Boutet de Monvel's illustrations in color, and two beautifully upstanding bows for her "scalp lock." She rushed home from school, happy in the prospect of birthday cake and possible ice cream. Skipping up to the Ark for her new book, she halted in amazement—she had had no idea of further presents, and yet there on the floor sat a big, "presenty"-looking parcel.

She looked inquiringly at Muddy Dear, who stood near with expectant face.

"No," laughed Mrs. Lane, "I haven't an idea what it is nor who has sent it. Do open it quickly, for it has been waiting here for you fully an hour, and I am perishing of unsatisfied curiosity."

Betsy tore at the strings excitedly and parted the paper wrappings. She turned pale with emotion—then a vivid red overspread her face, and with a shriek of joy she clasped Jo-An in her arms.

"Oh, Muddy Dear! Muddy Dear!" she cried, rocking back and forth on her knees, her face close to Jo-An's.

Among the wrappings lay the little grass suitcase, and on top of it a square envelope. Betsy stopped hugging her child long enough to open it.

"You read it, Muddy Dear; I can't read tall, sharp, grown-up writing."

"Dear Little Betsy," (read Mrs. Lane):

"When my brother sent you to see me, he did so hoping you would teach me a lesson I was needing—and you did. When I found that Josephine-Annabelle had been won by a young man in Mr. Corson's store, I had no difficulty in buying her from him, as he had only taken the chance because of his interest in the Red Cross. I kept her with me for a while so that, by keeping me constantly in mind of you and your mother, she could finish the work that you began. Last week I let my boy go the front in the same spirit you and your mother gave up those dear to you. And now, on your birthday, I want to send her safely back to you as I hope my boy will be returned to me.

"Lovingly,
Helen Stanton."

"Did you ever read anything so sweet?" beamed Betsy. Her face suddenly clouded. "Do you think I ought to keep her? You know I wanted to make a sacrifice."

"I'm sure you made your sacrifice, dear, and without this hope of reward, and the fact that it was hard for you to make it only made it of greater value. It is all right for you to keep Jo-An now that she has been so kindly returned to you; for all of us mothers, however willingly we may let our babies go, want them back—we want them back!"

Week-days in Dolly's House

by John Bennett

On Monday morning Dolly's clothes
   All need a thorough tubbing;
So Prue and I put in the day
   With washing, rinsing, rubbing;
With boiling, bluing, bleaching, too,
   As all good washerwomen do,
Till Dolly's clothes are clean as new
   And we have finished scrubbing.

On Tuesday comes the ironing,
   The starching, sprinkling, pressing;
For doing gowns up prettily
   Is half the charm of dressing.
And from our irons all the day
   We have to coax the cats away,
For with them they will try to play—
   And that would be distressing!

On Wednesday thread and needle fly
   With basting, whipping, stitching;
With hooks and eyes and buttonholes
   To keep our fingers twitching.
And while the scissors snip, snip, snip,
   We patch and darn and mend and tip,
Till all is trim from tip to tip,
   And Dolly looks bewitching.

On Thursday afternoon we take
   A recess from our labors,
Dress Dolly up in all her best
   And call upon the neighbors;
So she may learn to sit up straight,
   Nor come too soon, nor stay too late,
And always think to shut the gate
   At Tompkins's and Tabor's.

On Friday, dusting-rag in hand,
   We hurry up the sweeping,
And air the household furniture
   While Dolly still is sleeping.
We dust the mantels and the chairs,
The closet-shelves and kitchen stairs,
   And shake the rugs and portières
Like truly-true housekeeping.

On Saturday we bake our bread,
   Enough to last till Monday,
With sugar-pies and apple-tarts
   For Dolly's dinner Sunday;
With doughnuts round as napkin rings,
   And cookies fit for queens and kings—
For oh! it takes just lots of things
   To feed a dolly one day!

Are you giving any presents this year?

Anna Belle's Christmas Eve.
by
Josephine Scribner Gates

It was Christmas Eve. Anna Belle had had a very exciting day, and now, curled up on the window seat, her head pillowed on downy cushions, she sat watching the sleighs as they went flying by.

It was a glorious night. The moon shed its silvery glow on the busy scene, and Anna Belle drowsily noted the people passing with arms filled and pockets bulging.

"I wish I could see what's in those packages," she murmured. "I think Christmas is queer anyhow."

"Why?" came in the prettiest tinkling tones to her ears.

Anna Belle jumped, for there beside her was a beautiful fairy, holding on high a silver wand, on the end of which gleamed a star.

"Why?" persisted the fairy creature, determined to have an explanation.

"Well, I ask for a lot of things I never get, and I get a lot of things I don't want."

"You do?" said the Fairy, inquiringly.

"Yes, every year I do. In the attic are boxes and boxes of things I did n't care for at all. Somehow I'm never very happy at Christmas time."

"Are you giving any presents this year?"

"Oh, yes, Papa always gives me money for that, but I did n't spend it all. I've asked for a bracelet, and if I don't get it I'm going to buy one with what I have left."

The Fairy glanced about the beautiful room, where there appeared to be everything to make one happy, then she gently asked:

"Are the gifts you bought gifts you feel sure are wanted by those who will receive them?"

Anna Belle flushed as she replied:

"Perhaps not. Papa always says, 'You can't get something for nothing,' and you see I did n't want to spend all my money."

"Did you have a happy time buying these gifts?"

"Well, no. Do you think any one is *very* happy at Christmas time?"

"That depends. Some are very, very happy."

"Yes, I know. People who receive bushels of gifts are, especially if the gifts happen to be what they really want."

"Oh," laughed the Fairy, "I know people who have scarcely any money to buy presents and yet are having a lovely Christmas with presents out of nothing. People who are as poor as crows, and yet are bubbling over with joy this very night."

Anna Belle opened her eyes very wide at this statement.

"Making a Christmas out of nothing, and as poor

as crows!" she echoed. "Just how poor is that? I'd like to see them."

"You would? Come with me then," and after a wave of the silvery wand Anna Belle found herself floating along in mid air like a bird.

"Oh!" she cried. "What fun! I wish I could always be a fairy!"

"If you wish it hard enough you may be. Now follow me very closely, for we are n't the only fairies abroad on Christmas Eve."

"Oh, how lovely it is!" she exclaimed. "How different it all looks from above!"

"Yes, dear, everything looks different from above. Do you see that wee brown house far over in that meadow, all alone?"

"Yes," replied Anna Belle; "are they poor as crows?"

"Poorer; they have n't even any feathers," laughed the Fairy, as they gently floated down, down, till they could peer into a window of the little house.

A mother sat by a table sewing. Anna Belle watched her and saw that she was making dolls from bottles.

She fashioned heads by placing a wad of cotton in a piece of muslin. Giving the cloth a twist, she had a perfect round ball, which she shaped and tied down over a cork. On this she skillfully painted a face,

then tied a trim little bonnet about it, and behold, there was a smiling bit of a creature awaiting the next move.

She then made for it petticoat, dress, and coat, and stood it in a corner while she fashioned another. As she worked, she smiled so sweetly the whole room seemed aglow.

"Come and see whom they are for," whispered the Fairy.

Anna Belle followed and peeped into an upper window. There she saw a number of little children all snuggled up fast asleep.

"Look!" whispered the Fairy, and pointed to a stand upon which stood a pincushion made of bits of ribbon from a scrap-bag and a work-box fashioned from a cigar-box. Pockets had been tacked inside, and on the bottom of the box lay a spool of thread.

"Looks lonesome, does n't it?" whispered the Fairy.

Anna Belle nodded as she thought of her own beautiful work-box of carved ivory, with a gold thimble and all sorts of exquisite fittings. And then she remembered another laid away in the attic, one of the things she did n't want.

The two crude gifts on the little table were marked in a childish hand, "For Mother with much love."

"Love is sticking out all over those things," said

"ALL SNUGGLED UP FAST ASLEEP."

the Fairy. "Come down and see how she is getting on with her bottle family."

They went below to find the dolls nearly finished, and a fine ready-made family it was.

Father, mother, children—and even a weenty, teenty pill-bottle doll, dressed as a baby in long clothes, was pinned to the mother, the tiny head nestling close to where her heart should be.

"They are lovely!" declared Anne Belle.

"They are, indeed, and they can do what many of the finest dolls you buy cannot. They can stand, and so you can have great fun with them."

"I'm going to make some," said Anna Belle. "I think they are cute. What is she doing now?"

"Why, don't you see? Some one has given her a branch from a Christmas tree. She is fastening the dolls to it. Now she's poking the coals; she's going to pop corn and string it for the tree. That cost one penny. She's also going to make molasses candy. See it bubbling in that kettle. Molasses is very cheap and it will be the only candy they will have, but they will be wild over it, just because they have it only at Christmas time.

"Now come and let us see crow number two."

Anna Belle was loath to leave this interesting window, but she obediently followed on.

"Look in here," whispered the Fairy as they paused by another humble home.

Anna Belle looked, to see an empty stocking swinging from the mantel, on which was pinned a paper, and Anna Belle read the printed words:

Dear Santa Claus—If you have enuff things to go round wont you give my sister a musick box and a reading book. She is lame and cant play like me. You neednt give me anything. I can hear the musick and read hers.

JAMIE

Anna Belle's eyes filled as she read, and followed the Fairy to see two children fast asleep dreaming of what they hoped they might find in the morning.

"They have no mother. The father is n't much good, but does his best to feed them. In the morning those stockings will be as empty as they are now."

"Dear! Dear! Why does n't some one know about it?" asked Anna Belle, tearfully.

"Some one does—now," replied the Fairy with a wise nod as they floated on.

"I hope they'll do something then," said Anna Belle.

"I hope so," whispered the Fairy. "Look in here," and again Anna Belle peered in a window.

Here a child of perhaps twelve or fourteen was seated at a table working busily. Anna Belle watched to see her making paper-dolls. She cut them out, painted faces and hair, then made a number of cunning dresses, coats, and hats, placed them in envelopes, and marked the outside.

They watched till she had three ready. Then she slipped them into the stockings that hung waiting.

The love light in her eyes was sweet to behold, and, as she stood over the lamp, Anna Belle noticed the rare delicate beauty of her face.

Then all was dark, and the Fairy moved on.

"She did n't hang up her own stocking," said Anna Belle.

"No one to fill it. She mothers those three little ones, and it's all she can do to get along. But did you ever see any one look happier? See the card on this door-knob."

Anna Belle paused to read:

Dear Santa—Please bring me a sleeping doll. If you would just let me hold one and sing it to sleep once, I will be glad. I am a good girl. I never had a doll.

ELSIE.

"See her! Is n't she dear?" cried Anna Belle, as she peeped in the window to see a beautiful plump little girl fast asleep. "She looks like a sleeping doll herself. Will she get the doll?"

"I hope so. It all depends," said the Fairy.

They floated along for some time and presently went down to hover over some children looking in the window of a toy store. Wistful little faces they had, and their clothes told Anna Belle they must get their fun out of just looking. Farther on, in front of the candy store, huddled another shabby crowd, gazing at the sparkling goodies.

"Come away, please, I don't want to see any more. Surely they are n't happy!" cried Anna Belle.

"They are as happy as they can be. Each one of them has a penny in a tightly closed fist, wondering what to buy to take home and put in an empty stocking. Let's stop here a moment," whispered the Fairy, poising on the top of a Christmas tree in front of a big store.

Anna Belle, standing beside her, noticed that as she held her wand on high the star shone out so bright and beautiful the people below paused and gazed in wonder. The happy faces beamed even brighter and the unhappy ones changed instantly.

"What does it mean?" whispered one and another, while one dear little girl cried:

"Why, Mother, it's the Star! Don't you know?"

"A CHILD WAS SEATED AT A TABLE WORKING BUSILY."

"Yes," whispered the mother, clasping more closely the little hand and passing on.

"What made the cross ones look so glad, and the happy ones look more so?" asked Anna belle, as she watched the throngs below.

"Don't you know really?" asked the Fairy.

Anna Belle pondered a while, then looked at the sky to see it thickly dotted with stars, and saw that one shone more brightly than any of the others. She then turned to look at the star on the end of the wand, but lo, it had vanished!

"Where is it?" she asked in surprise.

"It came down and did its work and then went back where it belongs," replied the Fairy with a roguish twinkle, and Anna Belle stared for a moment at the splendid bright star, then said softly: "I understand now why it could do it, but I had forgotten what Christmas really means. For a long time it has seemed to mean only things. Gifts—and not only gifts, but certain *kinds* of gifts. Oh!" she said wistfully, "I wish I could do something to help. Was that what you meant when you kept saying, 'That depends'?"

"That was just what I meant. Now you have seen the Star, and I know all will be well."

Anna Belle seemed busily thinking, and the Fairy waited.

"The attic is full of presents I did n't want, and I have a lot of money I was going to use for the bracelet."

"*If* you did n't get it," laughed the Fairy.

"I don't want it now. I'd rather use it for these poor little children. Elsie must have a doll. I have one, and a music-box, and many 'readin' ' books with pictures. But how can we get them to the places?"

"Fairies are stronger than you think. I will summon my helpers."

Anna Belle then heard a sound as of wind whistling around the corners. In a moment there appeared fairies without number. Such silvery sprites they were that Anna Belle longed to take one to her heart to keep for ever and ever.

"Come!" cried the Fairy, who seemed to be the leader.

As she floated away, all followed, and Anna Belle found they were headed straight for her own home and the attic. As she wondered how they would get in, she found herself flying easily through the tiny bird-window high up in the tower.

"How lovely!" she cried. "I never knew it was for fairies!"

"Show what we are to take," cried the Fairy. "We must hurry."

Anna Belle pointed out a music-box, books, dishes, balls, skates—in fact, toys of every description.

Then she opened one large box where lay a beautiful doll with eyes closed in slumber. "For Elsie," she whispered. Then she watched and saw each fairy gather up a gift.

"Are you really going to take them?" she asked.

"We would n't miss the joy of it for anything!" replied her fairy friend.

They floated away, Anna Belle among them, holding to her heart the sleeping doll. She tried to recall why she had n't wanted it, for it was so pretty. Then she flushed, for she remembered that she had been very cross over this very doll because she had asked for a brown-eyed doll and this one had blue eyes!

"I did n't deserve any doll, nor anything!" she said. "I did n't know I was so bad."

"Forget it!" laughed the Fairy. "We can't afford to be thinking over our wrong-doings. If we have started on the right track we have enough to do to keep on it. Here is the candy store. I know you want to buy something here. Give me your money; I'll get it for you. The man is our friend. He'll double what he gives me, for he well knows what I'll do with it."

In some mysterious way Anna Belle found in a moment that each tiny arm was carrying a basket of bonbons as they floated on.

"Here is Elsie," whispered the Fairy.

Anna Belle placed the doll in Elsie's arms, then filled the stockings with other toys and sweets. In the toe she placed a shining gold-piece.

The music-box, books, and other toys were left in the home of the lame child, and a gold-piece in the toe of each stocking hanging there, too.

The paper-doll girl was generously remembered, and the bottle dolls smiled gratefully at the load of gifts left at their feet.

Anna Belle's eyes shone as she thought of the joy this Christmas was to bring to so many hearts.

"How many?" asked the Fairy, who seemed to know what she was thinking.

Anna Belle pondered as they floated homeward. Presently she cried: "Why, just think, it's twenty-four!"

"Only twenty-four? I counted twenty-five."

Again Anna Belle went over them, then said: "I can't remember the odd one."

The Fairy sent forth a bubbling, rippling laugh, which puzzled Anna Belle for a moment, then she twinkled and cried:

"Why, *I'm* the odd one. I never was so happy. When did it begin? Oh, I know; it was when I saw the Star, was n't it?"

"Yes, indeed!" replied the Fairy, "and not only when you saw the Star, but when you remembered the meaning of it. The love that came in with the Christ Child and His spirit of loving and giving, not only of gifts but of Himself, has come down with the ages and will go on and on."

"I'm so glad I found out. I really don't care now whether I get the bracelet or not," declared Anna Belle, as they floated into her bedroom window.

"No, but see!" and the Fairy pointed with her wand, on the end of which Anna Belle again saw the shining Star sending a glow of light over her pretty dressing-table, and there, lying on its velvet bed, she beheld a beautiful circlet of gold.

As she leaned forward to look at it, she whispered: "Is it plain? I really wanted it jeweled." Then she laughed and added, "No, I don't care *how* it is. Just so it's a bracelet, for I'm afraid I *do* want it. Is it wrong to want it? If it is, I'll try till I don't."

The Fairy gently caressed her, then touched the golden circlet with her wand.

"No, it is n't wrong to want it, now that you remember the true meaning of Christmas, and will keep it with the true Christmas spirit. See!"

Anna Belle looked and saw a starry jewel embedded in the gold. Then she noticed that the Star had vanished from the wand.

She looked quickly out at the sky, where the steady light of the Star shone straight into her eyes.

"I'm glad you did n't take *that* Star," she whispered. "We could n't get along without it."

"My, no! I could n't take that Star. That's the Star of Bethlehem, you know. This is just a tiny shadow of that Star—that's why it is n't quite so bright."

"It's bright enough for me, and means a lot. How can I ever thank you for this night's work?" asked Anna Belle.

"Never again lose sight of the Star and I will be more than repaid. Good-by."

Anna Belle watched her out of sight, then turned and—dear me!—she opened her eyes. The sleighs were still flying past, for she could hear the bells ringing so merrily.

"How much sweeter they sound!" she cried. "They seem to be saying 'Merry Christmas! Merry Christmas!' I wonder why I did n't notice it before."

She ran downstairs to find Mother busily wrapping packages. She looked at Anna Belle and cried:

"Why, child! What makes your eyes so bright, and why do you look so glad? I heard you saying all sorts of things as you slept."

"Oh, Mother! If you only knew!" and thereupon she told the whole story of her dream, omitting the part about the bracelet. When she had finished, she

drew her mother to the window where together they gazed at the Star.

Mother's eyes were full of tears as she said gently, "Ring the bell, dear."

The maid appeared, and Mother asked that John bring out the double sleigh at once, adding:

"Then come to me; bring Annie also. We have work to do."

Wonderingly the maids followed to the attic and brought down many boxes lying there, waiting for they knew not what.

"Help me to tie them up separately in white tissue-paper. Use the prettiest ribbons."

They worked busily, and soon a more Christmassy lot of bundles it would be hard to find.

They placed them in baskets, and Mother added some warm clothing.

Presently Anna Bell, Mother, and the baskets, packed in the big sleigh, were dashing down the street. One stop they made, at the candy store, then on they went.

"Do you think you can find Elsie, and the little lame girl, and the house where the bottle dolls are?"

"I'm sure I can," replied Mother. "I happen to know them all."

And find them they did, and many others who were not in the dream.

"Oh, Mother! is n't it a happy thing to do this?" cried Anna Belle, her bright eyes shining up at the Star.

"It is, indeed, dear. I'm very glad you had the dream, for I fear I, also, was forgetting the real meaning of Christmas and almost entirely losing sight of the Star."

She held the child close till the wonderful ride was over, then kissed her, saying:

"I don't know when I have been so happy!"

"Nor I, Mother dear, and we owe it all to the Good Fairy."

"We do, indeed. May she never cease to wave her starry wand. Good night, my child, good night."

Soon Anna Belle slept; and, as she slept, the starlight beamed on her sweet face, and presently shone also on a golden circlet lying on its velvet pillow on the dresser.

The dream seemed really coming true, for there embedded in the gold gleamed a starry jewel.

When Anna Belle found it the next morning, she ran to Mother's room asking earnestly, "Mother, *do* you think the Fairy left it?"

"No doubt," replied Mother, with twinkling eyes. "At least, she must have touched it with her wand, for you see she has left her messenger."

"And the Star is shining."

A Dispatch to Fairy-Land

By Helen K. Spofford

Connect me with Fairy-land please, pretty Vine,
   With the Fairy Queen's palace of pearl,
And ask if her Highness will hear through your
     line
   A discouraged and sad little girl.

O Queen, I'm so grieved 'cause my dolly wont play,
   And so tired of pretending it all!
I must walk for her, talk for her, *be* her all day,
   While she sits still and stares at the wall.

Her house is so pretty, with six little rooms,
   And it has *truly* windows and doors,
And stairs to go up, and nice carpets, and brooms—
   For I do the sweeping, of course.

There's a tea-set, and furniture fit for a queen,
   And a trunk full of dresses besides;
And a dear little carriage as ever was seen,
   And I am her horse when she rides.

But never a smile nor a thank have I had,
   Nor a nod of her hard, shiny head;
And is it a wonder I'm weary and sad?
   For I can't love a dolly so dead.

   I thought I would ask you if, in your bright train,
     You had n't one fairy to spare,
   A naughty one, even,—I should n't complain,
     But would love it with tenderest care—

   Or a poor little one who had lost its bright wings,—
     I should cherish it not a bit less,—
   And, besides, they'd get crushed with the sofas
     and things,
   And be *so* inconvenient to dress.

   O Queen of the Fairies, so happy I'll be
     If you'll only just send one to try;
   I'll be back again soon after dinner to see
     If you've left one here for me. Good-bye!

DOLLY'S LULLABY
BY MRS. SCHUYLER VAN RENSSELAER

Sing, I must sing to my dear dolly, sing,
And tell her the stories of everything.
She is tired of my singing just "Sleep, dear, sleep,"
She is tired of the song about Little Bo-Peep,
Of Little Miss Muffet, and all of the rhymes
I have sung from my picture-book dozens of times.
Sing, I must sing to my dear dolly, sing,
And tell her the stories of everything

Slumber, my dolly! I'll tell you to-night
Of trees that are blossoming rosy and white,
Of brooks where the ripples of brown water run,
And tinkle like music and shine in the sun;
Of nests where the baby birds sit in a heap,
And the mother sits over them when they're asleep.
Sing, I must sing to my dear dolly, sing,
And tell her the stories of everything

The summer is green and the winter is white,
There is sunshine by day and starshine at night;
The stars are so many it cannot be told;
The moon is of silver, but they are of gold;
The clouds are like ships, and the sky like the sea,
Only turned upside down over dolly and me.
Sing, I must sing to my dear dolly, sing,
And tell her the stories of everything

Pensez vous qu'elle ressemble à sa Maman?

Little Daughter of the Revolution
(THE STORY OF GREAT-GRANDMOTHER'S PLAYHOUSE.)

By Mary Bradley

Yes, it 's truly true, you know—
Dear old granny told me so;
And this very doll (who 'd think
That its face was ever pink?
But it *was*, long time ago!)
Was a present sent to her
By the Yankee officer.

It was in the old, old days
When King George had funny ways,
Interfering with the plans
Of us free Americans.
(Or, if not exactly free
At that time, we *meant* to be!)

Well, my granny's father then
Had a farm on Medford Hill.
Wish we had that farm again,
with the old tree on it still!
Such a dear old hollow tree,
Overgrown with vines and things—
Just the greatest place for swings
And all kinds of jollity!

Granny kept her rag dolls there,
And her kittens, too, she said,
When there was no room to spare
In the kitchen. Overhead
There were squirrels chattering,

Birds that used to build and sing,
Grapes all purple-ripe and sweet,
Nuts so nice to crack and eat!

Dear me! I 've a doll's house here,
Full three stories from the floor—
Staircase, hall with chandelier,
Double parlors, big front door,
Every kind of furniture;
But it is n't half so good
As that playhouse in the wood.

One day, rummaging around
In the hollow, granny found
There was something like a pit
Far in at the back of it—
Just a sinking of the ground,
I suppose, among the roots,
Handy for the nuts and fruits
That the squirrels hide, you see;
"But 't would hide a man," thought she.

So she hurried down the hill,
Told her mother what she thought;
And that night, when all was still,
To the hollow tree was brought
Meat and drink to feed—
And the man himself, indeed!

'T was a "rebel" officer
(That was what they called us then,
When we fought King George's men),
And to make him prisoner,
As my granny was aware,
Men were hunting everywhere.
It was only just that day
Officers had come to say
That whoever hid the man
Fed, or helped him on his way,
British of American,
He would have King George to pay!

So it was a risky plan
For her father, don't you see?
British constables and kings
Must have been right awful things!
But he was n't scared—not he!
Neither granny, you would judge,
If next day you 'd see her trudge
Up the hillside to the tree!

There, with playthings spread about,
Acorn cups and saucers set,
Kittens running in and out,
She amused herself—and yet
Was n't likely to forget!
Like a pious little maid,
I am sure she watched and prayed,
But was frightened all the same
When at last the soldiers came.

For they did come—oh, of course!—
Two afoot and one on horse,
All to catch one Yankee man!
And the biggest one began
(You should see my granny frown
As she tells it) to pull down
All her beautiful green bowers
Till they tumbled at her feet—
Purple grapes and yellow flowers,
Clematis and bittersweet.

Oh, I would have liked to see
That man's face as out she came,
Flashing eyes and cheeks aflame,

From the hollow of the tree!
And (as if against the cat,
Tooth and nail, had sprung the mouse)
"Shame!" she cried, "for doing that—
Now you 've spoiled my baby-house!"

How her heart beat in her dread!
But she bravely stood her ground,
And the burly man in red,
Casting watchful eyes around,
Saw within the hollow tree
Just her rag dolls, two or three,
And her kits, a sleepy pair,
But, except the pretty child,
Not another creature there.
So half sheepishly he smiled,—
Having children of his own,—
Said a kindly "Never mind!"
Turned about, and left behind
Kits and dolls and child alone.

How that "rebel" officer,
Under his thick coverlid
Of dry leaves so snugly hid,
Must have praised and petted her!
Fancy what a grateful kiss
Paid the little maid for this
When, the anxious hour past,
She came gaily home at last.

For, as afterward they knew,
There were papers that he bore
Worth their weight in gold, and more—
Papers planned to serve the State
When its need, they said, was great,
That were only saved to it
By her ready mother-wit.

So I truly think—don't you!—
That we "Daughters" ought to claim
And be proud of our fine name;
And I hope, if ever need
Comes again, that daughters still
May be brave in words and deed
As was she on Medford Hill.

119

Only a Doll!

By Sarah Orne Jewett

Polly, my dolly! why don't you grow?
   Are you a dwarf, my Polly?
I'm taller and taller every day;
   How high the grass is!—do you see that?
The flowers are growing like weeds, they say;
   The kitten is growing into a cat!
     Why don't you grow, my dolly?

Here is a mark upon the wall.
   Look for yourself, my Polly!
I made it a year ago, I think.
   I've measured you very often, dear,
But, though you've plenty to eat and drink,
   You have n't grown a bit for a year.
     Why don't you grow, my dolly?

Are you never going to try to talk?
   You're such a silent Polly!
Are you never going to say a word?
   It is n't hard; and oh! don't you see
The parrot is only a little bird,
   But he can chatter so easily.
     You're quite a dunce, my dolly!

Let's go and play by the baby-house;
   You are my dearest Polly!
There are other things that do not grow;
   Kittens can't talk, and why should you?
You are the prettiest doll I know;
   You are a darling—that is true!
     Just as you are, my dolly!

A Book-Lover

By Annie Willis McCullough

"I do love books!" said Marjorie,
  One morning as she played.
And so she did, as you can see—
  This literary maid!

The dictionary was her chair;
  The atlas big, her table;
The dolls sat up on other books
  As straight as they were able.

And then they all partook of tea,
  And did as they were bid.
"I do love books!" said Marjorie.
  Now, don't you think she did?

A Doll on Mount Etna

By E. Cavazza

On the doorstep of the house sat little Lucia with one hand in the other. Within she heard the voice of her baby sister who was cooing with pleasure to see the mamma's broom sweep across the floor. Near the doorstep the speckled hen was scratching in the warm, black earth with her chickens around her. At the door of the stable stood the bay mare, snuffing the April air, and beside her was her colt, unsteady on his long legs. Two little pigs had found a cabbage-stalk, and in the middle of the road shared the dainty with soft grunts of content. The cat on the window-sill blinked her drowsy eyes in the sun, with the calm of a good conscience; in the hay-loft, among the grain, no rat dared venture—she could be surety for so much! From the road sounded the anvil of neighbor Memmu the blacksmith; and, farther away, the soldiers were at drill, and the officers were heard shouting, *"Per fil' a destr'-marche!"*

The young leaves of the Indian fig trees and the olives, of the vines and the maize, were bright against the side of the mountain, like countless points of cool, green flame. In the sky, the continual smoke of Etna waved like the plume of a giant's cap. Lucia's papa and her twin brother, Giuseppino, were at work, away there in the fields. If she were there, too, weeding between the rows of maize, it would have been a pleasure for her. She only had nothing to do—the little one, and the idleness wearied her. Finally, a cloud of dust and the noise of wheels drew her attention. It was a carriage that seemed to belong to a baron at least, she thought, with the fine horses and harnesses. it came to a halt at the door of Memmu's forge. The driver dismounted, and afterward a gentleman, a lady, and a little girl of Lucia's own age—about seven years. Lucia could hear all that they spoke, but could not understand a word. The driver, who was from Catania, explained to Memmu that one of the horses had cast a shoe. The blacksmith set himself to make another, while his boy Neddu blew the bellows and the coals reddened. The lady and gentleman were not unlike others; Lucia had seen many travelers pass through the village. They would come up the road from Catania, and look in the sky at the smoke of the crater, and down at the black earth, and point here and there,

and talk in such strange tongues that Don Ambrogio had more than once said it was indeed a renewal of the confusion of Babel—these travelers. But the little lady—she carried in her arms a most beautiful doll! Lucia could not help going forward, timidly, and at a respectful distance, to admire it; while her serious, black eyes were round as the beads of a rosary, for wonder at this magnificent image of fine porcelain, with hair blonde as wheat, in a traveling gown of brown plaid wool, with the relative bonnet, bag, umbrella, even tiny, high-heeled bronze boots. The owner of the doll, however, appeared discontented.

"Mamma," she said in English—and Lucia, not understanding her language, thought it sounded like the idiom of the squirrels in the oaks of Belpasso. "Mamma, what was I thinking of, to buy this horrid doll?"

"Don't interrupt Papa, darling. As you were saying, Frederic?"

"At the time of the eruption of 1669, the group of hills called the Monti Rossi suddenly appeared, and from these new craters came a flood of lava which spread over the southern slope of Etna, like the black waves of a sea, petrified in a moment of tempest."

"I don't like light hair for a doll, mamma; it is too common. All the girls have light-haired dolls. When we go back to Naples, can't I buy one with chestnut hair?"

"Even more dismal than this region, is the Valle del Bove. Clouds hang and twist continually above its black masses. It seems like a dead city of Dis—"

"Mamma, can't I? Say, can't I buy—"

Professor Alleyn forgot his descriptive eloquence and turned quickly toward his little daughter, who, it must be admitted, was a trifle spoiled.

"Gladys, I will not have you so petulant. Since you do not care for your doll, you shall give her at once to that little Italian girl."

"I think Gladys is tired," said gentle Mrs. Alleyn. "She is not usually so silly." The mother drew her little girl to her side, while the professor went on to speak of the chemical composition of lava, and to wish that it might be possible to examine a quantity of it while still heated, in order to determine the nature of its crystalline deposits. His wife heard his discourse with interest, yet her mind was a little preoccupied by the effect likely to be produced upon Gladys, by the sudden command to give up her doll, bought a few days before in the largest toy-shop of Naples. Gladys waited for her papa to finish speaking; then:

"I am sorry I was naughty," she whispered. "But I wish I loved my dolly more, if I am to give her away."

Mrs. Alleyn comprehended that her little daughter's words came partly from a tenderness for the doll, partly from a curious penitent wish to make a little sacrifice. Gladys went toward Lucia.

"Little girl," she said. Lucia understood nothing. Neighbor Memmu had shod the horse and was helping the coachman put him to the carriage. "Little girl, this doll is for you."

Lucia, encouraged by the smile of Gladys, came timidly, touched with her brown forefinger the hem of the doll's dress, then kissed it seriously. Gladys thrust the doll into Lucia's arms.

"*È tua questa—*" here the professor paused, not having learned, in course of his correspondence with the Italian scientists, the word for *doll*.

But Lucia understood now. She kissed alternately the gown of the doll and the small gloved hands of Gladys.

"Her name is Margherita," said the American girl.

"Si, si—Margherita—bella, bella, bella!" answered Lucia with more kisses.

"Come, Gladys, we are ready to go now," said the professor. And as he seated the little girl beside her mamma, "Did you think Papa a little severe with his chatterbox?"

"I am glad you told me to give that little girl my doll. She is just perfectly delighted. And I have twenty-six dolls, and a hundred and seventy-nine paper dolls, anyway."

"When they come down the mountain," said Lucia to herself, "I shall offer to that little lady one of my hen's eggs. It is little, but one does what one can."

The doll seemed to her a worthy namesake of the good and beautiful queen whose photograph had been shown her by the corporal of the garrison. She did not yet dare treat the doll familiarly—to play it was her little girl.

"Signora," she said to it, "do me the favor to accommodate yourself on the doorstep while I seek the egg. Mamma, Mamma, come and see!"

Lucia's mamma, whose name was Marina, appeared at the door.

"See my beautiful doll!"

"Oh, what a doll! She looks like the images of the saints in the church, and is dressed just like a queen. Who has given her to you?"

"A little lady, that was passing in her carriage,

"Her name is Margherita," said the American girl.

with her papa and mamma, and the horse lost a shoe so that Compare Memmu had to make another."

"And what had you done for her?"

"Nothing. I was only looking at her. But I shall tell my hen to let me have a fresh egg to give her."

The doll was laid carefully upon the doorstep while Lucia hastened to search for the egg. But, unfortunately, that day the hen had forgotten to leave one in the nest for her little mistress. Lucia returned, with empty hands, to find her doll. What had happened? The beautiful blue eyes, blue as flowers of the lavender, were closed. The doll appeared to sleep. "She is tired with the journey from Catania," thought Lucia, and sat down to watch the slumbers of the doll. At last it seemed to her that the doll had slept long enough.

"Wake, Signora Margherita!" she said, very softly. The porcelain eyelids did not move. Lucia spoke again, and louder; but without effect. Marina came again to the door, at the cry: "Oh, Mamma, Mamma, my doll is dead!"

"What did you do to her?"

"Nothing. When I came back, her eyes were shut and I thought her asleep. My doll is dead!" sobbed Lucia, with the corner of her apron at her eyes.

"I do not believe her dead; no," said Marina. "Such a fine lady, however, might very well faint away, to be brought to the house of poor people."

Marina lifted the doll to its feet; the mechanism of its eyes worked as usual, and Margherita, wide awake, seemed to look with content upon her squalid surroundings.

The doll soon became the talk of the neighborhood. "It will be a thousand years before I can make one like that on my anvil," said Memmu the blacksmith.

The women never tired of wondering at its fine clothes, all but *Zia* Caterina, who shook her head with its yellow kerchief and said, "It seems like witchcraft. It is not an image of a saint—well, what is it then, to do the miracle of winking its eyes? I wish it may not bring you bad luck, *Comare* Marina." The other women contradicted her, and would have justice for the doll, shaking their distaffs in the face of *Zia* Caterina. Don Ambrogio, the parish priest, admired the doll; and the archbishop himself was reported to have smiled to see Lucia seated on the doorstep with Margherita in her arms. After that, *Zia* Caterina might say what appeared pleasing to her!

The month of May was more than half passed. Marina sat at her door spinning; while, near her,

Lucia rocked the cradle occupied by baby Agatuzza at one end, and the famous doll at the other. The mamma sang one of the popular songs of the country, which ran somewhat like this:

> "I lost my distaff on Sunday,
> I looked for it all day Monday,
> Tuesday, I found it cracked and split,
> Wednesday, took off the flax from it,
> Thursday, I combed the flax quite clean,
> And Friday sat me down to spin,
> On Saturday I must spin it all,
> For Sunday is a festival!"

Marina's husband, whose name was Celestino, came along the road, together with the corporal. They were looking with some anxiety at the sky. A column of thick, black smoke arose from the crater, and, higher in the air, separated into great whirling masses that waved like banners.

"There is the smoke of the enemy," said the corporal. "Let us hope that we may not have to feel his fire!"

That night the neighbors, assembled at the inn, watched the smoke. As it grew darker, red, glowing streams of lava were seen to run down the side of the mountain from new openings, near the crater of Monte Nero. The windows of the village rattled with the explosions which took place more and more frequently. A reddish vapor spread itself upward from the stream of lava. The bells of the town rang mournfully, while the people cried, "The lava, the lava!"

In the morning it was no better. The lava seemed to make its way in a sluggish current toward the towns of Nicolosi and Belpasso.

In a few days news came that the *oliveto* of neighbor Brasi, a few miles above the village, was on fire. "And the trees cry out for pain, like so many living souls, so that it is a pity to hear them," said Bellonia, his wife.

In truth, either because the sap was become suddenly heated, or for some other reason, the poor olive trees made a whimpering sound as the lava scorched them. Bellonia, Marina, and the other women took down from the dingy walls of their rooms the colored pictures of the saints, and fixed them upon sticks, at the edge of the vineyards. At the northern limit of the fields the vines already began to burn, although the lava was not yet near the village of Nicolosi.

"If the wells should burst," said Celestino, "as that pond did that the good soul of my father used to tell of, we are lost."

"Glowing streams of lava were seen to run down the side of the mountain."

"The water must be drawn off," recommended neighbor Turiddu.

"Eh! One can't live without water, for man and beasts. It is an ill death to die of thirst."

"I tell you, better drain the wells! Who knows if Heaven will not send us a little rain, afterward?" said a more hopeful person.

"Better quit the town, and then if the wells burst, they burst," said the corporal, who was of the group.

"And I am ruined, I am," said *Compare* Brasi, he of the olive-trees. "I and my family, we shall be in the middle of the road, asking alms."

The terror lasted for nearly a fortnight. The noise of the lava was like the rattling of great hailstones upon tiles, with frequent explosions like the firing of cannon. The images of the saints, Sant' Antonio and the others, were taken from their quiet shelter in the churches, where candles were burned and the floors and doorways were strewn with rose-petals and bunches of sweet herbs and the yellow flowers of the broom, that sent forth delicate odors. The images had to come out and stand in the *piazza* to encourage the people. The daylight was not flattering to their appearance. Their wooden faces painted in not the palest tint of pink, their round glass eyes

without intelligence, and the tinsel and jewels of their robes looked gaudy enough in the open air. Then Turiddu and Celestino and Memmu gave a hand to the litter whereupon the image of Sant' Antonio was carried up the hill, while the people cried, "Viva Sant' Antonio!" "Do us the favor, Sant' Antonio!" With banners and psalmody, they took him up to the Altarelli—which is a small structure of three arches painted, in the Byzantine manner, with curious stiff figures of saints. They set the image in front of the lava; the glass eyes stared at it in vain. "All the saints together could not work this miracle," said Brasi; and soon the image was brought back into the *piazza*.

Before the close of the second week, the telegraph operator received official notice to remove. Many of the people were gone to Pedara, to Trecastagni; but more remained, unwilling to leave their homes. The officers and soldiers of the garrison counseled the peasants to depart, since from day to day the lava threatened the village. Those who still remained packed their goods, and great cart-loads were sent along the road eastward. Marina, full of care, had no more time to admire Lucia's doll. With the aid of her husband, she had taken out of the house their small stock of furniture, bedding, dishes, and clothes, and arranged them in the cart, which was painted in vivid colors. Also Giuseppino and Lucia did what they could. They put the cat into a basket made of rushes, and tied a piece of cloth over, so that she could not escape. Giuseppino made a slip-noose to catch the little pigs, that soon after, squealing, with their feet tied, were thrust into a sack and placed among the other valuables in the cart. Lucia stood near, with her doll in her arms, dismayed by the confusion of carts and carriages, some taking into safety the inhabitants of Nicolosi, others bringing strangers to see the lava, as if it were a festival with Bengal lights.

Giuseppino, near the hen-coop, was trying to secure the hen and her brood. "Eh, how she runs, the poor little beast!" he said. "Come, Lucia, she is your hen; come and catch her."

The hen ruffled her wings as if she would defy not only the children, but Etna itself. Lucia seated her doll on a little hay behind the hen-coop, and helped her brother to reduce the hen to discipline. They had not yet succeeded when Marina called her daughter.

"Come here, Lucia!"

"Yes, Mamma. I'm coming, coming."

"Run quick to the house of the *nonna,* and tell her we shall come in a half hour to take her; and you, Lucia, do what you can to help her."

"Oh, willingly."

The *nonna* was not really Lucia's grandmother, but her father's. She was old, and had seen many things, of which—and also of giants and princesses and sirens—she knew how to tell famous stories when the Christmas *ceppo* was lighted on the hearth. She never came to an end of her stories and rhymes, and had a dried fig and two kisses, always, for good children. And to help the good *nonna,* Lucia left her hen and ran along the road like a fawn. Then, remembering her doll, she called back over her shoulder, "Giuseppino, oh, Giuseppino-o-o! Take care of Margherita-a-a!"

"*Brava!* With that voice we will have you for trumpeter!" commented the corporal, as she ran past him. But, alas, in the uproar of the road and the bombardment of the mountain, her brother could not hear her. and, being a boy, he forgot the doll in the glory of the conquest of the hen. At last, the *chioccia* and her brood were in a basket on the cart. Celestino had taken off the shutters, the latches and hinges, even some of the tiles of the roof and the floor of his house; and these, with similar belongings of other persons, were loaded upon an ox-cart.

Marina had put a halter on the neck of the colt, thereby the more easily to lead him behind the cart to which his mother was harnessed.

"Are we ready, Marina?"

"Yes. Oh, my little house! Who knows if I shall ever see again my poor little roof? We were so content, were we not, Celestino?"

"Yes, yes, indeed. But Lucia; where is she?"

"With the *nonna,* waiting for us."

"*Su,* Maddalena, come up!" This was to the mare.

The cart began to move. The colt trotted weakly, not to fall behind his mother, who walked with long steps. Marina sat on top of her goods, her baby in her arms, while Celestino guided the mare on foot, and little Giuseppino kept pace behind with his friend the colt. Arrived at the house of the grandmother, they found her standing at the doorway, with Lucia at her side, and dressed in her best plaid cotton gown, and clean apron and kerchief, content as if she were going to mass. Marina gave the *nonna* her own place on the cart, while she herself, with Lucia by the hand, walked, carrying her baby on her shoulder.

The road to Pedara was blocked with carts and with persons on foot, with goats, and sheep, and cattle, straying to this side and that, driven by men and watch-dogs. The people were in a panic terror; some wept, some prayed, some moaned, beating their arms, and others appeared stupefied. Trumpets were blown as a signal that the village should be cleared, officers and soldiers were everywhere to help, cheer, and advise the peasants. "Truly," complained the corporal, "I make myself into four, I make myself; but even so, I can't do everything!"

The archbishop caused the relics and the images from the churches to be carried toward Pedara; and the mayor and other officials ran here and there to direct things as the procession moved.

It was only by slow degrees that Celestino and his family approached Pedara. Marina wept like a fountain; and the grandmother repeated, "We must have patience," while the sighs came from her heart to think of the village that would soon be buried under the lava. They encamped for the night among the yellow broom that grew in tufts, in bushes as far as one could look, so that it appeared endless. Through the early hours of the night, people were passing, and added their shouts to the crashing bursts of the volcano.

Suddenly little Lucia awoke to the consciousness that her dear doll was not in her arms. Where was

Margherita? Was she safe in the cart, or had she been left in the village, a prey to the lava? Tears came into Lucia's eyes. "No, I must not wake mamma, who is so tired, nor the dear *nonna*, nor papa who has worked so hard," she said to herself. But she could not refrain from giving a gentle push to her brother. He awoke and said, "What is the matter, Lucia?"

"Margherita—did you bring her with you?"

"Oh! what should I do with a doll?" answered the boy, a little roughly—precisely because he was so sorry.

"I called to you, while I was running to the house of the *nonna*."

"And I did not hear you."

"You might have brought my poor Margherita."

"It is true, Lucia. Will you forgive me?"

She kissed him in token of pardon. Lucia crept back to her place beside the *nonna;* both children lay still, but it was only Giuseppino who slept. Lucia had in time come to love her doll like a little mamma; Margherita no longer seemed to her a great lady. Lucia could not bear the thought of the deserted doll; perhaps at that very moment the lava was entering the town. Margherita would be covered deep with the hot lava!—at the idea Lucia herself felt suffocated. She was resolved. Without noise, she arose and moved softly away toward the road. She knew the way, and was not afraid; the road was lined with wagons, near which mules, horses, and donkeys were tethered, while the peasants slept under or beside the carts, as it might chance. Many were awake, but none would harm a little girl, or even notice her in the apathy which followed their alarm and toil. Lucia made her way toward Nicolosi, with her head and limbs heavy with sleep, so that she often swayed from side to side as she walked, and could hardly lift her feet from the ground. Her mind was confused with dreams. Then a new explosion and a fresh thought of her doll impelled her, and she hastened forward.

At last she reached Nicolosi. Was this her own town? A light rain of warm sand and ashes was falling, the streets and the *piazza* were deserted.

Now and then she heard the howl of a vagrant dog. She put her hand against the wall of a building to guide herself. By the broken corner of a stone, she knew it to be the house of neighbor Nanni. Her own home would be the next house. She half saw, half felt her way to the hen-coop.

"Margherita, are you here?" she said, and was frightened to hear her own voice in the solitude. She groped with her hands behind the hen-coop, caught the doll in her arms, and kissed it many times.

Then came a great explosion. It seemed to Lucia as if the end of the world were come; the shower of ashes and sand fell thicker; and the little girl, clasping her doll, ran as fast as she could from the town. When she had reached the first encampment of people, she felt quite safe. The corporal, with some soldiers, came by.

"Who is this? Little Lucia! What are you doing here?"

"Signor Caporale, I returned for my doll."

"Via! You are worse than Lot's wife. What will your mamma say? Have you thought of that? It seems to me that she will be capable of scolding you a little. Run along to her!"

Before dawn the weary Lucia was not far from the place where she had left the family. Marina, with her white *mantellina* over her head, was running up and down the road among the people, crying like one possessed:

"My child, my Lucia! Who has seen my little Lucia?"

"Here I am, Mamma."

Marina caught her little daughter in her arms, and hastened back to the *nonna*, who sat tending the baby. Giuseppino was still asleep.

"Here she is; she is safe!" exclaimed Marina.

The boy awoke and opened his eyes, still full of sleep.

"Oh! you found your doll, Lucia?"

"You did wrong, little one," said the grandmother, but not until she had kissed Lucia. "Do you know you have caused a great fright to us who love you so dearly?"

"Nonna, I could not, no, leave my dear Margherita all alone. Don't you remember, she fainted only to come to the house of poor people? Alone, with no one to speak a good little word to her. Indeed, she might have had a fulminating apoplexy."

"Oh, we admit," said Lucia's papa, "that the doll is a great lady, and so delicate that you are right to keep her as if in cotton-wool. But, another time, think also a little of the rest of us!"

"I did wrong," answered Lucia. "I know it."

"And you proved yourself a brave girl," said Celestino, who, having done his paternal duty in the mild reproof, now gave himself the satisfaction of pride in his daughter. "You have a good heart—and good little legs, Lucia."

After their breakfast of black bread and a few olives, the family set forth again on their way to the house of a brother of Marina, who lived beyond

Marina caught her little daughter in her arms.

Pedara, on the road to Tremestieri. There they would remain until the fate of their own town should be decided.

Day by day, the stream of lava grew more sluggish, and finally came to a standstill, barely touching the wall of the Altarelli, three hundred kilometers from the northern outskirts of the village of Nicolosi. A fortnight after the abandonment of the town the trumpets blew joyfully, as a signal for the people to return to their homes. It was a fine procession. First went the archbishop and the priests, with the images and relics and brilliantly colored banners; and the people came after, led by the civil authorities and the soldiers, with psalms and shouts and military music.

The streets and the *piazza* were readily cleared of the layer of sand and ashes rained upon them from the volcano; shutters and doors were hung again upon their hinges, tiles were replaced, and household goods set in order. The town had never

seemed so dear, and all were happy and content.

"It is a fine thing to be able to end one's days where one was born," said the *nonna* to Lucia.

Lucia had not thought of that; but she felt it to be a fine thing to live when one has a mamma, a papa, a grandmamma, a brother, a baby sister,—and a doll.

It only remains to say that Professor Alleyn and his family returned one day, before the lava was cooled, and made the ascent of Etna as far as Monte Albano, in company with some distinguished Italian scientists. It is now thought—the professor told me at a reception—that incandescent lava is not to be regarded as an uniformly fused mass, resembling the *scoria* of a foundry, but owes its crystalline deposits to the chemical results of a gradual process of fusion. It may be so. Who among us has enough polysyllables at command to refute the theory? But more interesting to me was the story of the doll, which one of the Italian professors heard at Nicolosi. He told it to Gladys, and she told it to me.

A Queen

by
Faith Van Valkenburgh
Vilas

My mother made a pasteboard crown
   With points, to fit my head,
And then she crayoned jewels on
   In green and blue and red.

She let me wear her flow'ry dress,—
   It's sweet as sweet can be,—
In which she used to make believe,
   When she was small like me.

And then she found a long pink veil
   And pinned it to my crown;
I saw it follow on the floor
   Whenever I looked down.

I marched about the living-room
   All traily-proud and slow,
While Mother played a queen's own song,
   So dignified and low.

I sat upon my throne awhile
   Quite haughtily and grand,
And ruled my dolls that stood about
   On squares in Carpet-Land.

When I grew sleepy, Mother dear
   Just sat and held me tight;
A queen is fun for daytimes, but
   I'm glad I'm me at night.

The Tea-Set Blue

By Rose Mills Powers

When Tillie brings her tea-set out,—
    Her lovely set of blue,—
And lays the dishes all about
    The table, two by two,
        The little doll-house people all
        Begin to wonder who will call.

For 't is a signal, beyond doubt,
    That visitors are due,
When Tillie brings her tea-set out—
    Her treasured set of blue.
        So all the dollies watch and wait,
        And sit up very nice and straight.

And Pierrot forgets to tease
    In hopes to be a guest;
The Japanese doll from over-seas
    Tries hard to look his best;
        While Mam'selle French Doll, all the while,
        Wears—ah, the most angelic smile!

For all the nursery people know
    As well as well can be
That dollies must be good who go
    With Tillie out to tea.
        And would not that seem fair to you,
        If you possessed a tea-set blue?

ELIZABETH SHIPPEN GREEN

Kittie's Best Friend

By M. Helen Lovet

amma! Mamma!" cried Kittie Perry, running into the house early one afternoon and throwing down her school-books, "the new people are moving in next door."

"So I see, Kittie," said Mrs. Perry.

"And, Mamma, there's a little girl there just about as big as me. I just saw her going in. I've awfully glad! I'm 'most crazy for some one to play with since the Cooks went away. May Kingsley's the only other girl on the block, and we're having a tiff now. I'm going right in to see that girl and find out what her name is."

"Kittie!" said her mother, catching her just in time as she was flying out of the room, "you must not go. The little girl's mother would n't like it. I'm sure I should n't have wished the neighbor's children to come in here the day we moved. We had confusion enough without that."

"But, Mamma, I *must,* for I need some one to play with, and May Kingsley and I are angry at each other and I can't speak to her for a week."

"I'm afraid you will not be able to do that, Kittie," said Mamma, laughing.

"I'm afraid not," said Kittie, with a sigh. "I'll tell you how it was. I wanted to play jackstones, and May wanted to play paper dolls, and—" Mamma was trying to write a letter, but Kittie's tongue kept on pitilessly for ten minutes. Then she paused to take breath. "Well, that's the reason I can't speak to her for a week, Mamma, and I must have *some one* to play with. So, Mamma, why can't I go in and see the girl next door?"

"I've told you why, Kittie. And now you must not talk to me anymore until I've finished this letter."

But Kittie kept on talking as she stood by the window, for to talk to herself was better than nothing. "There's a sled; that's a girl's sled, and I don't see any other, so I suppose it's the girl's. There are a doll's carriage and two dolls' trunks. Why does n't the man turn them so I can see better? There! Why there's a name on the end! C-a—oh, I see, Carrie; no, Clara,— Clara L. Parsons. That's a pretty name. Oh, dear! I wish to-morrow'd come."

To-morrow did come,—that is, the next day did (some people say "*to-morrow* does n't"),—but it rained, and Kittie could n't go out in the afternoon.

Thursday, however, when she came home from school, her new little neighbor was sitting on the piazza with one of the trunks open before her, and a beautiful doll on her lap. Kittie glanced at her, and the little girl looked so friendly that Kittie nodded. Her neighbor nodded in reply. Kittie went up the steps. "Would n't you like me to come and play with you?" she asked.

The little girl looked as if she would, but did not make any reply.

"She's shy," said Kittie to herself. "How funny." Then aloud; "I'll get my doll; only it is n't nice as yours. Shall I?" The girl nodded.

Kittie ran into her own home, and up to the play-room, where she snatched up her best doll, rejecting the second best as not grand enough to associate with Clara L. Parsons and her family.

"Mamma," she called out, "I'm going to play with the girl next door."

"Did she ask you, Kittie?" said Mrs. Perry, coming into the hall.

"Yes, Mamma; at least, I asked if I should come, and she said yes. She would have asked me, I know, but she seems shy!"

"Well, you can go for a few minutes. Don't stay long." Kittie rushed off.

The little girl was sitting with her back turned, and did not move until Kittie came all the way up the steps; but then she gave a pleased look of welcome.

"Here's my doll," said Kittie, sitting down. "It is n't as nice as yours, is it?" Clara nodded. Kittie thought her a very polite girl, for Bella was only two-thirds the size of Clara's doll. "Her name's Bella," she announced. "What is your doll's name? I suppose Clara Parsons is your name, is n't it? I see Parsons there on your door-plate. Oh, may I look at the things in your trunk? What a lovely party-dress! Did you make it? No, I guess you did n't, 'cause I see part of it's made on the machine, and I don't suppose you can sew on the machine. Mamma won't let me touch ours. I made that blue dress, though,—almost all myself. What darling dolls' handkerchiefs, and oh, what lovely little visiting cards! 'Stella Parsons'; is that her name? Stella rhymes with Bella, does n't it? they ought to be friends; let's introduce them."

132

She held Bella up toward Stella, and Clara held up Stella and make her shake hands with her visitor and then kiss her.

"Now they're acquainted," said Kittie. "Let us pretend they have taken a great fancy to each other, as I have to you. I wish you'd be my best friend, for I have n't one now. Fanny Cook used to be, but she's moved away; she lived in that yellow house across the way; and May Kingsley is n't; we get mad at each other; and she talks so much; if you tell her a secret, everybody is sure to know it. Oh, my name's Kittie Perry; I did n't tell you, did I? My brother's name's Frank, and my sister's name is Amy, but they 're both big, nearly grown up, so I don't have any one home to play with. That lady at the second-story window is your mother, I suppose? That's my mother in a blue dress—on our stoop just now. That lady in brown that went in with her is Mrs. Fraim. She can't speak and she's deaf. Did you ever know anybody who was? It's so funny to see them talk. I can say a few words. See. This means man; this means woman; this means dinner; this means bouquet of flowers."

Kittie made the motions as she spoke, and Clara, smiling brightly and looking pleased, made them too, but much more deftly and gracefully than Kittie.

"And this means a baby with long clothes," continued Kittie. Clara shook her head, and made a motion a little different.

"Oh, yes, that *is* it," said Kittie. "How quick you learn! I'll teach you some more some day; then, if you ever meet a deaf person, you can talk to them. But it must be dreadful, must n't it?—to be deaf, and not to be able to talk. Why, *I'd* die!"(I almost believe Kittie would.) "And their language—why I could n't talk as much in a minute as in a week in our way—no, no, I mean a week as in a minute. Oh, what are you doing?"

Clara had taken Bella and removed her dress. She then picked up the dress that Kittie had admired, and holding it against Stella showed that it was too small; then buttoning it on Bella she laid the doll back in Kittie's lap and looked up with a smile.

"Do you mean to give it to me?" cried Kittie, delighted. "Oh, you darling! It's awfully pretty. Kiss the lady, Bella, my child. Now I ought to do something for Stella. Let me see,—when she has the measles, you send for me, 'cause I've had experience. She'll be sure to get them; they're very *relevant* this spring. Oh, dear, there's Mamma calling me. Wait here, and I'll be back soon."

Mrs. Perry had called Kittie to go upstairs and try on her new dress, and this occupied nearly half an hour. When she returned to the piazza next door, Clara had gone and so had Stella and her trunk. Only Bella remained, sitting on the doorstep in the party-dress which had been presented to her, and holding in her lap a piece of paper on which was written, in a round, childish, but neat and legible hand: "I can't wait any longer for you. I'm going out with Mamma. Come again tomorrow."

Kittie came late to the tea-table that evening, and did not notice at first that everybody was very much amused at something.

"Kittie," said Frank, "did you get acquainted with the girl next door?"

"Yes; she's awfully nice; her name's Clara Parsons. What made you call me in, that time, Mamma? She said she could n't play much longer, she had to go out with her mother; and when I came back she was gone."

"Did you have much conversation with her?" asked Papa.

"Yes, Papa; I think I was there half and hour."

"It was more than an hour," said Amy. "I saw you. But I think you did all the talking yourself."

Kittie was indignant at this accusations, although it was not a new one. "It would n't be very polite to go and see a person and never say a word, would it?" she said.

"You'll never be so impolite, certainly," said Frank.

"And she gave me the prettiest dress for Bella. It was one that was in her doll's trunk, but it was too

small for her doll. I'll show it to you after tea."

"Now, Kittie," said Mamma, "try to remember the exact words she said about the dress, or about anything else you talked of."

"The exact words," repeated Kittie, slowly. She looked thoughtful, then perplexed. "It's queer, but somehow I forget the exact words."

"Well, Kittie, we don't blame you. Mrs. Fraim was here this afternoon, and she was speaking about the family next door, the Parsons. She knows them very well; and this little girl—her name *is* Clara—is deaf and can't speak a word."

Kittie dropped the biscuit she was eating, and the blankness which overspread her face was too much for the gravity of the family. They all laughed.

"So, Kittie," said Papa, "you *must* have had all the talk to yourself, and, if I know you, you must have enjoyed it exceedingly!"

Kittie still looked so dazed that Mamma came to her assistance.

"What did she say about going out with her mother?"

"Why—she wrote that; but that was because I was away."

"And what did she say when she gave you the doll's dress?"

"She put it on Bella and handed it to me. *Maybe* she did n't say anything."

"And did she tell you her name was Clara Parsons?"

"Yes—why—well, I asked her and she said yes;—no, I believe she nodded. She nodded quite often. But if she can't hear how could she tell when to nod?"

Kittie asked this triumphantly.

"Mrs. Fraim says she is a bright little thing, and often can tell what people are saying by watching their lips; and then perhaps she thought it was polite to agree with you even when she did n't understand."

"Now perhaps you'll believe how much you talk," said Frank. "I promise you ten cents if you keep quiet all the rest of tea-time, because I know you can't."

"Yes, I can," said Kittie; "but I'm not going to."

The other day, when I was calling on Mrs. Perry, I asked, "How is the little girl next door whom I heard about, Kittie?"

"She's lovely," said Kittie. "I'm going to have her for my best friend; I don't care who laughs. I can tell all my secrets to *her.*"

"I wonder what's in here!—it smells like cheese."　　　　But it was n't.

Hetty's Letter

By Katharine Kameron

Miss Thankful White's "keeping-room" was as prim and proper as herself. Hetty Williams glanced about her, as she knitted briskly. Long practice had made this easy to her. The chairs stood stiff and straight against the wall in rows. The ancient sofa held itself severely erect, while its long lines of shining nail-heads made her arms ache to look at them. She had polished their bright brass every day of her life, as long back as she could remember. The square-figured carpet was speckless, even the feathery asparagus that filled the fire-place never dropped a grain. The great pink-lined shells on the high chimney-shelf, and the scraggy coral branch, had stood in the same places always, and the tall bunch of peacock's feathers, with their gorgeous colors and round eyes, nodding over the whole, were worst of all—"They stare so," she said softly under her breath. The dismal green curtains were down, to keep the sun from fading the carpet, but the summer wind fanned them in and out, and brought to Hetty bright flashes of golden-rod along the road-side, and the sweet scene of the buckwheat and the drone of the bees above its white blossoms. The door to the kitchen was closed. Miss Thankful had a visitor, and was enjoying a good gossip.

"Take your knittin', Hetty, and run into the keepin'-room, and shut the door after you," were Miss Thankful's instructions, when Widow Basset had seated herself comfortably in the flag-bottomed rocker. The session was longer than usual, and Hetty grew desperate.

"Miss Thankful," said she, clicking the latch, and putting her small head into the kitchen, "may I take my knittin' out under the big tree in the orchard?"

"I'd jest as lief's not," was the answer, "if only you don't get to witchin' and forget your work. The mittens must be done afore Sat'day night, you know."

For a while the needles flashed in and out, the mitten grew longer, and the work went on steadily and quietly, as if Hetty had been one of the newly patented knitting-machines. The sunshine made shadow pictures on the grass, the leaves over her head rustled pleasantly, and the leaves at her feet waved silently in a tangle of light and shade. The bees went humming by, and the butterflies brushed her face, but still the little maid worked faithfully at her task. The last mitten was nearly finished.

Presently the sudden sound of chattering voices and merry laughing caused her to look up in surprise. Three little girls were coming toward her, and one of them said, quite politely:

"We saw you here, and thought it looked such a nice shady place for our dolls' picnic. Should you mind if we staid with you to play?"

"I should be very glad, indeed," answered Hetty, heartily; but she scarcely looked at her little visitors—her eyes were fixed on the dolls which two of them carried. Hetty had a rag-doll of her own make, hidden away in a box under her bed, and it was one of her most precious possessions. She had seen prettier ones at the store, and had long dreamed of saving pennies to buy one—but these dolls! these were so unlike anything she had ever seen or imagined, that they "took away her breath," she said. They had dainty waxen faces, with cheeks like rose-leaves, and great blue eyes with dark, silky lashes, and real golden hair, wavy and long. "They must be meant for dolls' angels," she thought, but said not a word. Hetty was not given to speaking her mind, Miss Thankful White's motto being: "Little girls must be seen, but not heard."

While she stood lost in admiring wonder, the little strangers, with a busy chatter, set about preparing their picnic. Before long, Hetty knew that they lived in Boston, and that they, with their mamma, were boarding at the Maplewood Farm, near by, for the summer; that two of them were sisters, and one a cousin. All this, and much more, was told to their new neighbor.

Presently Hetty said, thoughtfully: "I guess little girls are heard in Boston."

They looked at her a minute in surprise, and then one answered:

"Why, yes, of course; are n't they in Patchook?"

"Miss Thankful says they should only be seen," was the reply.

"Who is Miss Thankful?"

"Why, she's Miss Thankful White; and I live with her."

"Is she your aunt?"

"No; she's the one who took me to bring up, when

"Should you mind if we staid with you to play?"

Mother died—to help 'round, and save her steps, and do the house chores." Hetty made this long speech quite rapidly, as if she had heard it, or said it, so often that she knew it by heart, and then she fell to knitting busily.

Her little playmates looked at her and at one another, but did not answer. This was a kind of life they knew nothing about. They could not imagine a little girl without a papa and mamma, auntie and cousins, plenty of toys and playtime, and lots of laughing and talking.

Soon one of them, with a bright thought, said quickly: "Would you like to hold my dolly, while I help set the table?"

This was delightful. Hetty dropped her mitten, and taking the dainty creature gently in her arms, she lightly smoothed the long, soft dress of finest frills and laces. What a wonder of beauty! Hetty sat silent and happy, stroking the golden hair and touching the little hands and pretty kid shoes.

"Where did it come from?" she asked at length.

"Uncle Charley bought it for me at one of the Boston shops," answered the little owner, carelessly. A wax doll was nothing strange to her.

Then Hetty took up the other doll and compared them—"a brown-eyed beauty and a blue-eyed angel," she thought.

Suddenly she heard Miss Thankful's voice calling: "Hetty, Hetty Williams! Can't you see it's near sundown? How are the cows to get home if you don't spry up and start after 'em?"

Sure enough, the day was nearly done, and when the little strangers started for Maplewood Farm, long, spindling shadows, with long, spindling dolls in their arms, ran alongside of them. Hetty saw this, as she stopped to look back after them on her way to the house.

Then off she trudged after Sukey and Jenny, but

she passed by the flaming goldenrod, the purple asters, and the creamy buckwheat without ever once seeing them. It was like walking in her sleep. Her eyes were open, but she saw nothing except the pretty doll-faces she was dreaming about.

After the cows were home, and the milk in the bright pans, she finished the last mitten and bound it off in the fading light. Before she slipped into her little bed, she took her dear old rag doll from the box for one look.

It was dreadful. She shut her eyes tight and put it back quickly out of sight. Those lovely doll angels! She could not quite keep them out of her prayers, even. It took a long, long time for Hetty to go to sleep that night. Her restless head tossed from side to side. When, at last, it lay quite still, and she was fast asleep, it was still full of rosy dreams. Blue-eyed dollies, with pink faces and wavy hair, crowded about her pillow.

The first beams of the morning sunshine found Hetty standing in the middle of the floor, with a brand-new idea caught tight and fast in her tangle of hair. Miss Thankful had not called her. She was not even stirring yet, and Hetty spoke aloud:

"Miss Thankful will take the mittens to the store to-day—that makes six pair—and Mr. Dobbins will send them to Boston. That is where the doll came from."

In a minute more Hetty had found a pencil and some scraps of paper, and was seated by the low window, busily writing. It was clearly something very important. She wrote one note and tore it up; and then another and did the same; the third time it seemed to suit her. Next, she folded it very small and flat; then she took the new mittens from the drawer, and tucked the folded paper close up into the tip of the right hand.

"She took one look at her dear old rag doll"

"Good mornin', Miss Thankful," said Mr. Dobbins; "want to trade fur mittens agin, do ye? Well, that little girl o' yourn makes 'em 'mazin' spruce. None o' the knittin'-machines beat Hetty much. We kin get rid o' all ye kin fetch. A Boston man was in here yist'day and spoke fur a dozen pair. So help yerself, Miss Thankful; got some extra fine cotton cloth, very cheap, and some hansum caliker as ever you see."

Hetty was at the south door as the old chaise drove up, and took the parcels from Miss Thankful. She saw the mittens had not come back. "Gone to Boston," she whispered joyfully, as she turned into the house again.

So they had—started that very day. They did not stay long in Boston, however. The city was full of western merchants, buying for the fall and winter. Among the rest, stacks of woolen gloves and mittens went off over the iron tracks, up into the great, cold north-western country, where Jack Frost has jolly times playing his Russian pranks, and nipping noses, ears, and fingers.

Time went by, and winter came in dead earnest. Jack Frost enjoyed his rough jokes and found his way through all kinds of gloves. The clerks of a great store up in Minnesota were tired of saying to customers, "We are out of woolen mittens, sir—all gone long ago—not a woolen glove left in the house, sir."

"Hello, Mike, what is this?" said a pleasant-faced young fellow to one of the porters, as he drew out a packing-box from a dark corner in the cellar.

"Shure an' I dun'no, sir. I'm thinkin' it's sumthin' that's hid itself away, unbeknownst loike."

"We'll find out quickly," said the young man. Mike's hatchet went splintering and cracking through the dry wood till the cover flew off.

"Wullun gloves! Misther Tom, and it's the lucky foind, sir. Shure the paaple 'll be twice gladder to have thim now, sir, than in the warrum wayther whin they come, sir."

Tom laughed at Mike's sharp way of dodging the blame, and ordered them brought upstairs to be put on the counter at once. As he turned away, he took up the top pair. "First come, first served," he said; "these are my share. My old ones leak the cold everywhere." Sitting down by the glowing stove, he examined his prize at his leisure. "Good, thick, warm wool," said he. "No thin places; honest work, first quality."

By this time, two or three others had gathered around him, each with a pair of the new "find." When Tom tried the fit of his new gloves, his fingers touched something in the very tip of the right hand. Turning it wrong-side out, he found a carefully folded paper, like a note. Smoothing it out on his knee, he read it aloud:

"My name is Hetty Williams. I am eight years old. I live in Patchook, Mass. I knit these mittens for Mr. Dobbins's store. I wish the gentleman who buys them would send me a wax doll. I have only a rag doll, and I want one with a wax face and blue eyes, and pink cheeks and real hair. I want her very much indeed."

"Hurrah for little Hetty!" said Mr. Tom; "she shall have her wax baby for Christmas-day." And then he fell into a brown study. The fact was, Tom had been born "away down East," and he had worked a while in a country store there. He knew in a minute just what Mr. Dobbins's store was like. He fairly smelt the soap, and fish, and coffee, and could see the calicoes, and dishes, and woolen socks, and gray mittens. It did not take long to think all this, and then he cried:

"Who wants to help get a stunning doll for little Hetty? I'm glad Mr. Dobbins sent her gloves along this way."

The boys who did not get notes in their mittens tried to think that Hetty had knitted them all the same, and when Tom passed around his hat, the halves and quarters rattled in, then a trade-dollar thumped down, and a greenback or two fluttered in silently. Tom took the proceeds and went to the gayest toy-shop in town, and found a famous wax

Tom reads the letter   J.Mᶜ D.

dolly. It was as big and as plump as a live baby, and much prettier, he thought. It had a long white frock, and shut its eyes properly when Tom laid it down to count out the money to pay for it. It did not take long to pack it snugly in a smooth box. Then Tom pasted Hetty's open letter on the cover. He went down himself with it to the express, and told the boys it must go free, and that every one might send a Merry Christmas to little Hetty till the lid was full of good wishes. I doubt if there ever was so much writing outside of one box. Every man who handled it seemed to think at once of some little sister or daughter or niece, and for her sake sent a greeting to the little girl in Patchook.

The day before Christmas, Miss Thankful White's old chaise stopped at Mr. Dobbins's store and post-office, and that lady, with Hetty to carry the parcels, came up to the counter.

"Good mornin', Miss Thankful—wish ye Merry Christmas—fine frosty weather, this. Le' me see: I think there's a letter for your little gal, Hetty there—came this mornin'. Get it out, Dan."

Hetty's eyes opened wider than ever before in her life. A letter for her! What could it mean? Mr. Dobbins must have made a mistake. But no, the red-haired boy, Dan, read the address, and handed it straight to her.

"Miss Hetty Williams, Patchook, Mass."

Her first letter! She never thought of opening it—she was too much astonished and too well pleased.

"Sakes alive! Hetty Williams, what be you standin' there for, like as if you was struck dumb? Why don't ye hev sense enough left to open that letter and find out su'thin' about it?"

But as Hetty did not stir, Miss Thankful took it from her hand, removed her glasses, wiped them and put them on again, then carefully opened it and slowly read aloud:

"There is a box for Hetty Williams, in the express office at Fitchtown. Will be kept till called for. This express does not deliver in Patchook."

"Wall, to be sure! Who kin it be from? how kin we git it?" queried that lady, helplessly.

"Why, bless ye, Miss Thankful, that's as easy as rollin' off a log. My boy Dan is jest hitchin' up to go to Fitchtown express for some store goods. He'll bring Hetty's box along with him, and glad tew."

Just after early nightfall that day, Mr. Dobbins's wagon rattled up to the south door. Miss Thankful and Hetty both rushed out to meet Dan, and it would be hard to say which was the spryer of the two.

Miss Thankful took the box from Dan with many thanks, and carried it into the house, saying:

"It's rather big and hefty for you, Hetty;" and then the good woman carefully pried off the cover with a claw-hammer and stove-lifter. The Christmas softness had, somehow, found its way to her heart, and so she quietly moved away to put up the "tools," and left Hetty to unfold the wrappings by herself and first see the sight, whatever it might be.

Hetty, when Miss Thankful came back, sat as still as a statue, with folded hands, looking only at her treasure. Miss Thankful settled her spectacles, took one good look, and then exclaimed: "Wall, I never! This does beat all natur'. Where upon airth did it ever rain down from?"

Just then, her "specs" grew dim, and the old lady took them off and wiped them well; then she continued: "Deary me, deary me! Well, I am right down glad that the Lord's put it into someun's heart to clap to and send that child a doll baby. I'm sure I never should 'a' thought o' such a thing, if I'd lived a thousand year, and yet how powerful happy the little creetur is over it, to be sure! She looks like a pictur', kneelin' there by the box, with her eyes shinin' so bright and so still, just as if the doll baby was an angel, come down in its long white frock."

I only wish Tom could have seen Hetty then, or afterward, when she sat by the bright wood-fire, looking with childish delight into the soft blue eyes of her waxen darling. Or if he could have taken one look at the two heads on the pillow of the little attic bed, that night—both pair of eyes fast shut, and Hetty's small arm hugging her treasure tight and fast in her soundest sleep—he would then have known to a certainty that little Hetty Williams was to have at least one happy Christmas.

"Hetty sat like a statue, looking at her treasure."

The Smiling Dolly

By M. M. D.

I whispered to my Dolly,
  And told her not to tell.
(She's a really lovely Dolly,—
  Her name is Rosabel.)

"Rosy," I said, "stop smiling,
  For I've been dreadful bad!
You must n't look so pleasant,
  As if you felt real glad!

"I took mamma's new ear-ring,—
  I did, now, Rosabel,—
And I never even asked her,—
  Now, Rosy, don't you tell!

"You see I'll try to find it
  Before I let her know;
She'd feel so very sorry
  To think I'd acted so."

Still Rosabel kept smiling;
  And I just cried and cried—
And while I searched all over,
  Her eyes were opened wide.

"Oh, Rosy, where I dropt it
  I can't imagine, dear;"
And still she kept on smiling,—
  I thought it very queer.

I had wheeled her 'round the garden
   In her gig till I was lame;
Yet when I told my trouble,
   She smiled on, just the same!

Her hair waved down her shoulders
   Like silk, all made of gold.
I kissed her, then I shook her,
   Oh, dear! how I did scold!

"You're really naughty, Rosy,
   To look so when I cry.
When my mamma's in trouble
   I never laugh: not I."

And still she kept on smiling,
   The queer, provoking child!
I shook her well and told her
   Her conduct drove me wild.

When—only think! that ear-ring
   Fell out of Rosy's hair!
When I had dressed the darling,
   I must have dropped it there.

She doubled when I saw it,
   And almost hit her head;—
Again, I whispered softly,
   And this is what I said:

"You precious, precious Rosy!
   Now, I'll go tell mamma
How bad I was—and sorry—
   And O, how good you are!

"For, Rose, I had n't lost it—
   You knew it all the while,
You knew I'd shake it out, dear,
   And that's what made you smile."

A Little Girl asked some Kittens to tea,
To meet some Dolls from France;
And their Mother came too to enjoy a view,
And afterwards play for the dance.
But the Kittens were rude and grabbed their food,
And treated the Dolls with jeers;
Which caused their Mother an aching heart
And seven or eight large tears.

An Idyl of the King

By Ernest Whitney

The carpet in the parlor is no better than the floor;
Of the carpet in the library one can say little more;
There's a good one in the dining-room, although it's
    rather small;
But the carpet in the nursery is nicest of them all.

There's a palace in the middle, circled with a wall of
    black,
With a moat of yellow water, four brown pathways run-
    ning back
Through a fearful, frightful forest from the windows to
    the door,
'Round four lakes of deep dark water with green griffins
    on the shore.

At the corners there are castles, and in one King Arthur
    reigns;
In the north one is a giant, and the south is
    Charlemagne's.
But the castle in the corner by the chest is the best,
And from this I rule my kingdom and reign over all the
    rest.

But the middle park and palace are a very wondrous
    place,—
Statues, vases, fairies, graces, flowers and bowers through
    all the space.
'T is a garden of enchantment, and the dreadful ogress
    there
Is my sister—You should see her when she rumples up her
    hair!

Now, it's very, very seldom that I'll play with dolls and
    girls,
'Cause I used to go in dresses, with my hair like Mary's
    curls;
But there's first rate fun in playing, on a rainy, indoor
    day,
That her doll's a captive princess, to be rescued in a
    fray.

So with Knights of the Round Table and with Paladins of
    France,
Charlemagne and I and Arthur through the wicked wood
    advance;
And we always have such contests, before all these wilds
    are crossed,
With the giant and the griffins, that half our knights are
    lost.

But at last we reach the portals, and the lovely princess
    see.
Then the ogress, with her magic, captures every one but
    me;
And transformed to wood and pewter in her dungeons
    they repine,—
But I bear away the princess, so the victory is
    mine.

The Story of a Doll-House

By Katharine Pyle

Seventy-five years ago, a little brother and sister had a play-house in a cupboard. It was a sheet-closet; and on the upper shelves were piled great rolls of home-spun linen, with bunches of lavender between their smooth folds to make them smell sweet. The two lower shelves belonged to the children, and there, for a while, their toys and boxes were neatly arranged side by side, and pictures were tacked up on the walls.

Boys are not so careful and orderly in their ways as little girls, and by and by the brother began to store all kinds of queer things in the play-house: bits of stick fit for whittling; an old dog-collar for which he had traded his jack-knife; pieces of string and fishing-line; a rusty key; and many other odds and ends, such as little boys love to gather together in their comings and goings.

It worried the little girl to have all these things littered about on their neat shelves; and the mother, as she sat in her cushioned rocking-chair, with her basket of sewing at the nursery window, saw it all, and felt sorry for the little daughter. So, one day after the children had started for school with their books tucked under their arms, and two red apples and some gingerbread in their baskets, she put on her bonnet and shawl, and went down the street to the carpenter's. She described to the carpenter exactly what she wanted, and he said:

"Yes, yes; yes, ma'am. A slanting roof, and six windows; yes, ma'am. And a wooden standard; yes, ma'am. I will have it done for you next week."

And next week the carpenter's boy brought something to the house on a wheelbarrow, while the children were away at school.

It was a play-house; a large play-house, a play-house with two chimneys and real glass windows. It was two stories high, and almost more than the boy could wheel.

The "downstairs" of the doll-house

144

The "upstairs" of the doll-house

The mother had it carried up to her room and put behind the high-post bed, where it was hidden by the white valance.

All that morning she was busy tacking and snipping and pasting and cutting; and all the while the children were at school, thinking of nothing at all but their lessons.

It was Saturday and a half-holiday, and about noon the children came home.

Upstairs they clattered and burst into the nursery, and then stood quite still in the doorway and looked.

The nursery was very quiet, with the chairs and tables in their places, and two squares of yellow sunlight on the carpet, but there, in the middle of the floor, stood a wonderful little house, painted to look just as if it were built of bricks, with chimneys, and glass windows, a slanting black roof, and a white door. It was the little house that the carpenter's boy had wheeled home on the wheelbarrow; but now it was furnished, and had black and yellow silk curtains at the windows, carpets on the floors, and one of Ann's own dolls was looking through the little square panes, for it was her home.

There was a key in a keyhole above the first-story windows of the doll house. The children turned it, and the whole front of the house swung open, windows and all. Then they could see just what was inside.

There was an upstairs and a downstairs. Upstairs there was a mantelpiece and fireplace, a round black tin stove, and a high-post bed with curtains and a valance. There was a clock standing on a chest of drawers under the looking-glass. There were pictures about the room, and a cosy stuffed chair stood by the bed for Grandmamma Doll to rest in when she came upstairs out of breath.

Downstairs there was another fireplace, a round center-table decorated with pictures, and a sofa. And there was Grandmamma Doll herself, sitting in the green rocking-chair. There was a folding table that was just the thing for dollies to sit around while they drank a social cup of tea.

While the little boy and girl were looking at the play-house their mother came in, and stood smiling on them from the doorway without their seeing her.

That is the story of the real doll-house.

Yes, of a real doll-house,—a dear old-fashioned doll-house.

As one opens the front of it a faint, delightful odor of long ago breathes forth, like the ancient fragrance that

Sister Hetty

The Mother doll

Aunt Jane

haunts the boxes and piece-bags of kind old ladies.

As one looks in the looking-glasses one thinks of all the little girls whose chubby faces have been reflected there,—Ann, in her short-waisted, long-skirted dresses; little nieces of hers, in pantalettes and pig-tails. And now others, with crisp white aprons and bangs, peer in with eager curiosity at the old-time doll-house.

What fun they had with it! How many times, on stormy days, when the rain beat on the nursery windows, and swept in whitening gusts over the wet trees on the lawn, the front of the dollies' house has swung back, and little folks have played happily with it for whole mornings at a time! How often they have pretended a dolly was ill, and have laid her in the fresh, white-sheeted feather-bed under the chintz curtains; and then, while the nurse warmed up her food on the tin stove, Grandmamma Doll has had her green rocking-chair brought upstairs, and sat at the bedside and rocked and rocked, while the other dolls went about very softly, and the nurse kept the baby quiet below.

Not long ago there was a fair in a certain city to raise a fund for a hospital. There, in a room special-ly set apart for them, were dolls by dozens and dozens, all standing in rows and dressed in their best; for the one that was the finest of all was to receive a prize. And there, too, among all the fine dolls and in the midst of the noise and glare of light, stood the dim old doll-house.

The key had been turned in the lock and the front had been swung back.

There was the round tin stove, the high-post bed,

and clock; there was the folding table, and the sofa, and there were the silk-covered chairs.

A crowd of faces peered in,—old and young; peo-ple pointed and smiled; it was a noisy crowd, and the yellow-faced dolls, in their old-fashioned dress-es, sitting in the quiet rooms, looked out strangely with their black wooden eyes, through the odor of long ago.

My face, too, peered in upon that old, Quaker doll-family. I too wondered and pointed with the rest, and then I thought how other children, old and young, might perhaps care to look through my eyes into those faded rooms. So I drew pictures of it all, and afterward I made portraits of the dear jointed and rag dolls, and here they are.

The Nurse and Baby

146

Wee Mother Hubbard,

The Great-Great-Grand-Daughter
of Old Mother Hubbard;
the same being a half-day-historie
here done in lines and many pictures
by one A. BRENNAN.

Wee Mother Hubbard
Ran to the Cupboard
But finding the Cupboard bare
Pulled out of the press
A gay satin dress
Just matching her golden hair.

She went to the Baker's
For Dolly's fresh bread
And when she came back
Her Doll was in bed.

She went to the Barber's
Tried on a white wig
And when she came back
Dolly danced a fine jig.

She went to the Fruiterer's
To buy her some fruit
And when she came back
Her Doll played the lute.

She went to the Tailor's
To buy a red coat
And when she came back
Dolly rode on a goat.

She went to the Cobbler's
To buy her some shoes
And when she came back
Doll was reading the News.

She went to the Doctor's
To get her some mustard
And when she came back
Doll was eating a custard.

She went to the Garden
For Peonies rare
And when she came back
Doll was dressing her hair.

She went to the Hatter's
To get her new hat
And when she came back
Doll was scolding the cat.

She went to ye Sempstress
To get bits of linen
And when she came back
Her Dolly was spinnin.

She went to ye Hosier's
To buy her some hose
And when she came back
Doll was dressed in new clothes.

The Darling did curt'sy,
The Doll made a bow,
The Darling said: "Nurtsy
I wants Dolly now."

"There's just a nice dinner for a baby lion."

"Whew! Sawdust."

—Kemble

Anna's Doll

By Lucretia P. Hale

Anna's doll was thought a very remarkable one by all of the family. It had now reached its third head, which could be washed in front, and could be curled behind, and, happily, was very strong.

For Anna, though she was very fond of her doll, whose name was Elsie, did often forget to take care of her. I am sorry to say she sometimes left her under the rockers of the chair, which is not a safe thing for a doll, or on the sofa in the parlor. And the way her first head was broken was, that somebody stepped on it, because Anna had dropped it in the front entry, one day, when she was hurrying off for school.

Anna had two older sisters and two very kind aunts, and that is the way her doll came to have so many nice things. Whenever they went away, they always brought home something pretty for Elsie. She was wearing now a pretty new hat, and a little parasol with fringe, that one of the aunts brought home from Paris.

Anna had a brother Jim, and it was hard to tell whether he was more of a help to her, or a plague, about her doll. On rainy days, when he had nothing better to do, he would make doll's chairs and tables for Anna's baby house. The legs were not very strong, and had a way of wobbling, but Anna was very grateful for them, and they made her forget that it was owing to Jim that Elsie had lost her second head.

This was a waxen head, and it was a very lovely one—there were light, golden curls, and you could move the head one way or another. But one winter's day Jim came in, and said he knew Elsie must be very cold, and advised Anna to put her in front of the crackling wood fire, to sit in her easy-chair and warm her feet. This might have done for a little while, but Anna left here there too long, and when she came back, all Elsie's sweet expression had melted away!

Jim was really very sorry, and he offered some of his next month's allowance to buy a new head for the doll, but one of the aunts had just come home with a new head, which she had bought, thinking Elsie might be in need of one, and this was number three. Anna began to think it was the most beautiful of all, though she loved her dear Elsie so much, she said she would not care if she had no head.

Jim then said he would write a book for the doll, a book that should teach her never to sit too near

The first of May is "Moving Day"

the fire, or to run into danger. The idea pleased Anna very much. This is the book:

About Dolls
By J. J.

Some dolls' heads are made of wood; these are called wooden dolls. Wood comes from trees, which are found in the country. Trees have leaves also; they grow up, but dolls do not grow. Some trees are pine, some apple, some pine-apple, and some murhoggany, a hard word to spell. These heads are very hard, and you can pound them without hurting.

Some dolls' heads are made of wax, and are called wax-dolls. The wax comes from a little animal called the bee, that has wings. Sometimes it is called the busy bee, because it buzzes. The bee does not make the dolls, but the wax. It goes in a straight line to a flower, and pokes the honey out with its sting. Then you feel glad you are not the flower, because the sting hurts—it does—that is the way it makes the wax. But it is not good to put these dolls in the sun or over a furnace.

Some dolls are made all over of India rubber, and you can fling them about anyhow. They grow on a tree, the India rubber does, in India, where they make India rubber boots. It is a good kind to have, because you can throw it about like a ball. But then the face is painted, and may rub off—some noses do.

Then there's China dolls, made of what tea sets are; but they don't come from the China where they make the fire-works, though they do make the tea. These might smash, if pounded with a hammer. There's another kind I don't know about, that Elsie's made of. It don't matter, any way. My aunt helped me about the spelling, except murhoggany—that I knew. I shall write another volume, telling more about trees and bees, and why dolls should take care of themselves.

This is enough for once.

The Rag Doll
By Junius L. Cravens

I
Liza's just a rag doll,
  Old and awful lookin';
I don't like her any more,
  She's going to get forsooken.
	II
	What I want's a jointy doll
	  With hair and pretty dresses,
	Instead of these old woolly things
	  That look such awful messes.
		III
		Yet, Liza is a good doll,
		  And such a quiet sleeper;
		She never breaks or comes apart—
		  I guess I better keep her!

How Bunny Brought Good Luck.

By Susan Coolidge

It was Midsummer's Day, that delightful point toward which the whole year climbs and from which it slips off like an ebbing wave in the direction of the distant winter. No wonder that superstitious people in old times gave this day to the fairies, for it is the most beautiful day of all. The world seems full of bird-songs, sunshine, and flower-smells; then storm and sorrow appear impossible things; the barest and ugliest spot takes on a brief charm and, for the moment, seems lovely and desirable.

"That's a picturesque old place," said a lady on the back seat of the big wagon in which Hiram Swift was taking his summer boarders to drive.

They were passing a low, wide farm-house, gray from want of paint, with a shabby barn and sheds attached, all overarched by tall elms. The narrow hay-field and the vegetable-patch ended in a rocky hillside, with its steep ledges, overgrown and topped with tall pines and firs, which made a dense, green background to the old buildings.

"I don't know about its being like a picter," said Hiram dryly, as he flicked away a fly from the shoulder of his off horse; "but it is n't much by way of a farm. That bit of hay-field is about all the land there is that's worth anything; the rest is all rock. I guess the Widow Gale does n't take much comfort in its bein' picturesque. She'd be glad enough to have the land made flat if she could."

"Oh, is that the Gale farm where the silver-mine is said to be?"

"Yes, marm; at least it's the farm where the man lived that, 'cordin' to what folks say, said he'd found a silver-mine. I don't take a great deal of stock in the story myself."

"A silver-mine! That sounds interesting," said a pretty girl on the front seat, who had been driving the horses half the way, aided and abetted by Hiram, with whom she was a prime favorite. "Tell me about it, Mr. Swift. Is it a story, and when did it all happen?"

"Well, I don't know as it ever did happen," responded the farmer cautiously; "all I know for certain is that my father used to tell a story that, before I was born—nigh on to sixty years ago that must have been—Squire Asy Allen that used to live up to that red house on North street—where you bought the crockery mug, you know, Miss Rose—come up one day in a great hurry to catch the stage, with a lump of rock tied in his handkerchief. Old Roger Gale had found it, he said, and they thought it was silver ore; and the Squire was a-takin' it down to New Haven to get it analyzed. My father he saw the rock, but he did n't think much of it from the looks, till the Squire got back ten days afterward and said the New Haven professor pronounced it silver, sure enough, and a rich specimen; and any man who owned a mine of it had his fortune made, he said. Then of course the township got excited, and everybody talked silver, and there was a great to-do."

"And why did n't they go to work on the mine at once?" asked the pretty girl.

"Well, you see, unfortunately, no one knew where it was, and old Roger Gale had taken that particular day of all others to fall off his hay-riggin' and break

153

his neck, and he had n't happened to mention to any one before doing it where he found the rock! He was a close-mouthed old chap, Roger was. For ten years after that, folks that had n't anything else to do went about hunting for the silver-mine, but they gradooally got tired, and now it's nothin' more than an old story. Does to amuse boarders with in the summer," concluded Mr. Swift, with a twinkle. "For my part, I don't believe there ever was a mine."

"But there was the piece of ore to prove it."

"Oh, that don't prove anything, because it got lost. No one knows what became of it. An' sixty years is long enough for a story to get exaggerated in."

"I don't see why there should n't be silver in Beulah township," remarked the lady on the back seat. "You have all kinds of other minerals here—soapstone, and mica, and emery, and tourmalines and beryls."

"Well, ma'am, I don't see nuther, unless mebbe it's the Lord's will there should n't be."

"It would be so interesting if the mine could be found!" said the pretty girl.

"It would be *so*, especially to the Gale family,—that is, if it was found on their land. The widow's a smart, capable woman, but it's as much as she can do, turn and twist how she may, to make both ends meet. And there's that boy of hers, a likely boy as ever you see, and just hungry for book-l'arnin', the minister says. The chance of an eddication would be just everything to him, and the widow can't give him one."

"It's really a romance," said the pretty girl carelessly, the wants and cravings of others slipping off her young sympathies easily.

Then the horses reached the top of the long hill they had been climbing, Hiram put on the brake, and they began to grind down a hill equally long, with a soft panorama of plummy tree-clad summits before them, shimmering in the June sunshine. Drives in Beulah township were apt to be rather perpendicular, however you took them.

Some one, high up on the hill behind the farmhouse, heard the clank of the brakes and lifted up her head to listen. It was Hester Gale—a brown little girl with quick dark eyes, and a mane of curly chestnut hair only too apt to get into tangles. She was just eight years old, and to her the old farmstead, which the neighbors scorned as worthless, was a sort of enchanted land, full of delights and surprises,—hiding-places which no one but herself knew, rocks and thickets where she was sure real fairies dwelt, and cubby-houses sacred to the use of "Bunny," who was her sole playmate and companion and the confidant to whom she told all her plans and secrets.

Bunny was a doll,—an old-fashioned doll, carved out of a solid piece of hickory-wood, with a stern expression of face, and a perfectly unyielding figure, but a doll whom Hester loved above all things. Her mother and her mother's mother had played with Bunny, but this only made her dearer.

The two sat together between the gnarled roots of an old spruce which grew near the edge of a steep little cliff. It was one of the loneliest parts of the rocky hillside, and the hardest to get at. Hester liked it better than any of her other hiding-places because no one but herself ever came there.

Bunny lay in her lap, and Hester was in the middle of a story, when she stopped to listen to the wagon grinding down-hill.

"So the little chicken said, 'Peep! Peep!' and started off to see what the big yellow fox was like," she went on. "That was a silly thing for her to do, was n't it, Bunny? because foxes are n't a bit nice to chickens. But the little chicken did n't know any better, and she would n't listen to the old hens when they told her how foolish she was. That was wrong, because it's naughty to dis—dis—apute your elders, mother says; children that do are almost always sorry afterward.

"Well, she had n't gone far before she heard a rustle in the bushes on one side. She thought it was the fox, and then she *did* feel frightened, you'd better believe, and all the things she meant to say to him went straight out of her head. But it was n't the fox that time; it was a teeny-weeny little striped squirrel, and he just said, 'It's a sightly day, is n't it?' and, without waiting for an answer, ran up a tree. So the chicken did n't mind *him* a bit.

"Then, by and by, when she had gone a long way farther off from home, she heard another rustle. It was just like—oh, what's that, Bunny?"

Hester stopped short, and I am sorry to say that Bunny never heard the end of the chicken story, for the rustle resolved itself into—what do you think?

It was a fox! A real fox.

There he stood on the hillside, gazing straight at Hester, with his yellow brush waving behind him, and his eyes looking as sharp as the row of gleaming teeth beneath them. Foxes were rare animals in the Beulah region; Hester had never seen one before; but she had seen the picture of a fox in one of Roger's books, so she knew what it was.

The fox stared at her, and she stared back at the fox. Then her heart melted with fear like the heart of the little chicken, and she jumped to her feet, for-

"The fox stared at her, and she stared back at the fox."

getting Bunny, who fell from her lap and rolled unobserved over the edge of the cliff. The sudden movement startled the fox, and he disappeared into the bushes with a wave of his yellow brush; just how or where he went, Hester could not have told.

"How sorry Roger will be that he was n't here to see him," was her first thought. Her second was for Bunny. She turned and stopped to pick up the doll—and lo! Bunny was not there.

High and low she searched, beneath grass tangles, under "juniper saucers," among the stems of the thickly massed blueberries and hardhacks, but nowhere was Bunny to be seen. She peered over the ledge, but nothing met her eyes below but a thick growth of blackish, stunted evergreens. This place "down below" had been a sort of terror to Hester's imagination always, as an entirely unknown and unexplored region; but in the cause of the beloved Bunny she was prepared to risk anything, and she bravely made ready to plunge into the depths.

It was not so easy to plunge, however. The cliff was ten or twelve feet in height where she stood, and ran for a considerable distance to right and left without getting lower. This way and that she quested, and at last found a crevice where it was possible to scramble down,—a steep little crevice, full of blackberry briers, which scratched her face and tore her frock. When at last she gained the lower bank, this further difficulty presented itself: she could not tell where she was. The evergreen thicket nearly met over her head, the branches got into her eyes and buffeted and bewildered her. She could not make out the place where she had been sitting, and no signs of Bunny could be found. At last, breathless with exertion, tired, hot, and hopeless, she made her way out of the thicket and went, crying, home to her mother.

She was still crying and refusing to be comforted, when Roger came in from milking. He was sorry for Hester, but not so sorry as he would have been had his mind not been full of troubles of his own. He tried to console her with a vague promise of helping her to look for Bunny "some day when there was n't so much to do." But this was cold comfort, and in the end Hester went to bed heartbroken, to sob herself to sleep.

"Mother," said Roger, after she had gone, "Jim Boies is going to his uncle's in New Ipswich, in September, to do chores and help round a little, and to go all winter to the academy."

The New Ipswich Academy was quite a famous school then, and to go there was a great chance for a studious boy.

"That's a bit of good luck for Jim."

"Yes; first-rate."

"Not quite so first-rate for you."

"No" (gloomily). "I shall miss Jim. He's always been my best friend among the boys. But what makes me mad is that he does n't care a bit about going. Mother, why does n't good luck ever come to us Gales?"

"It was good luck for me when you came, Roger. I don't know how I should get along without you."

"I'd be worth a great deal more to you if I could get a chance at any sort of schooling. Does n't it seem hard, Mother? There's Squire Dennis and Farmer Atwater, and half a dozen others in this township, that are all ready to send their boys to college, and they don't want to go! Bob Dennis says that he'd far rather do teaming in the summer, and take the girls up to singing practice at the church, than go to all the Harvards and Yales in the world; and I, who'd give my head, almost, to go to college, can't! It does n't seem half right, Mother."

"No, Roger, it does n't; not a quarter. There are a good many things that don't seem right in this world, but I don't know who's to mend 'em. I can't! The only way is to dig along hard and do what's to be done as well as you can, whatever it is, and make the best of yours 'musts.' There's always a 'must.' I suppose rich people have them as well as poor ones."

"Rich people's boys can go to college."

"Yes,—and mine can't. I'd sell all we've got to send you, Roger, since your heart is so set on it, but this poor little farm would n't be half enough, even if any one wanted to buy it, which is n't likely. It's no use talking about it, Roger; it only makes both of us feel sad.—Did you kill the broilers for the hotel?" she asked with a sudden change of tone.

"No, not yet."

"Go and do it, then, right away. You'll have to carry them down early with the eggs. Four pairs, Roger. Chickens are the best crop we can raise on this farm."

"If we could find Great-uncle Roger's mine, we'd eat the chickens ourselves," said Roger, as he reluctantly turned to go.

"Yes, and if that apple-tree'd take to bearing gold apples we would n't have to work at all. Hurry and do your chores before dark, Roger."

Mrs. Gale was a Spartan in her methods, but, for all that, she sighed a bitter sigh as Roger went out of the door.

"He's such a smart boy," she told herself, "there's nothing he could n't do,—nothing, if he had a chance. I do call it hard. The folks who have plenty of money to do with have dull boys; and I, who've got a bright one, can't do anything for him! It seems as if things were n't justly arranged."

Hester spent all her spare time during the next week in searching for the lost Bunny. It rained hard one day and all the following night; she could not sleep for fear that Bunny was getting wet, and looked so pale in the morning that her mother forbade her going to the hill.

"Your feet were sopping when you came in yesterday," she said; "and that's the second apron you've torn. You'll just have to let Bunny go, Hester; no two ways about it."

Then Hester moped and grieved and grew thin, and at last she fell ill. It was low fever, the doctor said. Several days went by, and she was no better. One noon, Roger came in from haying to find his mother with her eyes looking very much troubled. "Hester is light-headed," she said; "we must have the doctor again."

Roger went in to look at the child, who was lying in a little bedroom off the kitchen. The small, flushed face on the pillow did not light up at his approach. On the contrary, Hester's eyes, which were unnaturally big and bright, looked past and beyond him.

"Hessie, dear, don't you know Roger?"

"He said he'd find Bunny for me some day," muttered the little voice; "but he never did. Oh, I wish he would!—I wish he would! I do want her so much." Then she rambled on about foxes, and the old spruce-tree, and the rocks; always with the refrain, "I wish I had Bunny; I want her so much!"

"Mother, I do believe it's that wretched old doll she's fretted herself sick over," said Roger, going back into the kitchen. "Now, I'll tell you what. Mr. Hinsdale's going up to the town this noon, and he'll leave word for the doctor to come; and the minute I've swallowed my dinner, I'm going up to the hill to find Bunny. I don't believe Hessie'll get any better till she's found."

"Very well," said Mrs. Gale. "I suppose the hay'll be spoiled, but we've got to get Hessie cured at any price."

"Oh, I'll find the doll. I know about where Hessie was when she lost it. And the hay'll take no harm. I only got a quarter of the field cut, and it's good drying weather."

Roger made haste with his dinner. His conscience pricked him as he remembered his neglected promise and his indifference to Hester's griefs; he felt in haste to make amends. He went straight to the old spruce which, he had gathered from Hester's rambling speech, was the scene of Bunny's disappearance. It was easily found, being the oldest and largest on the hillside.

Roger had brought a stout stick with him, and now, leaning over the cliff edge, he tried to poke with it in the branches below, while searching for the dolly. But the stick was not long enough, and slipped through his fingers, disappearing suddenly and completely through the evergreens.

"Hallo!" cried Roger. "There must be a hole there of some sort. Bunny's at the bottom of it, no doubt. Here goes to find her!"

His longer legs made easy work of the steep descent which had so puzzled his little sister. Presently he stood, waist-deep, in tangled hemlock boughs, below the old spruce. He parted the bushes in advance and moved cautiously forward step by step. He felt a cavity just before him, but the thicket was so dense that he could see nothing.

Feeling for his pocket-knife, which luckily was a stout one, he stood still, cutting, slashing, and breaking off the tough boughs, and throwing them on one side. It was hard work, but after ten minutes a space was cleared which let in a ray of light and, with a hot, red face and surprised eyes, Roger Gale stooped over the edge of a rocky cavity on the sides of which something glittered and shone. He swung himself over the edge and dropped into the hole, which was but a few feet deep. His foot struck on something hard as he landed. He stooped to pick it up, and his hand encountered a soft substance. He lifted both objects out together.

The soft substance was a doll's woolen frock. There, indeed, was the lost Bunny, looking no whit the worse for her adventures, and the hard thing on which her wooden head had lain was a pick-ax—an old iron pick, red with rust. Three letters were rudely cut on the handle—R.P.G. They were Roger's own initials, Roger Perkins Gale. It had been his father's name also, and that of the great-uncle after whom they both were named.

With an excited cry, Roger stooped again and lifted out of the hole a lump of quartz mingled with ore. Suddenly he realized where he was and what he had found. This was the long lost silver-mine whose finding and whose disappearing had for so many years been a tradition in the township. Here it was that old Roger Gale had found his "speciment," knocked off probably with that very pick, and, covering up all traces of his discovery, had gone sturdily off to his farm-work, to meet his death next day on the hay-rigging, with the secret locked within his breast. For sixty years the evergreen thicket had grown and toughened and guarded the hidden cavity beneath its roots; and it might easily have done so for sixty years longer if Bunny, little wooden Bunny, with her lack-luster eyes and expressionless features, had not led the way into its tangles.

Hester got well. When Roger placed the doll in her arms, she seemed to come to herself, fondled and kissed her, and presently dropped into a satisfied sleep, from which she awoke conscious and relieved. The "mine" did not prove exactly a mine,—it was not deep or wide enough for that,—but the ore in it was rich in quality, and the news of its finding made a great stir in the neighborhood. Mrs. Gale was offered a price for her hillside which made her what she considered a rich woman, and she was wise enough to close with the offer at once, and neither stand out for higher terms nor risk the chance of mining on her own account. She and her family left the quiet little farm-house soon after that, and went to live in Worcester. Roger had all the schooling he desired, and made ready for Harvard and the law-school, where he worked hard, and laid the foundations of what has since proved a brilliant career. You may be sure that Bunny went to Worcester also, treated and regarded as one of the most valued members of the family. Hester took great care of her, and so did Hester's little girl later on; and even Mrs. Gale spoke respectfully of her always, and treated her with honor. For was it not Bunny who broke the long spell of evil fate, and brought good luck back to the Gale family?

Busy Saturday

By Fanny Percival

What a busy day for little May
    Every Saturday is!
There's so much to do, enough for two,
And how she ever can get through
    Is one of the mysteries.

You'd think she'd desire some help to hire,
    But times are hard, you know,
And she hardly knows how to get the clothes
For her two dollies, Lou and Rose—
    Her bank funds are so low.

The washing comes first, and that's the worst—
    The clothes for Rose and Lou;
She puts them in tubs, and hard she rubs,
And with her little fist she scrubs
    Till she thinks that they will do.

Then she ties a line of stoutest twine
    From the door-knob to a chair;
then quickly wrings the tiny things,
And in a little basket brings,
    And hangs them up with care.

Now while they dry, her hands must fly,
    And busy her feet must be;
First she must make some rolls and cake,
And put them in her stove to bake,
    For company's coming to tea.

Now her clothes are dry, and she must try
    To iron them very soon;
For there's's sweeping to do, and mending too,
And then her children, Rose and Lou,
    She must dress for afternoon.

And then in haste, no time to waste,
    Her children's beds she makes;
Then she must see that the dishes for tea
Are washed as clean as they can be,
    And with these great pains she takes.

Should you not think that she would sink
    With so much work to do?
But, strange to say, throughout the day,
Many an hour she'll find to play,
    And help her mamma too.

Troubles in High Life

By Mrs. J. G. Burnett

Two miniature mothers at play on the floor
　Their wearisome cares were debating,
How Dora and Arabelle, children no more,
Were twice as much trouble as ever before,
And the causes each had her own cares to deplore
　Were, really, well worth my relating.

Said one little mother: "You really don't know
　What a burden my life is with Bella!
Her stravagant habits I hope she'll outgrow.
She buys her kid gloves by the dozen, you know,
Sits for *cartes de visites* every fortnight or so,
　And don't do a thing that I tell her!"

Those stylish young ladies (the dollies, you know)
　Had complexions soft, pearly and waxen,
With arms, neck and forehead, as white as the snow,
Golden hair sweeping down to the waist and below,
Eyes blue as the sky, cheeks with youth's ruddy
　　glow,—
　Of a beauty pure Grecian and Saxon.

"Indeed!" said the other, "that's sad to be sure;
　But, ah," with a sigh, "no one guesses
The cares and anxieties mothers endure.
For though Dora appears so sedate and demure,
She spends all the money that I can secure
　On her cloaks and her bonnets and dresses."

159

Then followed such prattle of fashion and style,
   I smiled as I listened and wondered,
And I thought, had I tried to repeat it erewhile,
How these fair little ladies, without guile,
Would mock at my lack of their knowledge, and smile
   At the way I had stumbled and blundered.

And I thought, too, when each youthful mother had conned
   Her startling and touching narration,
Of the dolls of which I in my childhood was fond,
How with Dora and Arabelle they'd correspond,
And how far dolls and children to-day are beyond
   Those we had in the last generation!

Caught in the Act

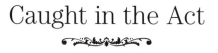

"Oh, you naughty, naughty dog! What *shall* I do with you?

A Letter from a Doll

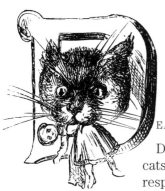

"The Nursery," February, 1887

DEAR CHILDREN:

Don't ever believe a single good thing you hear about cats. They are cross, ugly things, and they have no respect for dolls. I am a very nice doll indeed, and I have a lovely mother named Daisy. She is four years old. She likes me because she is a good girl, and she likes her ugly cat because she does n't know any better. Sometimes the cat gets mad at me and shakes me, and I can't shake the cat at all. I am too weak. I wish my mother had a fierce dog to fight for me. Don't you think I am good to let the ugly thing alone? We are both pets, but I am the nicest. This is all I have to say. I have a pain in my side to-day; and so would you if your little mother had a pet cat.

Your poor friend,
LUCY

THE CAT'S ANSWER TO THE DOLL'S STORY

DEAR CHILDREN:

My mistress's name is Daisy, too, and I think it must have been her doll that wrote the letter to you in ST. NICHOLAS, last March. She is a very selfish doll, for she never wants Daisy to pet me at all.

Cats can't help being cats, 'cause they are born kittens, and then grow to be cats. If I could have been born a doll, I think I would be a better doll than Lucy. Cats catch mice and rats, but dolls don't do anything. Daisy is good to me and I am good to Daisy. I never scratched her or bit her in my life. Isn't that a sign of a good cat?

You can see Lucy is a bad doll. If she was good she would n't say that her mother doesn't know any better than to like me. I don't believe your dolls talk about you in that way.

My name is Tillie. Is n't that a pretty name for a cat? I like children and I like good dolls; but I don't like Lucy, and you would n't like her either, if you knew her. I can purr poetry and Lucy can't. Here is some poetry that Daisy made for me.

I'm a little kitten cat.
Tillie is my name;
Mistress Daisy called me that,
'Cause I'm very tame.
Little children with me play.
And they love me, too;
This is all I have to say,
Good-bye, now, to you.

To the Very Little Folk, Care of
ST. NICHOLAS

Yours purringly,
TILLIE

Rosy

By Mary L. B. Branch

he very color I wanted, and just the kind I wanted!" said Louis, as he stood on the steps surveying his new velocipede. "Fire-red, and three wheels; you can't tip over on three wheels, you know."

"*I* could," said his brother Bertie, confidently.

"Oh, well, *you!* That's another thing. Here, Bert, help me buckle on my sword, and give me my soldier-cap. I'm a cavalry officer to-day, and I shall charge up and down the street exactly twenty times before I go to school."

Kitty and Willy boy watched from the window, and Bertie, book-strap in hand, waited on the steps, to see Louis' grand charge.

"Hurrah! hurrah!" he exclaimed, the first time he dashed by. "On, boys, and at them! Hurrah!"

A second and a third time he went swiftly and safely the whole length of the sidewalk, but the fourth time, just as he was shouting "Hurrah!" with a backward glance at Bertie, some one suddenly turned the corner ahead. There was a cry, a collision, and the next instant Louis and his velocipede lay flat on the ground, while a little girl of about ten sat near by, holding her ankle and crying bitterly.

Louis was on his feet in a moment, very sorry and very much ashamed; Kitty and Bertie flew to help the little girl, but could not reach her so soon as did a strong, broad-shouldered man who had been only a few steps behind her when she fell.

"Poor little lass!" he said, gathering her up in his arms. "Don't cry, for there's an orange in my pocket."

"My ankle hurts me," sobbed the child.

"I'm very, very sorry," said Louis, ruefully. "Please bring her into our house, sir, and my mother will put on something to cure her ankle right away."

"Oh, do please bring her in," joined in Bertie and Kitty, full of anxiety, and just then mamma herself appeared at the door, having been summoned in great haste by Willy boy. That decided it, for no one ever could resist mamma, and as soon as they were all in the house, she took the stranger child tenderly in her lap, and drew off the shoes from the little aching foot.

"There, move your foot now, dearie," she said, "That's right, move it again. It is n't sprained—only bruised a little. Run, Kitty, and bring my arnica bottle."

The little foot was bathed, the tears were dried, and then they all began to notice what blue eyes, and what pretty golden hair the stranger had.

"Is she your little girl?" asked Mrs. Neal of the broad-shouldered man.

"I guess I shall have to claim her," he said, good-naturedly, "though I never set eyes on her till yesterday. Her name's Rosy. She's the daughter of an old messmate of mine who died off the Ivory Coast, and I promised him I'd keep a lookout for her. So when the 'Laughing Sally' dropped anchor yesterday, I made for head-quarters straight off. We thought we'd have a walk this morning, but the little craft kept sailing ahead, and first thing I knew, she ran among breakers."

At this point Kitty, who had disappeared for a moment, returned with a rather dingy-looking little pie in her hands, which she insisted on giving to Rosy.

"I made it myself," she said, radiantly. "Bridget let me. I was saving it for my dolls, but now I would rather give it to you."

Rosy received it in the same spirit in which it was given, and regarded it with great admiration.

Meanwhile Louis and Bertie reluctantly gathered up their books and started for school, while Mrs. Neal pursued her conversation with the kind-hearted sailor. She found he had neither kith nor kin in this world, and had decided to adopt Rosy as his own little girl. He had found her not quite happy in the rough boarding-house which was all her home, and what do you think he was going to do about it? Kitty fairly lost her breath when she heard him say:

"I shall take her along next voyage; she'll be happier aboard the 'Laughing Sally.'"

Mrs. Neal involuntarily pressed the little waif closer, thinking of her own Kitty as she did so. What would become of a little, motherless ten-year-old girl, on a three years' whaling voyage?

"Do you want to go, dear?" she asked.

"Oh, yes," said Rosy, brightly. "Papa was going to take me next voyage himself; he wrote me a letter that said so, after mamma died. Papa always lived on the sea, and it will seem nearer to him if I live there too."

Mrs. Neal considered. It comes so natural to us to

"She took the stranger child tenderly in her lap."

shelter our children, to want them safely housed and guarded at every point. And the sea seemed to her so strong and terrible. But then her family had always been lands-people. She recalled a verse of Rossetti's:

"Three little children
On the wide, wide sea,—
Motherless children,—
Safe as safe can be
With guardian angels."

"The captain's wife promised Uncle Ben she'd take care of me," continued Rosy, "and I'm going to have a little hammock put up for me down in her cabin!"

"Oh, mamma, I wish I could go too!" exclaimed Kitty.

"Let Rosy stay here to-day," said Mrs. Neal to Uncle Ben. "Her ankle will pain her a little, and she should let it rest. Let her remain to-day and to-night with Kitty, and to-morrow you may come for her again."

"Well, ma'am, I will," said the good-natured sailor, glad to leave the little lass in so snug a harbor. And he went, but not before he took the orange out of his pocket.

Was n't that a great day for Rosy! To sit in an easy-chair in Kitty's room, and be made much of, to have picture-books heaped around her, and toys and bits of fancy-work; to have white grapes brought to her on a lovely china plate; and for dinner such delicious chicken pie. Then not only did she have Kitty for company, but all Kitty's dolls sat in order before her, dressed in their best. She said she wished her own dolly was there; and when Kitty inquired and found that the absent dolly had only one dress, what a hunting there was through mamma's piece-bags, until silk and lace had been found for Rosy to take home, to make a party-costume for her, fully equal to that worn by Kitty's own Florietta.

"I like dolls better than any other playthings," said Rosy, "because they seem just like folks. I should be real lonesome without mine."

So the two little girls played and talked all day long together, and liked each other better and better.

"If you were not going to sea, we could be friends all the time," said Kitty, regretfully.

"We'll be friends when I come back," replied Rosy, "and I'll bring you pink corals and shells."

Louis and Bertie were very much impressed when they found out the destiny that lay before Rosy; and hearing the children talk it over with so much enthusiasm, Mrs. Neal grew reconciled. After all it would make life broader and richer. Just think what it would be to any of us who have led quiet, uneventful lives, if we had three years to look back upon, of life on the broad blue ocean, under other skies, with strange stars overhead at night, sailing from zone to zone, stopping at tropical islands, catching the spicy breezes, seeing fruit-laden palms, seeing birds of bright rare plumage, and gathering wonderful shells on coral strands. Louis brought out his atlas, and all the children bending over it, marked out a voyage for Rosy, in which no sea was unvisited, no coast untouched, no island unexplored.

When Uncle Ben came for his little girl the next day, he found her bright and eager, quite willing to go with him at once, and begin to make ready for her ship-life. Mrs. Neal made some sensible suggestions in Rosy's behalf, which the bluff sailor gratefully accepted.

Louis and Kitty went once to visit Rosy at the boarding-house before she left it, and brought home a vivid account of its dreary discomfort.

"Not one bright thing about it, mamma," said Kitty, "only Rosy and her doll; and oh, mamma, she has made a dress for her dolly out of that blue silk I gave her, a great, *great* deal prettier than Florietta's!"

At last the "Laughing Sally" sailed out of port, with a little smiling figure on deck, waving a farewell to the group of friends who stood on the shore to see her depart. It was to be a three years' voyage. When they could no longer distinguish Rosy, the Neals went home, and from day to day tried to imagine how her new life must seem to her, and what was happening.

The months slipped by, and season followed season. The children talked often of Rosy, and wondered how she fared. Sometimes, on the very coldest, stormiest nights they would picture her walking at that moment on some sunlit shore, gathering curious shells for them. But their mother was haunted by the thought of a little shrinking, trembling creature, with only a few boards between her and the raging, cruel waters.

A year went by, two years, and the third was almost gone. Louis was now a tall boy of sixteen, and Kitty was growing a great girl. They wondered if Rosy would know them when she came back; she must be growing a great girl now herself. When the third twelvemonth had quite passed, they began to study the shipping list in the paper, expecting every time to see the "Laughing Sally" reported. But she was never even named. Month after month rolled by, and still no news. No "Laughing Sally" came sailing into port, with a little smiling figure at the bow waving a glad salute. No one seemed to know anything about Rosy's ship. The owners lived in some far-off city, so there was no one who could answer their inquiries. The Neals only knew that the ship never was hailed, never was sighted, never came to shore. So many ships went down each year, could it be that Rosy's was among the doomed?

At last it was five years since she sailed away. The Neals no longer spoke merrily and gayly of Rosy, but always gently and gravely. They had moved now from the house which had so long been their home, to another even pleasanter in the distant suburbs. Louis was almost ready for college, and Kitty was almost a young lady. Even Bertie had grown past belief, and Willy was the only one who now cared for velocipedes.

Still another year was slipping away, times goes so fast, and Mrs. Neal's birthday, which the family always celebrated, was close at hand. Louis and Kitty, in search of something lovely enough for a present, came into the city one day together, and went among all the stores. Louis complained that they should not get through before night, Kitty kept stopping so before all the show-windows.

"I can't help it, when everything looks so pretty," she said, laughing; "now just see that windowful of lovely dolls. If I live to be sixty, I shall always stop to look at dolls. If you feel too big and grand, Louis, you can be looking at that other window of books while you wait for me."

So Louis stood before the window of books, and

Kitty grew absorbed in the charming groups of gayly dressed dolls. She said afterward she felt impressed that she must look at them all. There was a bridal party, and a group at a ball, a cunning little tea-party, and a comical sewing society. In a corner of the window was a family group, at which finally Kitty found herself gazing with intensest interest. She could not make out its meaning at first. There was a sweet-faced lady-doll, holding a little girl-doll

There she sat at work.

in her lap while other doll-children stood around. Then there was a great, good-natured man-doll, with a big coat and long beard, looking on. Suddenly it all flashed over Kitty.

"Louis! Louis! come over here quick!" she cried excitedly. "See, only see those dolls!"

"I see them," said Louis, casting an indifferent glance that way.

"But you don't notice. Oh, Louis, don't you remember the day your velocipede knocked Rosy down, and how we children all stood around while mother took her shoe off, and Uncle Ben? There we all are, there you are yourself, with a sword at your side! I am going right in to find out who dressed those dolls."

And impulsive Kitty, followed by her bewildered brother, rushed into the store at once, and made her inquiries.

"We have two girls who dress dolls at work now in the back room," said the forewoman of the establishment. Kitty went eagerly to the glass door and peeped through. Alas! both were brunettes—no Rosy there.

"Who arranged the groups in the window?" she asked, pertinaciously.

"Ah, that," said the forewoman, "was done by our most skillful worker. She does the most of her work at home, then brings the dolls here and groups them. Her name is Ferguson."

"Her address?" demanded Kitty, breathlessly.

"No. 16 Weir Street," said the woman, referring to the books.

Louis was now interested too, and ordering a carriage, he and Kitty in a moment more were on their way to the place designated.

"Oh, Louis, Louis! can it be Rose?" said Kitty, as they alighted, and began to ascend the narrow stairs. A little boy showed them the door, Louis rapped, and a pleasant voice said, "Come in."

There she sat at work. It was she—dear, sweet Rose! Six years older, of course, and paler than when they saw her last, but it was Rose. Kitty threw her arms around her, with a storm of questions and tender reproaches, while Louis, much moved, made his way to the bed where poor Uncle Ben lay, evidently ill, and grasped his hand.

Then it all came out, the story of the delay and the long silence. The "Laughing Sally" had made out her cargo of oil in good time, and had started on the return, when she was met at Tahiti by another ship of the same owners, commissioned to take the oil, and to order the "Sally" back for another cruise. Uncle Ben's health had even then began to fail, he was becoming subject to rheumatism, and after five years' absence from his native land, he exchanged ships, took one homeward bound, and he and Rosy had now been back in the city for five months. Of course his little funds were soon exhausted, but Rosy luckily had been able to find work, and so they had lived. "But why did n't you come to us? Why *did n't* you come straight to us?" Kitty asked again and again as the story was told.

"I did go," said Rose, "but there was another family in the house, and no one could tell me where you lived. It was not in the directory either."

"Because we had moved out of town," exclaimed Kitty, "and there we were lost to each other, though less than five miles apart!"

"And did you reach the Fortunate Islands and find the coral strands, and the palm groves, Rose?" asked Louis.

Rose laughed merrily.

"I have kept a log," she said, "and you and Bertie shall read it. But whatever I found, there was nothing fairer than my native land!"

The Doll that Couldn't Spell Her Name

By Sophie Swett

om was really at the bottom of it. It very often turned out that Tom *was* at the bottom of things.

In the Belknap household, when the pot of jam tumbled off the top shelf of the pantry, when the cream was all drunk up, when the Sevres china cups were broken, they never suggested that it was the cat; they merely groaned, "Tom!"

Sometimes there was mischief done for which Tom was not accountable, but, being proven guilty of so much, of course he was blamed for all.

Bess had Tom for a brother. She had no sister and no other brother, so, of course, she had to make the best of Tom. And sometimes he was really quite nice; he had once taken her out into the park, and let her fly his kite—a beauty, with Japanese pictures all over it, and yards and yards of tail; once in a while he would draw her on his sled—though I am sorry to say he generally did n't want to be bothered with girls; and now and then, though not often, he had more caramels than he wanted.

He put on as many airs with Bess as if he were the Great Mogul, and, if he had been, Bess could not have had greater faith in him, or obeyed him more implicitly. When you are a boy thirteen years old and study Latin, it is easy to be the Great Mogul to a little body not quite eight, who is only a girl, any way, never went to school in her life, and can't go out when it rains, because she is delicate.

Bess was sure that a boy who studied Latin and could ride on a bicycle, as Tom could, must know everything. So when Tom told her that, if her doll was going to give a kettledrum, she (the doll) ought to write the invitations herself, she did not think of questioning it. She could n't quite see how it was to be done, but it must be the proper way, if Tom said so.

"It's the fashion now for ladies to write their own invitations," said Tom. "Have n't you noticed that Mamma writes all her cards? Never has them engraved, as she used to. It would n't be at all stylish, or even proper, for your doll to have a kettledrum, unless she wrote the invitations herself."

"But Lady Marion can't write," said Bess, mournfully. "I was going to ask Mamma to write them."

"Oh, you have only to put the pen in her hand, and guide it slowly, and she will write them well enough. I will tell you what to have her write. And she must draw a kettle at the top of the sheet and a drum at the bottom, like those that Miss Percy sent to Mamma, you know."

"It would be beautiful, Tom, but Lady Marion never could do it in the world!" said Bess.

"Oh, pooh! I'll show you just how, and you can help her. It will be just the same as if she did it all herself. There! that is the way to draw a kettle, and that's a drum," and Tom drew, with just a few strokes of his pencil, a kettle that was just like a kettle, and a drum that you would have known anywhere, while Bess looked on in breathless admiration, and thought Tom was almost a magician.

"And this is what you're to write—to make the doll write, I mean." And he repeated a formula several times, until Bess had learned it by heart.

"Oh, Tom, it will be perfectly splendid! How good you are to me!" said Bess, gratefully. "You shall have my new Roman sash for a tail to your kite!"

"Mamma would n't like that, and she would be sure to find it out; but I'll tell you how you can pay me: you can lend me your two dollars and fifteen cents. I am awfully short, and I must have a new base-ball bat."

Bess's face fell at this suggestion. She had been hoarding that two dollars and fifteen cents for a long time, to buy Lady Marion a new traveling trunk, her old one being very shabby, and having no bonnet-box in it, so that her bonnets got frightfully jammed whenever she went on a journey; and Nurse advised her never to lend money to Tom, because his pay-day was so long in coming; and when he got to owing too much he often went into bankruptcy, and paid but very little on a dollar.

But when one has been very kind, and shows you how to get up beautiful invitations, it is not at all easy to refuse to lend him your money. And, besides, if Bess should refuse, Tom would be very likely to tear up the beautiful kettle and drum that he had drawn, and, without a pattern to copy, Lady Marion could never draw them.

So Bess produced her purse, and poured its contents into Tom's hand.

"I'll be sure to pay you, Bess, the very first money I get," said Tom, as he always said.

"I hope you will, Tom," said Bess, with a sigh, "because Lady Marion is suffering for a new trunk. She'll have to stay at home from Saratoga if she does n't get it."

"Oh, you'll get the money long before summer. And, I say, Bess, I shall expect you to save me some of the goodies from that kettledrum—though I don't suppose you can save much, girls are such greedy things!"

"I will, Tom," said Bess, earnestly. "I will save lots of meringues and caramels, because those are what you like. And I'm very much obliged to you."

"Well, you ought to be! I don't know how you'd get along without me." And Tom went off, singing, at the top of his voice, about the "ruler of the queen's navee."

Left alone, Bess went to work diligently. Lady Marion's kettledrum was to come off next week; it was high time that the invitations were out.

Lady Marion had been invited out a great deal, but she had never yet given a party. She was well fitted to be a leader of fashion, but hitherto her mamma's health had prevented her from assuming that position. Nature had been very bountiful to her, giving her cheeks just the color of strawberry ice-cream, eyes like blueberries, and truly hair the color of molasses candy that has been worked a long, long time. She was born in Paris, and had that distinguished air which is to be found only in dolls who have that advantage. She had, it is true, been out for a good many seasons, and looked rather older than several of her doll associates; her cheeks had lost the faintest tinge of their strawberry ice-cream bloom, and her beautiful hair had been so tortured by the fashionable style of hair-dressing—bangs and crimps and frizzes and Montagues and water-waves and puffs—that it had grown very thin in front, and she was compelled to wear either a Saratoga wave or a Marguerite front to cover it. The Saratoga wave was not a perfect match for her hair, so she wore that only by gas-light. She had also been in delicate health, the result of an accident which strewed the nursery floor with saw-dust, and made poor Bess fear that her beloved Lady Marion would be an invalid for life. The accident happened at the time when Tom had decided to be a surgeon, and had bought three new knives and a lancet to practice with, and the dreadful cut in Lady Marion's side looked, Bess thought, very much as if it had been done with a knife.

Tom, however, affirmed that it was caused by late hours and too much gayety, and Bess did not take Lady Marion to a party again for more than two months. The accident destroyed her beautiful plumpness, but Mamma thought that slenderness added to her distinguished appearance, so Bess was comforted. This kettledrum was intended to celebrate Lady Marion's return to society, and Bess was anxious that it should be a very elegant affair. It was to be held in the drawing-room, and Bess had permission to order just what she liked for refreshments. There was to be more than tea and cake at that kettledrum.

And the invitations must be in the very latest style. Bess felt as if she could not be grateful enough to Tom for telling her just what was the latest style.

She aroused Lady Marion from her afternoon nap and forced a pen into her unwilling fingers—being such a fashionable doll Lady Marion had neither time nor taste for literary pursuits, and I doubt whether she had ever so much as tried to write her name before. But at last the pen was coaxed to stay between her thumb and forefinger, and Bess guided her hand. After much patient effort and many failures, a tolerably legible one was written, and Bess thought it was a great success for a doll's first effort, although the kettle and drum were not by any means perfect like Tom's, and, indeed, she felt obliged to write their names under them, lest they should not be understood.

They did not all look quite so well as the first. After one has written twenty-five or thirty invitations, one's hand grows tired, and one is apt to get a little careless; but, on the whole, Bess thought they did Lady Marion great credit. Not one was sent that had a blot on it, and Bess was satisfied that the spelling was all quite correct. Before six o'clock they were all written and sent, and Bess had a great weight off her mind. But she was very tired, and Lady Marion was so exhausted that she did n't feel equal to having her hair dressed, and was not at home to visitors.

Bess guided her hand.

Before she slept, however, Bess made out a list of the refreshments she wanted for the kettledrum, and she gave especial orders that there should be plenty of meringues and caramels, that Tom need not come short—he was so fond of them, and he would make such unpleasant remarks about the girls if they were all eaten.

And having settled all this, Bess felt that there was nothing more to do but to wait for that slow coach of a Tuesday to come around; party days always are such slow coaches, while the day on which you are to have the dentist pull your tooth comes like the chain-lightning express! There was nothing more that she could do, but there was one little thing that did n't quite suit her: she wanted to invite the nice little girl who lived around the corner of Pine street, and when she had asked leave, Mamma had said:

"Oh, hush, dear! No, no! you must n't ask her. You must n't speak of her! Papa would be very angry!"

Bess thought that was very strange. She was a very nice little girl. Bess had made her acquaintance in the park; they had rolled hoops together, and exchanged a great many confidences. Bess had told her about her parrot that could say "Mary had a little lamb," and about the funny little mice that Tom had tamed, and described Lady Marion's new dresses that Aunt Kate had sent her from Paris; and the strange little girl told her that her name was Amy Belknap,—Belknap, just like Bess's name, which Bess thought was very strange,—and that she had three brand-new kittens, as soft and furry as balls of down, with noses and toes just like pink satin, with dear little peaked tails, and the most fascinating manners imaginable; and she had invited Bess to come and see them. But her mamma would not let her go, and told that if she ever talked to the little girl again her papa would be angry. And Mamma looked very sad about it; there were tears in her eyes. It was all very strange. Bess did not know what to think about it, but Papa was very stern when he was angry, so she did not say anything more about Amy, although she met her two or three times at parties. But she did so want to have Lady Marion invite her doll to the kettledrum that she could not help asking; but it was of no use, and Mamma said "Hush! hush!" as if it were something frightful that she had proposed. And last night she had heard Nurse talking with Norah, the parlor maid, when they thought she was asleep, and Nurse had said that Amy Belknap's father was Papa's own brother, but they had quarreled years before about a will,

and were so angry still that they would not speak to each other. And Amy's mother was Mamma's cousin, and had been brought up with her, so that they were just like sisters, and Mamma felt very unhappy about the quarrel.

It did not seem possible to Bess that her papa would quarrel, when he always told Tom and her that it was so wicked, and when he got down on his knees and said, "Forgive us our trespasses as we forgive those who trespass against us," just as if he meant it!

Just what a will was, Bess did not know, but she had a vague idea that it had something to do with money. Surely her father would not quarrel about money! She had heard him say that it was very wrong to think too much of it.

There must be a mistake somewhere, Bess thought, and she wished very much that it might be set right, so that Amy and she might be friends.

Tuesday came at last, and long before four o'clock Bess and Lady Marion had their toilets completed, and were perched up on the windowseat to watch for the coming of their guests. It was not very dignified, certainly—Mamma never did so when she expected guests; but then Lady Marion was of a nervous temperament, and could not bear to sit still.

Lady Marion had on a lovely "tea-gown" of Japanese foulard over blue satin, trimmed with beautiful lace, and carried a new Japanese fan, with pearl sticks and lace, and her hair was arranged in a new style that was extremely becoming.

The refreshments and flowers had all come: there was nothing wanting to make the kettledrum a complete success—nothing but the guests. Strangely enough, they did not appear! Four o'clock came, and half-past four, and not one of the dolls that Lady Marion had invited came, but all the time a stream of carriages had been going around the corner of Pine street, and stopping at Amy Belknap's door; and Bess could see gayly dressed little girls tripping up the steps, every one with her doll in her arms!

Had Amy Belknap sent out invitations for this afternoon, and did all the girls prefer to go to her party? It was very strange. And a doll's party, too, apparently! Amy's best doll, Flora McFlimsey, had been left carelessly on the mantel-piece when a very hot fire was burning in the grate, and there was nothing left of her when Amy found her but a pool of wax, a pair of lovely blue glass eyes, and some locks of golden hair. And Amy declared that she never would have another doll that looked in the least like Flora; it would break her heart. But she had another doll, who, strange as it may seem to you when I tell you how she looked, was very popular in society. She was a funny-looking doll, and her name was Mary Ann. A very comical doll indeed she was, with the reddest hair that was ever seen, eyes that would roll up so that you could see only the whites, and lips that were always smiling and showing her white teeth. She looked so jolly that it made one laugh just to see her. She could turn her head from side to side and give you a friendly little nod, and if you pulled a string she could walk and dance. It was not a dance suited to polite society that she danced—indeed, I do not think that Nature had intended Mary Ann for polite society, but for all that she was very popular in it. No doll's party was thought to be complete without her, and her mamma paid as much attention to her toilet as to the lamented Flora McFlimsey's. Was Mary Ann having a party this afternoon? A suspicion darted into Bess's mind. The names were a good deal alike—Marion and Mary Ann. Could they have made a mistake?

She rushed up to the nursery, and found one of the invitations which had been discarded by reason of many blots. It seemed to her that the *o* was plain enough, but, oh, dear! Mamma had told her once that Marion was spelled with an *i* and not with a *y*.

"It was Lady Marion's fault! If I had been writing by myself I should have thought. It does look like Mary Ann, and Amy's Mary Ann had so many parties, and goes so much, they thought it must be her kettledrum, and they have all gone there!"

Bess wrung her hands, and hid her face on Lady Marion's sympathizing bosom. Only for one moment; in that moment she decided that she could not bear it. She rushed to the table, in a little ante-room, where the refreshments were spread, and taking up her over-skirt, apron fashion, she filled it full of goodies, tossing them all in helter-skelter, never minding that the candied fruit was sticky and the grapes juicy. Then she seized Lady Marion upside down, actually with her head downward and her feet sticking up in the air, so that she was in imminent danger of apoplexy—not to mention her feelings, which were terribly wounded by such an indignity—and ran out of the street door, not waiting for hat or cloak!

Mamma was away, and would not be home until night, but if Nurse saw her she probably would not allow her to go, so she closed the door very softly behind her. In her eagerness she quite forgot that there was a mysterious reason why she should not

She ran out, not waiting for hat or cloak.

go to Amy Belknap's house; she only realized that Lady Marion's kettledrum had gone astray, and she was fully determined not to lose it entirely.

The servant who opened the door had been surprised at the appearance of so many little girls and dolls, when none had been invited, but she was still more surprised when she opened the door to a little girl without hat or cloak, with her over-skirt full of bon-bons, and her doll's legs waving wildly in the air!

Amy had thought it a surprise party, and there had been no explanations until Bess and Lady Marion appeared. The girls were all very much surprised at the mistake, and said they did not understand why "Lady" was prefixed to Mary Ann's name, and some of them thought they ought to go at once to Lady Marion's house, since the invitations had really come from her; but Bess was quite willing to stay where she was, and Lady Marion made no objection.

The only difference was that there were two hostesses instead of one, Lady Marion and Mary Ann being seated side by side in state. Lady Marion was very elegant and polite, and was greatly admired; and as for Mary Ann, she fairly outdid herself, setting everybody into roars of laughter with her dancing; and the refreshments were not so *very* much mixed up.

Bess and Lady Marion staid after the others were gone. Bess wanted to see the kittens and the other

Lady Marion and Mary Ann seated side by side in state.

pretty things that Amy promised to show her; and, besides, she had begun to realize by this time that she had done wrong in coming, and she did n't want to go home and tell how naughty she had been.

If it were wrong merely to mention Amy's name, how dreadfully wrong it must be to have run away, without asking leave of anybody, and stay so long in Amy's house! She must be as bad as Tom was when he got acquainted with the circus clown, and went home with him and staid all night. Tom was kept shut up in his room all day, on bread and water, and Papa said he would "rather have no boy at all than a boy he couldn't trust." Would he wish that he had no girl at all? That was a dreadful thought.

But why should n't she visit Amy, who was the very nicest little girl she knew, and never got cross and said she would n't play if you did n't do just as she wanted to, as some of the girls did?

Bess turned it over and over in her small mind, and decided that it was very unjust. But she was very tired, and while she was puzzling over it her thoughts got queerly mixed up, and, before she knew what she was going to do, she had "taken the boat for Noddle's Island." They were sitting on the

warm, fluffy rug, before the fire, in the nursery. Amy's nurse had given them some bread and milk, and then she had hinted, very strongly, that it was growing late, and Bess had better go home.

Bess did n't choose to pay any attention to the hints. She dreaded going home, and it was very pleasant where she was. They had the three kittens, who were twice as furry, frolicsome, and fascinating as Amy had said; a toy mouse, with a spring that, when wound up, would make him run and spring so like a "truly" mouse that it made one's blood run cold, and nearly drove the kittens frantic; a music-box that played the loveliest tunes, and a Jack-in-the-box that fired off a tiny pistol when he popped out; all these delightful things they had on the hearth-rug, besides Lady Marion and Mary Ann, who were a little neglected, I am afraid, but so tired and sleepy that they did n't mind.

After such an exciting day as Bess had spent, one can't keep awake long, even when there is so much fun to be had, especially when it is past one's bed-time.

Nothing but politeness had kept Amy's eyes open so long, and when she saw that Bess was asleep she gave a great sigh of relief, and she, too, got into Noddle's boat. The three kittens, finding it very tame to play with a mouse that would n't go for the want of winding up, curled up together in a little furry, purring heap, and went fast asleep, and the Jack-in-the-box, losing all hope of getting another chance to pop out, did the same. Lady Marion had long ago been lulled to sleep by the soft strains of the music-box, and, last of all, Mary Ann, who ached in every joint from so much dancing, and whose eyes were strained and smarting from continual rolling up, but who never left the post of duty while there was anybody to be entertained, stretched herself comfortably out on the soft rug and, like the others, forgot her weariness in slumber.

The nurse stole out to have a chat with a crony. Amy's mother was out, and there was no one to notice that it was very quiet in the nursery, or think that it was time for the strange little girl to go home. But in the strange little girl's own house they were thinking that it was time for her to *come* home!

They had discovered her absence two or three hours before, and had been seeking her far and near, in the keenest anxiety and distress. They had visited every house where they thought she would be at all likely to go; they had given notice of her loss at several police stations, and secured the aid of two or three police officers in the search. Last of all, having heard that Amy Belknap had had a party that afternoon, they came there: Papa and Mamma almost beside themselves; Nurse never ceasing to weep and wring her hands; Tom outwardly stolid, and with his hands in his pockets, but inwardly wishing heartily that he had been a great deal better to Bess, and resolving that, if they ever found her, he would pay her that two dollars and fifteen cents right away.

"I am sure she is n't here," said Bess's mamma, as they rang the door-bell. "Bess never does what she knows I would not wish her to."

But when the door was opened the servant said she thought she was up in the nursery. And upstairs rushed Bess's father and mother immediately, scarcely remembering whose house they were in, but thinking only of their lost little girl who might be found.

It happened that they opened one door into the nursery just as Amy's papa opened another. And when Bess opened her eyes, almost smothered with her mother's hugs and kisses, there stood her papa and Amy's papa, looking at each other, as Tom, afterward, rather disrespectfully remarked, "just as his big Newfoundland Rover and Bobby Sparks's big Caesar looked at each other, when they had n't made up their minds whether to fight each other, or go together and lick Dick Jefferd's wicked Nero!"

Bess discovered that she was not going to be scolded, but was the heroine of the hour; even Tom, who hated "making a fuss," was actually crying and kissing her; and Bess began to feel very important and thought she might set things to rights. She tugged at her father's coat-tails to gain his entire attention.

"Papa," she began, "don't you know 'Birds in their little nests agree,' and 'Let dogs delight to bark and bite'? I'll get Nurse to say them to you, if you don't. It is n't right for you to quarrel just because you're big! And he's your brother, too—just like Tom and me. And he's Amy's father, and Amy's my pertikler friend. You kiss him, now, and say you're sorry, and—and I'll buy you something nice!"

In her eagerness, Bess had fallen into Nurse's style of bribery.

There was one very good thing about it—it made everybody laugh; and sometimes a laugh will swallow up more bitterness than tears can drown. They did not kiss each other, to Bess's great disappointment; but the very next day Amy came to see her, and Amy's mamma, too, and she and Bess's mamma kissed and cried over each other, just as if they were school-girls; and they called Bess "a blessed little peace-maker;" so Bess is quite sure that it is all coming out right, and that she shall always have her cousin Amy for her "pertikler friend."

When Bess's mamma heard that it all came about because Lady Marion could n't spell her own name, she praised Lady Marion, and said her ignorance was better than all the accomplishments that she ever knew a doll to have!

But as for Tom, who was really at the bottom of it, nobody thought of praising him.

But Bess had saved a great many meringues and caramels for him—more than anybody but a boy could eat—so he did n't mind.

Dolly Takes Tea

By Albert Bigelow Paine

When dolly sits down to the table,
 And ev'rything's ready, you see—
With cookies and water for Mabel,
 And water and cookies for me,

We nibble and chatter with dolly,
 And offer her "tea" from a spoon,
And often our meal is so jolly
 It lasts through the whole afternoon.

Till Mabel jumps up in a hurry
 And says that she really must go,
And I say, "Oh, truly, I'm sorry,
 And dolly's enjoyed it, I know."

Then gaily we clear off the table
 When dolly has finished her tea,
With cookies and water for Mabel,
 And water and cookies for me.

Thirteen and Dolly

By Mollie Norton

Oh Dolly, dear Dolly, I'm thirteen to-day,
And surely 't is time to be stopping my play!
My treasures, so childish, must be put aside;
I think, Henrietta, I'll play that you died;
I'm growing so old that of course it wont do
To care for a dolly,—not even for you.

Almost a young lady, I'll soon wear a train
And do up my hair; but I'll never be vain.
I'll study and study and grow very wise—
Come, Dolly, sit up now, and open your eyes;
I'll tie on this cap, with its ruffles of lace,
It always looks sweet round your beautiful face.

I'll bring out your dresses, so pretty and gay,
And fold them all smoothly and put them away;
This white one is lovely, with sash and pink bows—
Ah, I was so happy while making your clothes!
And here is your apron, with pockets so small,
This dear little apron, 't is nicest of all.

And now for your trunk, I will lay them all in—
Oh Dolly, dear Dolly, how can I begin!
How oft of our journeys I'll think with a sigh—
We've traveled together so much, you and I!
All over the fields and the garden we went,
And played we were gypsies and lived in a tent.

We tried keeping house in so many queer ways,
Out under the trees in the warm summer days!
We moved to the arbor and played that the flowers
Were housekeepers too, and were neighbors of ours;
We lived in the hay-loft, and slid down the ricks,
And went out to call on the turkeys and chicks.

Now here is your cradle with lining of blue,
And soft little pillow—I know what I'll do!
I'll rock you and sing my last lullaby song,
And I'll—No, I can't give you up! 'T will be wrong!
So sad is my heart, and here comes a big tear—
Come back to my arms, oh, you precious old dear!

175